The Elephant's Footprint

Joan Zawatzky

First published in Australia in 2011 by: Veritax. Victoria, Australia

Website: www.placeofbooks.com

Cover design: Brennen Lukav: Rank One
Printing and typeset by BookPOD

ISBN: 978-0-9871340-2-8

Praise for the Scent of Oranges

"The elegance of Joan Zawatzky's writing is a big part of what makes this story so memorable and delightful. Her words flowed right through me and led me into a story so full of life, nature and relationships. I never wanted it to end."

Ashley Merril, Front Street Review

"The Scent of Oranges by Joan Zawatzky is the first book I've read by this author but hope to read more. Right away I was transported to South Africa. I could picture everything that Linda saw as if I was her. Joan captures the essence of South Africa with the mystery and intrigue of murder."

Cheryl's Book Nook

"Zawatzky's style is wonderfully descriptive and I felt transported to South Africa through the pages of the book. I also loved learning more about South Africa and its people. The Scent of Oranges dynamically explores intense interpersonal relationships and I found it fascinating."

Tara's View on Books.

"The South African setting is beautifully recreated, with lovely descriptions of the landscape and people, and the author has written a thoughtful depiction of life under the terrible system of apartheid and its aftermath."

Book Buzz

"I think this novel will really appeal to people who like to sit and savour the writing and ...a mystery unfolding."

Peeking Between the Pages

"I was intrigued by the storyline and the uniqueness of the characters. It was fascinating to be taken to a new place, into a culture so different from anything I have known. I was just as curious as Linda, as she continued to push through dead ends and as she discovered astonishing things about her family. The ending did not disappoint."

That Book Addiction

"I really enjoyed this book. It was so sad, yet poignant. So many lives were ruined all because people judged others by the colour of their skin and not the type of person they were. It was an excellent read. It gave me plenty to think about. So buy it!"

The Bluestocking Guide

About the Author

Joan Zawatzky was born in South Africa. After completing her studies, first in art and then in psychology, she moved to Australia, where she worked for many years as a counselling psychologist. Though painting remained a hobby, she decided to try her hand at writing. She wrote *There's a Light at the End of the Tunnel*, to help her clients overcome depression. *The Scent of Oranges*, her first novel, is set in South Africa and was shortlisted for the Australian Books Alive Programme in 2007. Recently she began writing full-time. The Elephant's Footprint is her latest novel, and the next in her South African series. She lives in Melbourne with her husband and their Siamese cat.

Other books by the author

There's a Light at the End of the Tunnel:
*Self -Help and Hope for Suffers of Depression. Stories, Solutions
and Strategies.*
Publisher: Hybrid 2002

The Scent of Oranges
Publisher Australia: JoJo publishing 2006
Publisher UK and USA: Garev Publishing International 2008

Acknowledgements

Prior to writing *The Scent of Oranges* and *The Elephant's Footprint*, I knew the history of South Africa and had read about the changes since the Apartheid years, but what I needed to know was current information to help me appreciate and understand the new South Africa. I am especially grateful to my sister-law, Estelle Zawatzky, for not only providing this information, but also for her invaluable help with the final draft of the book.

My sincere thanks go to each member of The Blackburn Writer's Collective, for their constructive criticism, suggestions and encouragement while writing the book. Over the years, I learned so much from them all.

To Reeva Metz, my thanks for her review and her support.

My thanks to Sylvie Blair for all her help and advice. I am grateful too, to Brennan Zukav for his electronic mastery and artistic expertise.

Finally, I thank my husband and my friends for their caring encouragement.

For my husband, Hymie.

Cast of Characters

The Van Wyks
Linda van Wyk, amateur detective and recently qualified private investigator.
Connie van Wyk, Linda's eldest brother and owner of the farm where Linda grew up.
Vince van Wyk, Linda's younger and favourite brother who is a physiotherapist.
Hannes van Wyk, murdered when he was fourteen, many years earlier. Linda finds the murderer.
Pa (Piet van Wyk), Linda's father, deceased three years earlier.
Ma (Gladys van Wyk), Linda's mother, deceased 20 years earlier

The Moeketsis
Kosigo Moeketsi, young ngaka or healer/diviner found murdered in the Pilanesberg Nature Park
Galani Moeketsi, Kosigo's middle sister who is also a ngaka
Thabang Moeketsi, Kosigo's eldest sister who is a healer and naturopath.
Mr Moeketsi, elderly wealthy father to the Moeketsi sisters

The Lagaris
Tansie Lagari, Linda's nanny when she was a child on the farm.
Nandi Lagari, Tansie's sister who is secretively a midwife and healer.
Rosie Lagari, Tansie's daughter. Grew up with Linda on the farm and is her closest friend and, despite great difficulty, became a doctor and then a paediatrician.

The police
Chief Detective Inspector Arnie Swart, Head of the Homicide Division, Rustenburg Police.
Detective Inspector Phineas Phefo, in Arnie Swart's team.
Detective Sergeant Amita Pradesh, a member of Arnie Swart's team.

Others
George Hughes, archaeologist and Linda's friend and lover.
Ivan Sherwell, archaeologist and George's friend.
Wil du Plessis, Linda's ex husband
Josh, Linda's cook and cleaner

Tobias, wise old man who lives on the mountain.
Jairus, sorcerer, witchdoctor
Jake, farm owner
Tagoe, the Moeketsi's next door neighbour.
Kenneth, Kosigo's boyfriend
Rethabile Letsebo, older ngaka, second healer found murdered.
Nathaniel, lived and worked for Pa and is now Headman of a
new farm.
Amos, tour guide
Stan, tour guide
Samuel, Headman at Connie's farm
Sunshine, the third person found murdered
Esiekiel, old man who was Headman of the farm prior to Samuel
Karel, Josh's partner

The landscape is different,
The forest is fading,
behind the naked oak trees
The mountain stands dry.

Why do I dream of the drought,
The desiccated days that had us bound
To a spot in the ground
where we fervently prayed
for water to be.

Why didn't the sun
scorch the injustice
stamped on our bodies,
marked in our minds?

From: *The Dry Days of my Childhood* in *I've Come to Take you Home,* Diana Ferrus 2010

Rustenburg, South Africa 2010

In the cherry dawn, a film of dew is the only moisture on the parched veld. Soon the sun will boil and with not even a breeze to stir the trees, animals will scour the veld for water and shade.

The Tswana guide claps his hands.

'Good morning everyone and welcome.' He smiles broadly at the tourists and taps the microphone.

'Everybody in seats now… and eyes watching!'

A weak sun rises as he drives into the heart of the Park. Excitedly the tourists point to swooping birds and a distant herd of zebra gathered around a cracked hollow, once a drinking hole. When he spots an elephant stripping the top leaves off a mopane tree, he pulls up.

'The elephants are eating breakfast. Come on everyone. *Out!*' The thud of the huge beasts on the move echoes through the bush. Politely he helps the older members of the group off the bus and holds down the crackling grass for them to move in closer.

'Look, there near the trees!' He raises his voice as he steers them past an orange anthill.

The tourists watch amazed as the elephants denude the trees of leaves and strip bark from trunks.

While looking out for danger, he notices unusual markings on the ground and branches ripped from a thorn tree. He bends to examine the earth and sniffs the dry grass, flattened in places. Shaking his head with concern, he mutters to himself.

'Sorry people, we have to leave immediately. Everybody

back in the bus, please.'

Protesting loudly the group clambers onto the bus. A count of his passengers and he turns on the microphone. 'Please stay in the bus. There is something important I must check. I'll be back in a few minutes.'

Hurriedly he follows the tracks, the fetid smell and swarm of flies. An amber haze hangs between the trees, swirls through branches and settles on leaves. After checking that he is alone, he treads warily towards a dark heap beneath a tree. A young Black woman is lying there in blood soaked earth, her head cradled in an indentation in the ground, a branch roughly torn from a tree pinioning her breasts. He does not need to feel her pulse or listen to her breath. Her frightened, staring eyes tell him she is dead. If the visitors were not waiting, he would examine her more closely.

In his haste, he snags his finger on a thorn tree. Cursing he licks the sprinkling of blood and glares at the offending branch. He frowns as he turns to confirm what he has seen. A dead black snake is draped on a tall branch. He is almost certain he is looking at the mysterious and deadly Black Mambo that Tswanas associate with spirits of the dead. Shivering he scurries into the sunshine. When he returns to his passengers, the elephants have moved on.

He wipes his brow. 'We *must* return to the camp. *Now*!'

Once the engine is humming, he clicks on his cell phone to contact the park ranger. No dial tone. After another quick count of his charges, he slams the door shut and roars off. With a dismissive wave, he ignores the group's complaints. They pass a troop of grey - brown baboons with pink bottoms, gibbering loudly to each other as they race across the dirt road. The largest baboon herds the troop into the veld.

'What's up with the baboons?' A man in the front seat asks.

'They see … smell something in the veld that makes them scared,' he replies, summoning all his patience.

One

The first purple light broke through the South African night sky as I set off for the Pilanesberg National Park. Dazzling Sirius and the dawn star Canopus hovered over the horizon. In past years many believed that those fortunate enough to see Canopus at sunrise were about to witness a significant event.

Only a few kilometres outside Rustenburg, well-maintained houses in tree-lined streets unravelled into a spread of makeshift shacks. Those with jobs, woke for work. Along the pavements, rows of hawkers arranged their goods on slabs of wood, hoping for sales that day. To improve the country's image to visitors, the hawkers would soon be gone, but nothing could make the slums disappear.

The traffic choked up as I reached the newly built soccer stadium, rising from the dawn mist like a primeval animal. The stadium was to be a key attraction for the 2010 World Cup soccer games in a few months. Practice matches were already being played there and those eager to secure seats for matches that day began to queue for tickets. Even that early, the piercing sound of the *vuvuzela* could be heard. Excited supporters blew their plastic horns that would become symbols of South African soccer.

By the time I drove through the *Bakubung* gate at the tip of the Park, the sun baked the scorched earth. I had dreamt of visiting the Park for years, but what I saw that day was nothing like my memories of lush undulating veld and wooded ravines. Now dust blocked my nostrils and caught the back of my throat. Everywhere, plants buckled in the heat.

Two modern tourist buses blocked the driveway to the lodge. I parked some distance away and strolled towards the reception area. There was no sign of a receptionist and after ringing the service button without result, I gathered some brightly coloured brochures and stuffed them into my handbag. I found shade outside under a striped awning, sat on my suitcase and waited.

A police car drove up and screeched to a stop. Two police officers, a man and a woman, climbed out and headed in my direction.

'Bugger of a case, this,' the man said.

'If the big boys hadn't pushed us to follow it up, who'd bother,' the woman replied. The man's voice was familiar.

'Detective Inspector Arnie Swart!' I called out.

'Chief Detective Inspector, now.' His grin was broad. He was as tanned as I remembered him but leaner, and he wore an expensive suit with a tie too wide to be fashionable.

'What's brought you here?'

'I've been promising myself a weekend at the Park for as long as I can remember. It couldn't wait any longer.'

'When I last saw you I was thinking of leaving the force. I'd had enough, but when the Chief retired two months ago I was offered his job, an offer I couldn't refuse.' He straightened his back with pride.

'Of course,' I said.

'You're looking well...very well,' he said as he gave me a practiced top to toe appraisal. 'A real coincidence, bumping into you here.' Before I could reply, he turned towards the police officer standing next to him. 'I'm sorry. I didn't introduce you two. Detective Sergeant Amita Pradesh ... Linda Van Wyk.'

'Pleased to meet you, Sergeant.'

Her ponytail bobbed as she nodded.

'It must be year or two since I last saw you. What've you been up to?'

'It's three years, actually. I've been back to Australia.' I laughed. 'I enrolled in an investigator's course there and now have my P. I. license. I haven't worked up to private detective yet but I've been doing some part-time investigation.'

He pursed his lips and nodded. 'I can't say I'm surprised.'

He waved away my attempt at an answer and glanced at his watch. 'We have to get back to the station. Right then, Sergeant, grab those cold cokes from the bar.' He wiped his brow. 'That bloody place is more of a madhouse than ever. More murders, more rapes every day.'

He lifted his hand in a half wave and half salute and walked to the car. 'See you around.'

The sergeant closed the door too hard and they were off in a dirt cloud. I stood watching their car disappear. A coincidental meeting? I didn't believe in coincidences.

🦂

The receptionist returned and attended to the long queue. At last it was my turn. She handed a key to an elderly man, who was to carry my suitcase to my room. I followed him along a flower lined path until he stopped at a hut on a rise. He was about to turn the doorknob, when he dropped my suitcase, '*Hau*! *Serurubele!*'

A Praying Mantis clung to the screen door. The brownish cricket- like insect lifted its triangular head and huge eyes in my direction, seemed to nod and then disentangling itself from the wire mesh of the door, hopped away.

'It is very special ... brings you message from ...' He pointed upwards and then looked at me. I was not certain if his look was one of respect or astonishment.

'Too dry. I not see one here for long time.'

I smiled. I liked the idea of the welcoming visitor.

The hut was made of mud bricks with a conical straw roof but contained all the comforts I needed. As I unpacked my bag, I thought of my visit to South Africa three years earlier and how I met Arnie Swart. I came to Rustenburg to attend my Pa's funeral. After the burial, I intended to spend sunny hours on the farm where I grew up, but my time was consumed by a task Pa set me before he died. Over the years, he became increasingly uncertain about the guilt of three Blacks charged in 1951 and later jailed for murdering my fourteen-year-old brother, Hannes. It was Pa's last request that I investigate the murder. It was a ridiculous request as the little I knew about crime investigation came only from books and movies. At the time of Hannes' murder Arnie Swart was a junior, a constable. I was a child and Arnie was my hero. I remembered his rugged handsomeness and vitality.

All those years later, when I returned to Rustenburg for Pa's funeral, Arnie had climbed the ladder and become a detective inspector. With no idea where to start my investigation, I asked for his help. At first, he refused to look into a case closed years earlier. With the overwhelming number of current crimes, there was no time for it. Fortunately, he fancied me and his desire to please me softened his attitude. Though he refused to be directly involved, he agreed to review any useful information I discovered.

Phineas Phefo, Arnie's junior officer together with workers on the farm, were the ones who helped me to find the clues pointing to Hannes' murderer. Though the then farm manager admitted to killing Hannes, he was too old and sick to stand trial. A month after my return to Melbourne he had died.

Thoughts of Arnie faded as I spread the brochures, snatched from reception, on the bed. Impulsively, I decided to splurge on a two-day tour that offered a visit to a volcanic crater, the discovery of ancient sites and game spotting. Most tempting was the idea of eating meals cooked on a campfire like a true tourist. None of these activities were new to me but I hoped that the reliving of them would meld with my sweet memories. With the tour starting the next morning at sunrise, the rest of the day was mine.

I felt a twinge of guilt. I had arrived in South Africa five days earlier and had barely moved into the house Pa had left me in his will. Instead of spending the weekend with my brothers and their families, I had rushed off to the Park. After our years spent apart, a whole weekend of togetherness was daunting. There would be all those questions about my future plans. Would I stay in the house or sell it? Would I stay in South Africa for a while or return to Australia? My excuse of longing to see the game park again, was a useful one and close enough to the truth. I told myself that there would be more than enough time to catch up with family.

Suddenly tired, I sank into the softness of the old fashioned, candlewick bedspread. I slept deeply. When I woke the air in the round room was cooler. I was aware of the silence and emptiness, the stark white washed walls and the faint smell of insect repellent spray. At least there were no mosquitoes or fleas. My idleness forced me to acknowledge my loneliness. I was an expert at blunting the edges of emotions. If I was honest with myself, I would have admitted how much I longed for a lover's touch, a shared word, an affectionate hug and the pleasure of sex.

After a shower, I dressed and ambled through the property. I came across several boreholes that helped to create the abundant garden paradise. Close to the reception area, a group of women weeded the lawn and sang softly as they worked. They were mainly older women, wearing traditional coloured scarves, wound around their heads. Only a few people sat near the pool, as most of the guests were out touring. I found a sunny spot and delighted in the sunshine before returning to the room.

Later, I changed my clothes and followed the sound of singing to the dining room. I arrived as a Tswana group were nearing the end of a traditional dance in the lounge. The lodge was putting on a show for an enthusiastic crowd of tourists. I had seen Tswana dancing many times in the past – the men wearing short, animal skin skirts, stomping and shuffling in the front line and the women gyrating and clapping in the background. The crowd applauded and I joined them.

In the dining room, a waiter showed me to the table I was to share with a family. We chatted amiably while we all studied the menu. It was an extensive menu and included international food as well as traditional Tswana dishes. I was hungry and ordered a starter of seafood cocktail. For the main dish, I decided to be adventurous. The chef's suggestion was a Tswana favourite, *Mashonzha* on a bed of *Amandunbe* and a side dish of *Morogo*.

The man at the table laughed as he read the description of my choice in English. 'Rather you than me. I think you're going to eat grilled caterpillar-like worms from the mopane tree, on a bed of creamed, mashed sweet potato with a spicy peanut sauce and a bed of leaves.'

My nanny had given me a few of the worms as a treat when I was little and I remembered liking them.

'Yuk worms,' one of the children said.

'They're large worms. And anyway, we all eat prawns,' I retorted. The food took ages to arrive, but it was hot and tasty and I ate the lot, even though the *Mashonzha* worms were a bit stringy.

That evening, I turned on the television for the news. During my going to bed ritual, I heard the newsreader report that a young woman had been killed in the Rustenburg area, but I missed further details. A momentary look at the screen and the face of a young Tswana woman, who could not have been more than seventeen, stared at me. Her round Tswana face and her large golden eyes bored into me. Too tired to ponder on the exceptional nature of such a report, when so many young women died weekly and unnoticed, I flicked off the television. As I curled into sleep, the girl's face was still with me.

Two

A fter two days of hot and cramped touring in a mini bus, the water in the swimming pool was deliciously refreshing. Once I'd wrapped a soft towel around myself, all I wanted was to lounge in an easy chair. *Mind blowing*, was the only description I could find for my two day tour of the National Park. Fourteen of us, togged out in our soccer team scarves and caps left at dawn. The advanced age of the few single men on the tour destroyed my hopes of a connection or casual sex. Most of my enjoyment came from our middle-aged guide who called himself Stan, though his traditional name was actually Kefentse. He enjoyed showing us around, smiled and laughed a lot and liked to talk about his people, the Tswanas who once inhabited the area. Stan left us in no doubt that we were in the midst of Tswana territory.

The tour began with a visit to an 800 year old, Iron Age Village. The incredibly small rooms were constructed by fitting stones together. I was holding a knobbly bit of quartz and wondering about the person who chose it and placed it in the wall of the hut, when suddenly my head spun. I was thrown into the past, in the midst of a jostling crowd of ancient Tswanas, each one at least half a metre shorter than they are today and so malnourished that their bones stuck out. A short distance away graves with tiny markers indicated dead babies and children.

The images receded and I rushed back to the bus. I found my bottle of water in the side pocket next to my seat, gulped down mouthfuls, wet my face with a sprinkle and then took deep breaths. Though I was accustomed to tuning into the spirits when I visited ancient places, this visit disturbed me.

Stan watched me. 'You saw them?'

'Mmmm.'

'This is one place when I stay in the bus,' he said with a few knowing nods.

≈

I had spent my childhood on a farm near the game parks, and the birds and animals in the region were not new to me. This time, I viewed the wild life with fresh, tourist eyes and each spotting of a giraffe, zebra or eagle in flight was a thrill.

From the start of the tour, I watched eagerly for elephants. On the first day, we saw rhinos and hippos, but not a single elephant. On the next day, I was satisfied. Stan drove onto a dusty path and from a distance, we saw four adult elephants and a mother with her calf, under a shady tree. Further on, a lone elephant stood menacingly in the centre of the road flapping its ears at us. Its eyes were wild and I rubbed my clammy hands on my shorts.

'He's an angry young bull,' Stan's voice was raised with concern. 'Hang on folks, this will be bumpy. I'm driving away … before he decides to charge.' He steered the bus onto the saddle of the road with a thump. 'Phew, that was a close one!'

There was silence before Stan spoke again. 'Those young bulls have been making one hell of a racket and causing plenty trouble in the Park…just like wild teenage kids.'

Stan pulled up in a cool valley. 'Lunch now,' he called out.

We waited expectantly for our camp lunch, but we were disappointed. We were served sandwiches and coffee. Stan waved away our complaints and promised us an authentic camp fire meal that evening. Later, I found him perched on a rock some distance away from the group puffing on a cigarette. I lit up and joined him. We drank our coffee and I waited for the right moment to ask my questions. Having lived with men - Pa, a husband and two brothers - I had learnt that choosing just the right moment was important.

When Stan lit his second cigarette, I asked my question. 'You said the rogue elephants caused big trouble. What sort of trouble?'

'Two rogue bulls killed a white rhino last month. It wasn't a pretty sight. They smashed her up real bad with deep cuts. You don't want to know.'

'Have they attacked or killed any people?'

He explained that a few weeks earlier, an elephant charged at some youngsters who had provoked him by revving their car too close. The elephant replied by thumping the bonnet with its trunk. The engine was destroyed and one of the young men was seriously injured.

'People forget that elephants are wild animals and so big. They think they are seeing the slow, happy animals in the circus… but they can change like this.' He snapped his fingers. 'If they're sick, injured or upset they can attack.' His tone became more serious. 'Only yesterday a young woman was killed near here.' He pointed southwards. 'Maybe elephants are the guilty ones. We don't know yet. The rangers aren't sure and the police are all over the place. Only God above knows'

After stubbing out his cigarette with the heel of his shoe, he stood slowly. Whistling softly to himself, he adjusted his khaki uniform, pulled the keys for the bus from his pocket and walked off to round up stray members of the tour group.

Once I was seated in the bus, I experienced one of those unique *ah hah* moments. In a flash I recalled my glimpse of the dead, young woman I had seen on television and connected it with Arnie and Amita's appearance at the Park.

🐘

A campsite for the night was prepared and our outdoor meal was already cooking on a blazing fire. Meat simmered on the slow burning section of the fire and tea boiled in a can much like a billy. I had cooked over a bush fire many times while camping in Rustenburg and later in Australia.

As we ate our meal, I was back with my nanny Tansie as she stirred a pot of *mielie meal* on the communal fire. Women gossiped and sang as they prepared the evening meal for their families. The beef stew with tomato and onions that Tansie made was almost identical to the camp fire stew I had just eaten. In those early days I learnt to roll the meal into balls and dip it into the stew, instead of using a knife and fork.

At the camp, the sharp night air drew us closer to the fire. We had an opportunity to talk and find out more about each other before retiring to the huts that looked primitive but contained essential amenities.

As I was falling asleep, a familiar smell permeated the hut. I opened my eyes. In the darkness, greyish- white smoke spiralled. I sniffed. It was Pa's special blend of tobacco, his calling card.

I lay in the dark mulling over my connection with the spirits. As a child, I was intuitive. When I was five or six years old, Ma told me that I would probably be like my great grandmother, who was in touch with the spirits. I was aware that I was different in some way. I was able to finish off the sentences of those close to me and sensed things about people that others did not. In those days, I knew there were strange creatures in the attic of our old farmhouse and greeted them like old friends each time I went up there. Others found the attic a dark, scary place but I rather liked it, that is, apart from the spiders. Though none of the creatures ever spoke to me directly or presented themselves visually, I knew they were there by their smell, their buzzing sound or a chill in the air.

Nowadays, family spirits rarely visited. When they did, I considered myself lucky. I had the link that in most people, died with childhood.

Three

From the sun deck at the swimming pool, I watched the orange sun slide behind *Thabayadiotso,* the Proud Mountain. I picked up a newspaper lying next to my chair. There was still sufficient light to make out the leading article, featuring the recent soccer qualifiers. I was thrilled. In only a few months, Australia would definitely be playing in the new Rustenburg stadium.

Too weary then, to even think about buying a ticket for the game, my eyes closed and the newspaper slid onto the tiles. When I heard my name called, I straightened up with a start. Arnie Swart was looking down at me. 'A hectic day touring, eh?'

'It was wonderful…'

He cut in impatiently. 'I was near here so I thought I'd pop into the lodge for a beer to stir up the brain cells… and anyway, I wanted to talk to you.'

'Ah hah.'

'A young Tswana woman, Kosigo Moeketsi was killed in the Park, only five miles from here. She was a popular young *ngaka,* a diviner just seventeen years old, brilliant at bringing rain. Ever heard of her?'

'I saw her picture on the television'

'Anyway, the pressure to find her killer is on, big time. She's from a wealthy and important family, and instructions have come from the top brass to find her killer. A new Chief Detective Inspector has to prove his worth, you know.'

I nodded.

'The story goes that even before Kosigo trained as an *ngaka,* she showed talent in making rain. Out of love and respect for her, the Blacks around here gave her the name of Rain Goddess.'

'She was young to have those talents. Very sad that she's dead.'

He threw his arms apart in a despairing gesture.

'You know that cattle are money to the Blacks, that they need rain to keep the cattle fat and healthy. They swore by her magic that brought the rain. Even some of the White farmers paid Kosigo to cast her rain spells.'

'But what's happened to the original Rain Queen, Modjaji?'

'She died recently, at only 27. Some people say that Kosigo didn't show the respect she should've to the late Queen... that she should've waited the traditional year before trying to take her place.'

He glanced at his watch and coughed.

I waited, knowing that last words can often be the most important ones. He scratched the stubble forming on his jaw. 'It all clicked for me when we drove away the other day. Here I am, battling to handle an escalating crime wave and to top it I've got this case to sort out. You've proved your skills as a detective and you're listed on our computers as a consultant to our division. You understand the Blacks better than I do... and now you have your P.I. license. Well, as I said, it clicked. Maybe, if you've got the time, we could work together on this case.'

I tried hard not to show my interest, but he must have noticed the flush of excitement spreading over my neck and face.

He squinted as he looked up at the darkening sky. 'We'll need a lot more than spirits or mumbo jumbo to squeeze moisture out of that bloody sky.'

'Mmmmmm.'

'So, I guess I'm asking if you're interested. I'm desperately short of staff with experience. Half our people are being trained to protect the crowds. We're expecting at least 450,000 visitors for the Soccer Cup. So, the way things are, we could do with someone with a sharp, logical mind to cut through all the crap,' he said with a wave of his arm.

I raised my eyebrows, but he would not have noticed. A young blonde woman in a low cut top walking past us distracted him. He shifted his feet under the table. 'It's a long shot, but I'm pretty sure I could organise it.'

His enthusiasm surprised me and I gave him my most quizzical look.

'Any clues to who killed her yet?'

'No hard leads. A lot of supposition.'

Now it made sense. Arnie was in a tough situation casting about for a lifeline. 'Complicated, eh?' I said, smoothing my crumpled shorts.

He was talking fast now and his face was taut with unease. 'The Minister of Tourism visited us last week. His message was loud and clear. Crime rates have to be reduced dramatically and undesirables removed from the streets. The city has to look safe to attract visitors. While all the dirt's being swept under the carpet, there's no time for crime detection.'

Did I want to be involved, I asked myself? Though the victim and her family were not known to me, I could not help being fascinated by the case. But I doubted whether Arnie would be granted the clearance. My knowledge of bureaucracies taught me that even the smallest thing asked of them took a very long time.

'Sure, I'd be interested. See what you can do.'

'I'm serious about this. I'll do the paperwork as soon as I get back to the station.' He stared at the ground for a moment. 'But this won't be an easy murder to sort out, I can tell you that,' he said standing to leave.

After dinner, I mulled over Arnie's suggestion. Recently, crime detection interested me more than my life-long career of nursing. My interest grew from my last visit to Rustenburg, with the enthralling hunt for my brother's murderer and my success in nailing him. When I returned to Melbourne, I could think of nothing else and gravitated towards a career change. I attended a lengthy course in private investigation and obtained my license. In the past year, I worked part time for a small investigation agency. Though the cases were inconsequential - marital infidelities or the tracking down of workers feigning illness, I had found my niche. To earn my bread and butter, I continued nursing. In spite of the extra hours, investigation work intrigued me.

A loud noise outdoors interrupted my thoughts and I went to the window. A trail of wailing, stamping farm workers packed the driveway from as far back as the entrance sign. When the manager appeared, he could not make sense of their questions and called for assistance from one of the restaurant staff.

'What the hell do they want?' he demanded.

The young man coughed and then hesitated before replying. 'They are asking us to tell them who killed the Great One who brings the rain.'

'For God sake, how on earth should we know?' the manager muttered. 'Tell them that it has nothing to do with us, that the police are looking for her killer.'

The young man relayed the information. Some of the workers spat, others clenched their fists and shook them in anger. 'Police are no good, do nothing,' some shouted. Then as one, the crowd turned about and formed a straggly, dejected mass down the hill.

I returned to my hut. The room was warm and I opened the screen door. I knew that I would never tire of watching the shutters of darkness close over the veld or listening to the animals' first calls into the night.

Four

I woke from an early morning dream with aching muscles and my pulse throbbing. I had dreamt that I was alone in the veld. I froze as a herd of elephants bellowed behind me. The sky suddenly iced over and turned a dynamic blue. A blustering wind wrenched twigs from dry trees and small stones sprayed me. Dust was everywhere. As the scene changed, the elephants charged, but not at me. Their target was a rhino standing forlornly next to a dried up drinking hole. Fearing a violent confrontation between the archenemies, I hid behind a bush. I was relieved that the rhino escaped, just in time.

Though a warm shower relaxed me, the vivid dream remained with me. I took my dreams and visits from my dead relatives seriously, while others may have laughed them off. They were a natural part of my life. I grew up with the Blacks who believed that spirits appeared in many forms - dreams were one of them. Then there was Tansie, my old nanny, who was a Christian but continued to follow her ancient ancestral rituals. On the surface Christianity was the religion of South African Blacks, but in times of crisis or death, they frequently reverted to their familiar tribal beliefs and practised the spiritual rituals their people had followed for generations.

I opened the door of the hut onto a perfect day, with the sky that exquisite African blue and in the distance the mountains a fringe of mauve. My tour was over. As the lodge offered me nothing more, I packed and was soon on the road home. Each time I approached *my* house, I was charged with joy. Built to face the mountains and bask in the sunlight, it was Pa's gift to me. Now I owned it. He must have known I would be happy there.

Josh rushed up to the car. He cared for the property while I was in Melbourne and I asked him to stay on to clean and cook for me. 'Welcome back! Did you have a nice time? See lots of lions and elephants?' He did not wait for my response. 'I'll take your suitcase.' The young, broad shouldered man disappeared around a corner, followed by his mongrel Stevie. I gazed out of the window at the once lush garden. It was a desert now, surrounded by a high security fence topped with hideous and deadly razor wire. My house in Melbourne was fitted with a security door and a deadlock as well as window locks and it seemed sufficient protection. In Rustenburg, I was forced to live in a high security prison.

Josh must have noticed my dissatisfaction. 'Security is mega important here. We've got to be careful these days. Crime in this area is going up and up. Plenty break-ins, some armed,' he said, as he resumed his work. 'I don't want to make you scared, but just down the road from here Lorrie Jansen and her teenage daughter were raped and murdered. Terrible. It happened about three months ago.' He gave the dog a quick pat.

I shut my eyes and shuddered. I didn't want to hear those awful things. I had met Lorrie and liked her.

'Don't worry, I'm here to look after you.' He flexed his broad chest. 'And there's Stevie,' he said with a grin.'

The little I knew about Josh was from my younger brother, Vince. He knew Josh when he worked on my eldest brother, Connie's orange farm. Vince wrote to tell me that Josh was gay, though he hid it successfully while working on the farm. That is, until his fancy for a fruit picker during harvest made it obvious. Though black homosexuals were accepted in the cities and towns, in rural areas they were not well tolerated. One night a group of workers attacked Josh. Though he was strong, they overpowered him and beat him so brutally that he ended up in hospital with broken bones.

Once he recovered, he could not return to the farm and his family ostracised him. The offer to work for me came in just in time.

He decided to complete his high school studies so that he could become a carer for the elderly and infirm. A fortunate grant from the government helped him to pay for his computer and night classes. A salary, the free room, food and a quiet place to study was fair exchange for any cooking, cleaning and gardening he would do for me.

※

I logged onto my computer to check my emails. One of the incoming messages was from Ivan Sherwell, an archaeologist, studying the early Rustenburg civilisations of the Tswana and Bushmen, or as he preferred to call them, the San. We became correspondents after I made enquiries on an archaeological internet site. I clicked on to his message.

Let me know when you've arrived so that we can get together. Looking forward to meeting the real you.

Ivan's emails were usually detailed, but interesting descriptions of his team's progress at their archaeological dig, accompanied by pictures of the artefacts or San rock engravings they had discovered. Though we wrote to each other for almost a year, he did not give me a glimpse of his personal life. I reacted by not revealing much of myself either. Nevertheless, I was curious to meet him and replied immediately.

That evening, I poured myself a generous glass of wine and sank into the old but comfortable couch. There were decisions I had to make. I owned two homes - this comfortable, rambling, ranch style house of Pa's and a cottage on the outskirts of Melbourne with its wild garden and old trees.

During my last three years spent in Melbourne, I had often thought of returning to South Africa for a few years. It seemed such an easy and logical choice. From a distance,

I indulged myself in daydreams, the idealist in me eager to contribute to the incredible changes in the new South African democracy. I romanticised my childhood in frequent reminiscences that I longed to recapture.

Beneath it, was the thick curtain I drew over my impending divorce from Wil, my childhood sweetheart. Though our marriage was now as dry and empty as my garden, I was used to his presence and could not imagine life without him.

An emotional and physical shift of home and even country was an option, and possibly a remedy. Of course, I had not considered the practical implications. If I moved to Rustenburg permanently, I would have to sell the cottage I loved. I would have to resign from my nursing job and give my pets away to friends, that is, if they would take them. The thought of this undertaking was gut wrenching and the cost unthinkable. I sighed, poured another glass of wine and closed my eyes.

Five

My day was free and I decided to visit my old friend Nathaniel. The heat was rising and red dust clung to my car as I turned into the farm road. As I pulled up, Nathaniel raced to greet me.

'Welcome to *Mosego*,' he said clapping his hands. The tall man's grin was broad and his teeth glinted in the sunlight. 'Ah! Missie Lindie. It is very good to see you again.'

Standing on tiptoe, I did what I wanted to do for years. I put my arms around him and hugged him, though I only reached just passed his middle. He looked down at me, shuffled his feet awkwardly and placed his hands on my shoulders. We formed an enduring friendship playing together on Pa's farm as children, but the barriers of apartheid prevented us from touching, that is apart from a handshake.

He tapped my shoulders awkwardly and nodded still smiling, 'Ja Linda, it is time.' My eyes were moist as he carefully pronounced and repeated my name. He swallowed and went on talking. When speaking Setswana his words rushed out, but his English speech was slow and he was mindful of error.

I was relieved that Pa did the right thing before he died. He returned the land our forefathers seized from the local inhabitants, Nathaniel's Tswana ancestors to its owners. In the 1830's, our Afrikaner forefathers trekked from the Cape, then under British rule, in search of a place where they could set up farming communities and practice their religion unimpeded. The fertile hills and valleys of Rustenburg was an ideal destination. Here our forefathers established two farms that were later passed on through our family. When Pa died, he left his own farm to my brother Connie, his oldest son. The other, he left in Nathaniel's care. I was certain that Pa would have been pleased that *Mosego* was thriving.

We sat on the large rocks near the driveway. Nathaniel sighed loudly.

'Last year everything in the farm was growing. I wish you'd seen it. Now, no rain for months.' His head drooped and his usually taut form buckled. '*Modimo* looks after us… but this time maybe we did something wrong.' He stared at the mountains.

I had known about the Tswana's belief in their ancestors and the supreme power *Modimo*, since childhood and respected it. When Nathaniel fixed his eyes on the mountains, it meant he was worried or upset.

'What's upsetting you Nathaniel?'

'Ai,' He sighed again. 'Kosigo is lying dead in the National Park.'

I nodded. 'Yes, it's very sad. Did you know her?'

'My brother Isaac married Lettie from her tribe, the *Bafokengs*. She is the sister of Jeremiah Moeketsi. Jeremiah is the father of Kosigo.'

Both Nathaniel and Kosigo and their families were from the same tribe, the Tswanas. There were many clans amongst the Tswanas, mainly named after animals or reptiles. Nathaniel and his family were from the *Bahurutshe* or Baboon Clan, while Kosigo's family came from the *Bafokeng* or Crocodile Clan. None of these divisions mattered when everyone was getting along but when there were disagreements, the smallest concern assumed importance. The *Bafokeng* clan was lucky. Platinum was discovered on their land and it made them extremely wealthy. Some of their money went towards building the soccer stadium in Rustenburg to be used for the World Soccer Cup.

'So, you must be related to the Moeketsis by marriage?'

He nodded. 'Kosigo was like the sun in my heart. I loved her from the time she was very little. Everybody loved her.'

I touched his hand.

'People say the police think that elephants killed her but how can that be true? I'm sure no elephant killed Kosigo,' he said emphatically. 'When I was maybe ten years old, I was riding on the back of a baby elephant. The mother did not like it in the beginning, but when she saw me give the baby food she let me ride.'

Though Nathaniel's stories about elephants were entertaining, I doubted their authenticity.

'Well then, who could've murdered her?' I asked.

He pursed his lips and stared at the mountain once more. The buzz of a mosquito arrested his attention. He slapped it dead on his arm and faced me. 'Tell me, how do *you* know Kosigo is dead?'

I explained that I met Arnie Swart at the Park and that he provided me with the details about Kosigo's murder.

'So, he's already asked you to help the police to find the murderer, eh?'

'We talked about it but I can't do a thing until the police department gives me permission to work on the case.'

'They will ask you to help, you will see. Then you must try extra hard to find who killed beautiful Kosigo.'

I agreed to help in whatever way I could. To Nathaniel, agreement meant a promise. The sudden wail of a police siren drowned the crackle of our footsteps on the dry veld.

He read my worried expression. 'Every day police are going somewhere in big hurry. We are used to it.'

My gaze swept over rows of silver tasselled maize almost ready for harvest and across the land edged by the mountains.

'We are very lucky we have some water from the mountain.' He rubbed his hands together. 'Come, I will show you the rest of the farm.'

He took such long strides that I struggled to keep up. In the narrow orange grove, the scent of citrus was in the air and the trees were laden with fruit soon to be picked. Nearby a group of workers sang as they tended to rows of young orange trees.

'It's good to be back.'

Nathaniel stopped and placed his hands on his hips. He looked hard at me. 'So, tell me, why have you come to Rustenburg this time?'

'I wanted to have a holiday and …'

'Maybe the land will hold you fast and you won't want to leave us again.'

'Maybe.'

I followed him through the veld where birds hovered over wild plum trees and then sloped down to the bottom of the hill. Bordering the highway, a line of roughly built kiosks stood with trestle tables in front of them. He laughed with pleasure at my surprise. Young people smiled at him and waved, older ones nodded in deference. 'This is how we make money to run the farm,' he shouted above the din. 'They're all unemployed people... making jobs for themselves.'

'Do they pay you to rent the space?'

'Ja, but the first month is free.'

Protected by a windbreak of tall pines, the strip of tightly packed kiosks and caravans spilled onto the road. Cars vied for parking on the rough apron of dirt, men heaved bags of oranges and oversized watermelons into car boots. Some bought only one or two oranges, holding the golden fruit carefully, while others lingered undecided over a selection of beads, leather ware and wooden masks. The atmosphere was lively, with Black and Indian traders calling out as they competed for passing trade. Aromas mingled: cut flowers, turnips, rich golden pumpkins, rosy apples, spinach, lettuce and crisp celery. Incense burned where bejewelled saris twinkled in the sunlight. Spicy dried meats and sausages hung to dry. To make themselves heard, people yelled over Elvis in one corner and an African beat blasting in another. Everywhere people haggled over price.

'What's behind there?' I asked, pointing at a colourful striped curtain.

'*Boloi*, a bad witch.' Nathaniel said, shaking his head.

'Bad witch?'

'Ja, he can make very bad things happen to people. He

also sells little bottles of muti. I don't know why the workers want him here. Next month I will chuck him out.' His face was a picture of displeasure.

I was confused. 'Tell me, what's the difference between *ngakas* and bad sorcerers or witches?'

'First come with me. Later I will tell you.'

I followed Nathaniel to a stall that sold refreshments, sandwiches and cookies. He bought cokes and dusted a bench next to the stall. 'Sit down and have your drink. Now, I will tell you about the bad witches.'

He explained that Tswanas believed that the *Baloi* seized the powers of evil and used it to destabilize and, ultimately, destroy a community. Those affected by witchcraft lost the protection of the ancestors, making them as vulnerable as open sores. Weakened, they may have poor crops, become prey to marital troubles, infertility, illness or injustice. The furrows in Nathaniel's brow deepened. '*Baloi* hide at night or in dark places so you cannot see them. Then one day, like a cat, they jump out to give you pain and trouble. They can make you sick in the body and the head or kill you with poison.'

'Horrible!' I pulled a lemon face. 'And what about *ngakas*?'

'Ah, *ngakas*!' He smiled his gentle smile and explained that they were respected members of the community, like western doctors. People turned to *ngakas* in times of crisis or illness. They were not only medicine men but rainmakers, mediums, psychics and, at times, virtual social workers. A *ngaka's* skill was passed down through generations, as were the ethics of healing and practice. To diagnose a client's problem the *ngaka* would seek guidance from their ancestors or *badimo*. The message came through trance states, bone throwing or the interpretation of dreams. The solution could be a prescription of herbs or the suggestion to talk through an issue. If the *ngaka* recommend that the *badimo* be appeased or their help evoked, often a chicken or sheep was sacrificed.

'Are there lots of bad witches around?' I asked.

'There's enough bad ones just waiting to bring trouble and make people scared but *ngakas* are looking out for them and chasing them away,' he laughed. 'I know some and they bring plenty trouble.' He clapped his hands. 'Now, enough talk about *baloi*.'

I was proud of Nathaniel. He was mature now and he walked with the tall firm tread of a confident man. When I lived on the farm all those years ago, the gossip then, was that Nathaniel's mother Lena spoiled him by keeping him home from school, when he pretended to be sick. Old women clicked their tongues with displeasure. Lena maintained that her Nathaniel's nature was the sweetest of all her children and so she fed him sweetness; sugar cane sticks from the Indian trader up the road and round chocolate coins in shiny paper she bought for a half penny. When no one was watching, she treated him to the creamy top of the milk and fatty bits of meat left in the dish after a meal.

It was not surprising that the workers on *Mosego* greeted his new status as headman with mixed feelings. Though Nathaniel was well liked, everyone on the farm knew that he found making decisions difficult, and they feared he would not take to his new role with the required responsibility. Over the months, working tirelessly with his men, he had proved himself and together they created a viable farm with thriving crops, in spite of the drought.

When the light began to fade and the final blazing orange rays disappeared over the mountain, he accompanied me to my car.

'I will do my very best for Kosigo,' I said.

'I know.'

'See you soon.'

'*Tsamaya sentle*. Go well.'

'*Sala sentle*. Stay well.'

Six

A visit from Arnie in the late afternoon, came sooner than I expected. Thinking that the bureaucracy would move too slowly to include me, I put all thoughts of involvement in the investigative team aside. Without his tie, his hair ruffled and his sleeves rolled up, he looked nothing like the chief inspector I had met only days before.

He sat with a tired thud. 'I managed to escape from the station earlier than usual today, and thought I'd come past with my news.'

'Yes…and?'

'We've got the green light… you're now a civilian aiding the police. That's if you're still interested?'

'Of course I am, but how did you manage to pull it off so quickly?'

'People in the right places,' he said with a smirk.

'Any leads yet?'

'So far we know that Kosigo received death threats in letters and emails, and we've started looking into the source of the threats. It's strange that a week before her death her wooden divining tablets, a pack of tarot cards and divining bones disappeared. Kosigo thought they'd been stolen but no fingerprints other than hers were found on the desk or in the side drawer where she kept them.'

'Do you think the threats and stolen items could be connected to the murder?'

'I suppose it's possible but I think it's more likely that an elephant killed her in a mad rampage – the cuts on her body substantiate that… but the rangers don't agree. We'll have to wait for the autopsy report.'

'Mmmmmm.'

'My sergeant will be back here tomorrow, to take some extra soil samples at the murder site and more detailed measurements for Pathology. You can join her if you like, to get a feel of the crime.'

'Good idea.'

'I'll let her know you're joining her. Amita's a good cop, graduated top of her year at the academy. You'll find her a smart detective.'

⁂

At exactly 9.00 A.M. the following morning, a police car roared to a halt in front of the *stoep*. As Sergeant Amita Pradesh was about to place her finger on the doorbell, I opened the door. She was framed in the doorway – a petite young woman with lustrous hair and sparkling brown eyes, rimmed in black kohl.

During the drive to the crime scene, our conversation was stilted at first. We focused on the drought and the latest statistics of violence, until holding the wheel with one hand, she sneaked a look at me. 'My, my, the boss has built up your reputation.'

'Really!' I retorted jokingly.

'So you're a licensed investigator … in Australia?'

'Soon I'll have my full private detective accreditation and a license to carry a gun, too.'

'All this in the three years since you've been away. I'm impressed.'

I laughed.

'Did you know that the boss has only been in the job for seven months? I wouldn't like to be in his position'

'Oh!'

'The Chief of Police in this region is a member of the *Bafokeng* clan. Apparently the Chief and Moeketsi, the victim's father, are brothers. He's promised his brother that we'll find his daughter's killer,' she rattled off the information.

'That's heavy pressure.'

'You said it. The boss and the Chief don't hit it off that well. I doubt if the boss would've been promoted if the Chief was the only one on the board,' she chattered on.

I would have to be careful what I said to Amita. 'What's this Chief like?' I asked, taking advantage of her loose tongue.

'He's quite intimidating. He has the usual background – an anti-government fighter during the apartheid years and I heard he's a mate of Mandela's.'

'A policeman's job is tough with crime on the up and up.'

'Now you can understand why the boss is looking for whatever extra help he can get.' She looked at me out the corner of her eye.

'Ah huh.'

'So, how're you finding things here?' she asked, changing the subject.

'Confusing.' I answered cautiously.

'That's what all visitors say. It'll take years for the new government to get their act together, but meanwhile Blacks and Whites with cash are living it up … and that's apart from shitting themselves over the rising crime here,' she said with a laugh.

'Poverty and crime have always been bedfellows,' I said, certain we would disagree. I did not want the discussion to move into politics. After so many years of living in Australia, I could not help expecting more to be done by the government to alleviate poverty, the major reason for crime. Then there were major health issues.

'If you like, you can look at the photos of the victim's body and the crime scene - grizzly if you're not used to looking at that sort of thing,' she said offhandedly.

I fanned out the photos on my lap. The first photo showed the dead young woman trapped under a branch, her eyes shut, her mouth purple. Others photos were of the branch lifted, revealing her entire torso bruised and punctured with deep wounds. I looked at her battered body from a range of angles and couldn't help shuddering. Beneath the group of photos were close ups of what looked like elephant footprints.

'Any information yet on the elephant footprints?'

'No. not yet.' The young sergeant flicked her long black ponytail as she negotiated a busy intersection. While the traffic demanded her attention, I examined the photos again, this time more carefully. Surprisingly Kosigo's face lay in repose. Once a warm and vibrant teenager, laughing and loving friends and family, she now lay on a slab in the mortuary. I thought sadly that once she had climbed the mountains, thrown handfuls of pebbles across the rivers, picked proteas and daisies in the veld and sniffed the fragrant orange blossoms in spring.

'Right, we're here!' Amita announced, pulling up under a wilted mopane tree.

The ancient volcanic bed in the National Park *interested* me but the idea of a dead young woman in the veld *intrigued* me. I was not obsessed with the macabre; it was solving a bizarre murder that fascinated me. Since solving my brother Hannes' murder, I scoured the Internet, read newspaper reports about murders and read several books on the topic.

'Follow me, but watch out for low branches,' she warned.

A high-pitched buzz, barely discernible at first, was amplified well before the putrid smell led us to the white outline marking the spot, where the body had bled into earth and grass. The veld was trampled on and twigs snapped. Amita held back the police tape as we approached a dark hollow. In a cool flash, I saw the shadowy bundle drained of all the plumpness of life. A glimpse of sharp vermillion and then the image faded. I searched for the source of the red but could not find it.

I stopped for a moment feeling unsteady. It was difficult to hear Amita over the buzz.

'Let's see,' she said, bending over the dark patch. 'According to the coroner, the girl was killed the day before yesterday. From her wounds and the torn branch, we think an elephant attacked her. It was that thick branch over there lying across her body,' she said, pointing to it. 'And there's the elephant's footprint but in this light it's difficult to make out.'

I bent to look more closely at the large, pudding bowl indentation. All I could see were ridges and bumps in the sand.

'I almost forgot to tell you that we found a few drops of blood on the ground here near the body. See how the bleeding starts from this big thorn tree and trickles down the bark of the tree to the ground. The Ranger says the blood was quite fresh, but we don't know yet whether it's animal or human blood. A murderer could have snagged his hand at any stage. Again, we'll have to wait for the results of tests.'

'Did you find her clothes or a handbag?'

'No, not a thing. She was naked. All we have is two cigarette butts. Benson and Hedges, from under the tree.'

'Ummm.'

More of my questions were taking form, when Amita interrupted my thoughts. 'The autopsy is being performed today. We should get the results fairly soon but the pathology tests always take a lot longer.'

'It's frustrating. Things take so long,' I added. 'I'm not used to it.'

She pulled back her shoulders and ignored my comment. 'One of the constables found a dead snake on that thorn tree - a six foot poisonous mamba. He handed it into pathology.' She took a breath before continuing. 'He said that the Blacks believe snakes are connected to witchcraft... and a lot more that I didn't want to hear about.' Her face was distorted in disgust. 'My God, I hate snakes.'

I shut my eyes, trying to retrieve from my memory bank what I knew of snakes in Black culture. The Tswanas talked with awe about snakes. I must have been little when Zacharias, the oldest Black man on Pa's farm, regarded as a seer, told me never to kill a snake, unless I was forced to for my safety. Snakes were revered in ancient Tswana belief as a symbol of speed, energy and immortality. Once I overheard Zacharias talking about a sorcerer who encouraged a snake to slip inside a man's body and devour him, leaving him depleted by diarrhea and dehydration until he died. Even though the story couldn't have been true, the gruesome idea of a snake inside a human body scared me enough to find a place for it in my memory.

'I'll just look around,' I said, wanting to absorb the atmosphere around the murder site, unhindered.

'Watch out!' I thought Amita said, as her voice melted into the background and the high frequency sound dominated once more. Suddenly, the branches of a wild fig tree shook wildly and a hail of fruit hit me. Amita laughed as I pulled the figs out of my hair and tried to brush my clothing.

'I told you to watch where you were going.'

I had company. I recognized the icy sensation. What did the spirit want?

'When you think of it, that's one hellava of a heavy branch,' she interrupted my reverie. 'The victim was on her back and the branch was lying over her chest, pinning her down. The assistant ranger was here. He thought that an elephant could've torn it off that mopane tree in fury during an attack.' She pointed to the almost bare mopane overhanging the spot that the body had occupied.

I bent to feel the scarred end of the branch with the tips of my fingers. Next to the flat scar was a sharp piece of protruding bark. The assistant ranger was in a hurry, I thought as I edged forward. Right up close I could tell, the branch over Kosigo's body could not have been ripped from the tree. The contours of the scar were entirely different. The two surfaces did not fit.

'Assistant ranger? How long has he been in the job?' I asked, while turning about and examining other trees close by.

'He's a newie, didn't seem to know that much. I told the boss to wait to talk to the older guy. He's on leave for a few days, but the boss is always in a hurry.'

'If you match the branch that was lying over Kosigo to… let's see now….' I walked deeper into the bush. 'To this tree here.' I pointed to a tree conspicuous in a surround of light.

She joined me and examined the scar on the trunk. 'I think

you're right. And you got it so quickly, too.'

'Just luck,' I said, with a grin.

'We'll take some photos back with us and I'll get the boys to come back here and hack off some of the trunk. Then we'll check if it fits the branch lying over Kosigo.' She took a camera from her inside pocket and photographed the trees, the branch and the ripped bits from several angles. I was certain that enlargements would give us verification.

'I suppose you realize what your finding means?' she said.

I nodded. 'Someone could've carried the branch and placed it over Kosigo's body, hoping we'd be in a hurry and assume an elephant ripped it from the overhanging tree. Or, I suppose an elephant could've attacked and dragged the branch with his trunk and placed it over her. Unlikely, but one never knows.'

Feeling in her pocket, she pulled out plastic bags and a spoon, and begun to dig the ground for soil samples. To back up Arnie's theory of an elephant killer, the pathology department was looking for traces of elephant pee in the soil. Once the bags were sealed, she went on to take measurements between the indentation where the body lay, the footprint and the trees. Then she was ready to leave. Why was she collecting soil samples and measuring now, days after the body was discovered? I had read and seen on TV that forensic evidence was usually collected in the early stages of a murder investigation. I doubted that the procedure was meant to be less efficient or different in Rustenburg. Someone had forgotten to take measurements and dig for the soil samples.

When we were back in the car, we talked about Kosigo's popularity at her young age. I asked whether she knew if Kosigo was any good at making rain. Amita's mouth twisted cynically. 'The Tswanas believed in her absolutely but who knows. She has a sister, Galani, who is also into making rain. But the story is that Galani is in Kosigo's shadow.'

The traffic was back to back all the way to Rustenburg. All Amita said as she drove me home was, 'Now do you see why our Chief Inspector needs help with this case?'

I did not reply. I was still under the tree, absorbed in the recent experience. Those spirits were nothing like the ancestral spirits that often visited me. I was used to the sudden chill in the air and the whoosh of energy, yet this was a different feeling. I felt dizzy and the surround of darkness was oppressive. I did not know whether Amita had noticed the spirits' dark presence or seen the deep red whirl. I doubted it.

During the last three years in Melbourne, since my earlier trip to South Africa, I became more sensitive to the glow emitted by all living things. Music, colours, sounds and natural beauty affected me more intensely than before, and my dead relatives were around me more frequently. My grandparents, Oupa and Ouma also appeared in my dreams and daydreams. Pets I loved when they were alive were there for me too, especially my cats – Zeke a champagne Burmese who lived to almost twenty and Petra an affectionate Siamese. I knew I was not imagining the presence of spirits. Experience taught me that if a spirit was trying to catch my attention, it would not rest until it achieved what it was after.

`Back home safe and sound,' Amita said, pulling up and breaking my reverie.

Seven

The ringing telephone woke me. I had been dreaming that elephants saved the devastated veld by uprooting large trees, in that way opening tracts of land for other animals to move more freely. The huge beasts brought down leaves from the tops of trees and tore up roots, providing food for many species.

The call was from Arnie Swart. 'Believe it or not, we might not need you for this case after all,' he chuckled.

'Explain... please!' I answered grumpily.

'Something interesting has turned up. We could have our suspect... Amos, a tour guide at the Pilanesberg National Park. He takes the overseas tourists on sunrise and sunset tours. While he was out with a group of tourists he came across the body, or so he says.'

'Why is he a suspect?'

'Phineas Phefo has been reviewing the case notes. You must remember Phefo. Well, he's been promoted since you were here last – he's Senior Sergeant Phefo now. He reckons there's more to this guy, Amos.'

'Mmmmm.'

'You might have noticed a few drops of dried blood on the grass, near where the body lay. Amos reckons he nicked his finger on a jagged branch the day he came across the body. Phefo being the good cop he is, somehow got the lab to do an express job and compare Amos' blood with the blood spatter on the grass. This time we have the results. It's Amos' blood, all right.'

'And what about the autopsy report … and, the pathology results?'

Arnie's sigh was deep and long. 'Still waiting. They move at their own pace… in their own disorganized way. It would make life easier if we had *all* the tests from the crime scene.'

I didn't reply.

'We've asked the coroner to check the body for any signs of the tour guide's blood. He's not at all keen on the extra work and I suppose it will probably take ages.'

I sighed. Melbourne's efficient police force was so far away.

He coughed before continuing. 'It's almost impossible to work under these conditions! I can understand why so many of our top people have left the country and are all over the world. But I'm not even thinking of going. This is my home – always has been.'

I ignored his dig at me and once again said nothing.

'Amos reckons that before his early tour on the day of the murder, he was in the canteen. To warm up, he drank a quick cup of coffee with one of his friends. This mate of his has taken leave to see his family, so we can't check Amos' coffee alibi. We've tried to contact him but God knows where he's gone to in Botswana. We'll have to wait until he returns in a day or two. I'll get back to you then.'

'We're running out of time.' I almost spat out the words. Everyone who knew anything about crime was aware that the first 24 hours was crucial in finding a killer. We were well past that, and still there was no clarity. Was it an elephant or a person who killed her? And if a person was our suspect, who was he?

When I returned home, I muttered to myself constantly about the fuss Arnie made about me joining his team, a team that was ridiculously inefficient. As I saw it, the cops minds were on the soccer, on their team Bafana-Bafana, and not on their job. The possibility that a rogue elephant was on the loose in the veld did not seem to bother them unduly. I would have to get used to it, the priorities of people in Rustenburg were altogether different, and they moved at a far slower pace.

Knowing Arnie, he was grasping at straws that would soon break in the wind. The last thing I needed right then was uncertainty. I closed my eyes and lay back on the pillow.

In the shower, my mind raced. Surely I did not have to wait for Arnie, I could start my own investigations. After all, I promised Nathaniel. Elephants! Elephants! As a start, I needed to build my knowledge base. I remembered that there was an Elephant Sanctuary nearby.

I found Josh emptying the garbage bin. When I mentioned that I wanted to visit the Sanctuary, he immediately offered to drive me there. It was far too isolated a place to visit alone, he said.

'I love elephants… I've loved them since I was a child.'

'Let's go, then.'

'One, two three, I'll change and be ready.' He was waiting for me next to the car, in black denim pants and a dark shirt, with a black leather cap sitting jauntily on his head.

'Your security guard.' He grinned, making a half turn to show off his outfit.

I gave an appreciative nod and handed him the car keys. I liked Josh and I knew how lucky I was to have him working for me. An added plus was that he enjoyed his protective role. With Josh driving, I felt safe enough to close my eyes and daydream. As we picked up speed, I was a child on the farm again with the rumble of elephant herds combing the mountains for trees with edible leaves. By sunset their trumpeting was loud enough to be confused with thunder. Only occasionally one or two wandered down to the outer edge of the farm. When they strayed, they turned about and joined the herd. In those days, there was no talk of attacks by elephants.

One of old Zacharias' charming elephant folk tales came back to me and I shared it with Josh. No man wanted the girl who was fatter and taller than all the others of her age, as a wife. Accused of witchcraft and ousted from the tribe, she was forced to survive alone in the veld. One day when she was thin and tired from digging up roots, her only diet, she met an elephant. The elephant helped her to dig with his trunk. Later he promised to help her to find wild cucumbers, tasty plants and berries to eat if she stayed with him. After a few years, she mysteriously gave birth to four sons, each taller and more powerful than the other. The sons then became ancestral leaders.

He laughed. 'I know that story... about the birth of the Zulu nation. My father told it to me as a kid. He said that we Tswana's should be careful of the powerful Zulus and of course, history tells us he was correct.'

Until then Josh had not asked why we were going to the sanctuary but his curiosity overwhelmed him. 'Are we here about Kosigo, the Rain Goddess killed in the veld... maybe by an elephant?'

I nodded.

At the entrance, a young guide greeted me but gave Josh a long look and disapproving sneer. He muttered edgily when I asked to see the elephants.

'I'll call the *Baas*.' He pointed to a gangly man dressed in khaki.

'Morning, I'm Johan Meintjies, manager. How can I help?'

'We've come to see the elephants.'

He beckoned us to follow. 'Mosadi, Moroela, Khumba, Thandi, Jambu. – all busy eating their breakfast,' he pointed each one out to us. 'Later they'll eat much more. A full-time job feeding them. Masses of food must be collected for them each day of the week.'

The immense grey beasts were still, only their trunks moved or an ear flicked as they suctioned up food. They ignored us and continued feeding from the huge piles of green that disappeared in minutes.

'If we gave it to them they'd eat double the amount. It's far better that they feed on this mix of leaves and vegetables than they strip all the trees. I don't think people have any idea that one of these large elephants consumes over 180 kilos a day and a herd of them can clear a field in hours.'

'Are they happy here?' I asked.

'Kumba can get cross sometimes and Thandi blasts her

trumpet when she's hungry but that's normal for elephants.'

'Do you think an elephant would kill a person?'

'You working with the cops?' he asked, lifting his chin questioningly.

'Alongside them.' I gave Josh a shut your mouth look. 'There's talk that elephants have attacked, even killed people in the past.'

'Oh, I suppose you're talking about that young woman who was killed in the veld recently. News gets round fast that the police think an elephant killed her.'

'Well, what do you think?'

'A lone elephant … it's unlikely that it would go crazy and attack a person.' Johan's voice was sharp. 'It's like this, if a person has hurt an elephant or his family, he'll remember for a bloody long time and then one day he could have a go at him.'

'Ah huh.'

'There is one time when the males go absolutely nuts and that's during *musth*. That's when we all keep out of their way.'

Musth sounded like a religious holiday. I listened while he explained that throughout their lifetime, male elephants have a once yearly rush of testosterone that is far higher than normal. The testosterone is so high then that it can cause swellings in the glands on both sides of their heads. The swelling secretes a pheromone that attracts elephant cows in heat. During this time of musth, male elephants can be erratic.

He lit a cigarette and inhaled pensively. 'A rogue elephant that has left the herd, was in musth and turned violent….is a possibility the police should consider.'

'But how can one tell. There's a dry footprint near the body… and that's all.'

'If an elephant was on the rampage in musth, his sticky secretions will be easy to pick up on trees and leaves and on the girl's body.'

'Thanks Johan. I can see how important the pathology tests will be.'

'Glad to help.' He flicked grass from his shirt and walked away as two trucks arrived to off-load more leaves and grass. While Johan was taking charge of the delivery, I examined the large footprints in the soggy soil and thought of the prints near Kosigo's body.

'There are millions of elephants in Africa and we don't often hear that they killed someone,' Josh said, speaking for the first time.

'That's true.'

When Johan returned, I asked him what one could tell about an elephant from its prints. He launched into a technical explanation I found difficulty in following, but I gathered that elephant footprints were as individual as our fingerprints. They revealed the size of an elephant, its approximate age and a lot more.

'I've made copies of some footprints. They're in my hut; I'll get one for you.' He returned with sheets of paper marked with shapes that reminded me of the painted potato cuts children made in nursery school. He pointed out the differences in front and rear footprints in both old and young elephants and then handed me a few pages. I thanked him and took the pages, wondering what use they would be to me.

It was late morning when we drove home. Children in rags begging at busy intersections took my mind off elephants. I felt in my purse and started to open the window, when Josh warned that the beggars at intersections were often a front for carjackers that roamed the roads like pirates. A tiny slit was all I needed to push all the change my purse held and some notes towards the children.

Josh was a mixture of practical wisdom, muscular strength and gentleness. During one of our drives he explained that he had his mother to thank for his practical side and that his father had encouraged him to develop his muscles. I imagined how shocked his parents were when they discovered he was gay.

We were halfway home when the traffic choked up. I craned my neck hoping to see a break but there was no movement ahead. Drivers shouting abuse, lent out of their car windows to find out the reason for the stoppage. Josh jumped out of the car to speak to the man in front of us. He returned with a worried face.

'We'll be stuck here for ages. The tar on the road has melted into the potholes. Of course the municipality didn't get round to fixing it. It's disgusting! Nothing works in this place.'

'They will have to do some repairs before the crowds arrive from overseas. Imagine what they will say,' I added.

Eight

I padded barefoot to the bedroom door.

'Sorry to wake you, a policeman is here to see you,' Josh said, giving me a concerned look.

'Ask him to come into the sitting room … and tell him I'll be down in a second.'

I heard Josh's mutters down the stairs.

A pee, face wash, a comb through my hair and I was downstairs in a tracksuit pulled over my nightdress and still in a daze. Arnie was waiting at the foot of the stairs holding a brown paper bag and smiling.

'I brought along some freshly baked scones, farm cream and raspberry jam for breakfast. All we need with it is strong coffee.'

I thanked Arnie, led him into the kitchen and gave the paper bag to Josh. With a flourish and bow, Josh placed the scones on a doily covering a colourful plate and placed jam and cream on the table. The coffee followed. His speed and style could have suited a posh restaurant.

Arnie waited until Josh was out of earshot. 'I see you've got a *moffie,* a gay guy, working for you.'

'He's a wonder.'

'He's well built … good protection.' He laughed, before biting into a cream scone. 'Do you know he was beaten up something terrible at your brother's place. Never found out who did it. The usual story, he wouldn't say.'

'I'm very happy with him. Couldn't be happier.'

Arnie sneered.

'Lovely scones, what a brilliant idea to bring them,' I said, licking my fingers.

'Tell me, how did your viewing of the crime scene go?'

'We're eating Arnie. Can't you wait?

'Sorry, I forget sometimes.'

I was keen to know whether he had charged Amos the tour guide but I waited while he wiped his mouth and crumpled his napkin.

He coughed dramatically, as if about to make an important announcement. 'Amos has a firm alibi which puts him out of the picture.'

I nodded and went on devouring the scones. Solving puzzles, crosswords, mysteries and detective stories, the more complex the better, had always interested me. Though I had not met Kosigo, her death touched me. There was more to this case than my selfish interest in solving a murder. I sensed that spiritual forces close to Kosigo were tugging at me, coercing me to find her murderer.

'We have another suspect now… Kenneth Sanele, Kosigo's boyfriend. Their romance started at junior school and they've been together all through high school. Apparently, he wanted to marry Kosigo even if she was too young for him. He's just completed his first year in engineering with distinctions. Apparently, he and Kosigo argued just hours before she died. I don't know much more than that.'

'He's a bright light.'

'At his books maybe, but stupid enough to have taken off when Kosigo died. Now the finger's pointed straight at him. No one's caught a whiff of him for the last day or so. His parents don't know where he is either. We're trying to establish exactly when he left.'

'But what about the story that a rampaging elephant killed Kosigo?'

'The rangers still won't commit themselves and we haven't got very far with our tests yet. You should know the situation by now.'

'I heard that Kosigo's sister Galani has filled the space left by Kosigo. She's apparently expanding her career. Isn't it possible that she was jealous of Kosigo and wanted her out of the way?'

He shook his head. 'Possible, but we can't handle more than one suspect at a time, we don't have the staff.'

I sighed. 'Working with you on this case isn't easy.'

He picked up crumbs and licked his fingers. 'At the same time as all this is going on we're rushed off our feet with a wave of robberies, murders and street violence... and there's the World Cup Soccer hanging over our heads. I don't know how we'll cope.'

I smiled sympathetically.

'We have to clean up the streets – get rid of the hookers, druggies and most of all the beggars, but as soon as we chase them away, they're back. We're spread thin but we'll keep going and somehow or other, we'll follow on up Senele,' he said, lifting his briefcase.

I pushed my chair back.

'Don't get up, I'll see myself out.'

He was driving off, when I realised that I had not mentioned my discovery of the mismatched branch over Kosigo's body. I put the thought aside and presumed his sergeant had given him the information.

⁂

I shifted my focus while logging onto my emails. A message from my archaeologist pen pal, Ivan Sherwell appeared on my screen. He suggested that we meet in Rustenburg at 6 P.M. at the Cosmo, a popular bistro.

Don't worry, I'll find you – tall, olive skinned, with lots of dark curly hair... wasn't it?

That's me, I answered quickly, surprised he remembered my casual description of myself in an email.

It was midday when Josh knocked on the study door. 'Lunch is ready on the *stoep* when you want it,' he said, with a twirl of a checked kitchen towel. Having a full time help made life more structured than I was accustomed. Meal times, cleaning periods and rest - all had to be adhered to if the system was to work. In Melbourne, I ate at odd hours - baked beans on toast for dinner if there was nothing else in the house or I stopped for take-out. If it was hot, I sat about almost nude. I entertained until late, drank and smoked when I felt like it. Now that Josh worked in the house, I dressed every morning and behaved more decorously. Having my meals served in my own home was still an uncomfortable notion. I was lazy and indulgence would soon take hold.

Josh placed my food on the table with a flourish. That day he wore a newly ironed apron over his matching light blue pants and shirt. A momentary look or gesture gave him a feminine look, yet the strength and speed he applied to cleaning and gardening chores was definitely masculine. Flowers filled the house and each meal he cooked was creative, though not always to my taste. I liked simple food and insisted he temper his preference for exotic and spicy sauces.

After my meal, I went into the kitchen to hunt for something sweet. Beginning with an apple, I finally capitulated and ate a small block of chocolate I had resisted until then. Still not satisfied, I rummaged in the pantry.

'I want to ask you something,' Josh hesitated. 'Would it be okay if my friend Karel stays with me overnight?'

'Of course.'

Josh told me that Karel saved his life. He visited Josh at the farm on the night of his attack and was the first to find Josh lying unconscious on the floor of his hut. He then carried Josh to his car and drove him to the hospital.

'The whole thing caused plenty trouble. My father and me…it's finished between us now. He had big plans for me… once.' He turned away and wiped his eyes.

I understood Josh's predicament and his anguish. Haltingly he spoke about his father's small farm where he kept a few sheep. He told me that he attended a good White school, meant to equip him in later life. When he finished his schooling his father wanted him to learn the practical side of modern farming, so that he could pass it on to his younger brothers. Josh explained how his father approached my brother Connie, to take his boy on. The idea was to train him while he worked on the farm. Josh worked for Connie for at least five years. During this time, his father was in the process of applying for government assistance to increase the size of his land so that he could grow tobacco. It was just then that Josh was attacked, his homosexuality exposed and the family's plans ruined.

'My brother won't make a farmer without me behind him. I've ruined everything.'

I pretended to look in the pantry, rummaging around, to give Josh time to wipe away his tears.

'Time fixes a lot of things, Josh.'

He sighed.

'I'll be out for dinner tonight,' I said. 'Cook your friend Karel something tasty. There's plenty food in the fridge.'

My Ouma would've been mortified that I gave Josh free run of the fridge and pantry. She lived in distrustful times, when the pantry door was locked. Each week she doled out sugar, soap, and cooking oil to the servants, as the domestic helpers were called then, and provided them with milk, bread and jam as well as the cheapest meat cuts that needed stewing for hours. They did not steal food but resentment drove them to take inconsequential items from the house - an occasional pillowslip or towel, a dish or cup. The more cupboards Ouma locked, the more little things disappeared. I must have been seven when looking for someone to talk to, I wandered into Betty, the house maid's room. Boxes of the soap Ouma gave her and tins of sugar were stacked under the bed. There were sealed boxes too. She told me she intended to take it all home to her family in a few months. How could I blame her?

Nine

That evening, I scanned the faces in the crowded bistro. A hand shot up, waved and a voice called out, 'Linda, it's Ivan. Over here.' He smiled shyly and fumbling, took my hand. He held it for some time before releasing it. We rested against the overstuffed seats, while he talked animatedly about the archaeological dig in the mountains. The tanned bald headed man was nothing like his description of himself as an ordinary bloke. From his handmade sandals to his intense stare as he pronounced his words in purposeful groupings, he was unusual.

I had bothered with my dress and wore a black slinky top with pants. My hair was styled and I wore a touch of lipstick. Ivan's emails were interesting but after being with him for only minutes, I knew that any hopes for romance were dashed. While he went to the bar, my ex-husband Wil's smiley face was in my thoughts. He became more appealing with age, even handsome, with those lines and crags. For that moment, our differences, the pain we inflicted on each other was forgotten.

Ivan returned carrying a bottle of red wine, and a carafe of water. He poured the water first and hastily cleaned all signs of the drips from the table with napkins. Ivan's finicky behaviour was irritating me when my cell phone rang. It was Arnie.

'I'll speak to you tomorrow morning,' I said a little sharply.

'Just a quick word. The Park rangers want to meet with us. They've performed their independent tests and want to discuss the results.'

'A huh.'

'Can I pick you up tomorrow morning, at nine?'

'Fine. See you then.'

'Something interesting?' Ivan put his head to the side and waited for my comment.

'Sorry about that... nothing important. You were telling me about the dig.'

He sat back in his chair and tediously explained the importance of 14th and 15th century Iron Age Tswana sites he was investigating. My attention drifted until he mentioned the San rock carvings he described in his emails.

His chatter slipped past me and my thoughts turned to Kosigo. Would the rangers have found anything conclusive to tie the attack and killing to an elephant? If they did, Arnie could wrap up the case. If not, it could be a protracted and inefficient investigation. Arnie's team had not interviewed her boyfriend, Kenneth yet. The excuse of the demands of the Soccer Cup were hard to swallow. Arnie was just coasting.

The clatter of Ivan's knife and fork drew me back to him. It was 8.45 P. M and the crowd had thinned. As we left the bistro, I agreed to meet with the crew from the dig for lunch. I kissed his cheek and we parted. Ivan was a rock but not my rock.

🐘

The next morning two senior rangers met us at the Park's administration block. They had conducted their own pathology tests and combed the area near the body. While they found the typical evidence of elephant urine on the sand and dried secretions on some of the branches typical of an elephant in musth, these signs were weeks old. On the other hand, they were certain that the footprints, though indistinct, were made only a few days earlier. The rangers could not provide suggestions as to how these two opposing pieces of evidence occurred simultaneously. Apart from the footprints, there were no other indications that elephants were recently in the vicinity.

I thought of the extra soil samples Amita had taken for the

pathologists when we viewed the crime scene and wondered what had happened to them.

'You've brought us all this way to tell us that,' was the only comment Arnie made to the rangers.

When I told Arnie that I was not surprised by the findings, he looked at me blankly. He was clearly unaware that that the branch holding down Kosigo's body came from a tree growing metres away from the scene of the murder. And he had no idea that both Amita and I thought it unlikely that an elephant could have dragged the branch to the body. If only I had phoned him and told him about my findings, instead of relying on Amita to pass on the message.

As Arnie pulled up outside my house, his expression was serious. 'We'll have to step up the investigation now. I'll give Amita a kick up the bum and get her to follow up the branch angle.'

'Right then,' I replied, lost for further comment.

'I'll get her to give you a call to fix a time for a visit to the Senele's, the boyfriend's parents. Let's hope they can fill us in on their missing son.'

Ten

When I went into the garden to scatter breadcrumbs for the birds, there wasn't a bird in sight. The strange thing was that I could hear loud chirping. Were the birds nesting in the roof? I went indoors to ask Josh.

He stopped vacuuming and placed his hands on his hips. 'Bird sounds!' He smiled his embarrassed smile. 'They're lovebirds. Karel and me own a pair each and we breed them to make extra cash. Come, I'll show you.'

I followed him behind a side wall to where an elaborate gold cage contained two lime and peach, small but stout parrots. They were beauties.

Later, when I was reading the morning newspaper over coffee and a croissant, I noticed Josh hovering behind me. 'Yes Josh?'

'I have something to tell you,' he hesitated. 'About Kosigo.'

'Yes.' I put the paper down and waited expectantly.

'I belong to a spiritualist group. We meet for séances every Wednesday night. Last session, I heard the people in the group talking about Kosigo. She wasn't a member of our group but they said she attended the Friday sessions run by Gabriel. '

When he stopped talking my questions flew at him. I wanted to know where the Friday séances were held and who the other people were who attended them. Who was Gabriel and what were his qualifications? I would have gone on asking questions if Josh had not raised his voice and held up his hand.

'Sorry to interrupt but there's a séance on tonight and we could go if you want to. Then you can ask all the questions you like. All I have to do is make a phone call.'

'Tonight! Yes, let's go.'

It was dark when we walked up the path of an ordinary looking house in the suburbs of Rustenburg. No one would have guessed that anything as unusual as a séance was to be held within its walls. Josh introduced me at the door, we paid the entrance fee and went inside. There were eleven of us of different ages and colours seated around an oval table. They knew each other and chatted easily, while we waited for the leader to appear. Sitting there, I felt like a child again, waiting to see a magic show. When the exceptionally tall and bony White man in a royal blue, satin Kaftan entered the room, my dreams came to a halt.

He welcomed us and introduced himself. The lights dimmed, he clapped his hands and then making dramatic movements, he lit three candles in the centre of the table.

His voice was resonant as he called on the spirits.

Let us join hands and begin our invocation. Dear spirits, as we sit here before you, we ask for your love and protection so that any evil forces can be released and negated. We speak as one, from the purity of our souls. We seek your guidance and healing.

I don't remember a lot about the séance, due to the incense and my dreaminess, but I do recall that Gabriel asked the question: *'Is there anyone with us in the room?'* The strange man did make contact with someone or something but I had my doubts that it was a spirit. I knew about genuine spirits. My gut warned me of a scam, yet Josh's face was clothed in rapture.

When the séance was over, I spoke to Gabriel. Close up he was pale and even more bony than from across the table. When I asked if he recalled Kosigo, he stared at his fingernails and then trotted out the line about confidentiality. When I told him that I was working with the police to find her murderer, he closed his eyes and placed his hand on his forehead.

'She was such a beautiful young woman and so in touch with the spirits. What a loss it is for us all!'

I persisted, asking if he noticed anything unusual in the sessions she had attended. He shook his head. When I inquired about her friends in the group, his expression was thoughtful.

His forehead wrinkled. 'Yes, there was an older Black man dressed up like a witchdoctor. And she did talk to him a lot.'

'Do you know the name of this person?'

'No sorry, I can't help you there.' Gabriel edged away from me towards one of the others.

I followed him and spoke in a firm voice. 'You said he was dressed like a witchdoctor. Can you describe his appearance?'

His reply was detailed, with a full description, from the man's arrogant walk to the leopard skin draped across his body. I found it strange that he remembered so much detail but not the man's name.

Though Josh was talking to friends and was keen to linger, I felt uncomfortable in Gabriel's presence and insisted on leaving. Josh was surprised and a little upset when I said that I doubted everything Gabriel had told me. 'I know he looks weird and he has some strange ideas but he's no liar. If he doesn't recognise a spirit during a séance he admits it. He's on the line.'

I said no more about Gabriel, and we drove the rest of the way in our own worlds of contemplation.

Eleven

Since the meeting with Ivan, I ached with loneliness. I could not help wondering if I would ever connect with a man who teased my intellect and captivated me sexually, as Wil had.

My thoughts shifted to Kosigo. It was two days since I had talked to Arnie and I wondered if the police were still attempting to find Kosigo's murderer.

With his usual energy, Josh mopped the slate floor. He held the mop in the air. 'Something biting you?'

'Ummm.'

'I guess the beautiful Kosigo is biting, eh?'

'Was she exceptionally beautiful?'

'Big, big eyes and a very sweet nature. Some people say the spirits sent her, like an angel. No one says bad things about her.'

'Have you heard anything more about that witchdoctor from the séance?' I asked.

'Sorry, no luck.' Josh kept on emptying a pail of suds in the garden and put the mop in the sun to dry. 'How about I make you a cheese omelet for lunch? You like cheese omelet. Maybe it will cheer you up.'

Josh made a perfect omelet, not too light or too brown, surrounded with delicately diced salad. He presented it with the pride of a master chef and to ensure that his creation was appreciated, peered over my shoulder now and again as I ate. After lunch, a flickering red light on my answering machine caught my attention. It was Arnie, inviting me to join him later when he visited the Senele's. Apparently Kosigo's boyfriend Kenneth was still missing and had to be found and excluded from the inquiry. I smiled as Arnie insisted that the situation was urgent, one he wanted to tackle personally.

Driving the short distance to the Senele's with Arnie that afternoon was not a pleasant experience. The wailing orange siren on the roof of the car gave him an excuse to speed from the town's centre through the barren landscape. Even though I knew he had trained to drive in pursuit, and every car on the road gave us right of way, I held on to the sides of my seat.

The car smelled predominantly of peppermint and my sensitive nose identified the trace of another smell as well. Brandy. Arnie was not looking well. His face had a yellow tinge and was as dry and lined as the landscape. Years of trying to stem murders in the homicide squad had obviously consumed the juice of his youth.

The Senele's lived in a new housing development close to Connie's farm. All the houses in the block were identical, characterless rectangles with a strip of a garden in front and a skinny *stoep*. We parked outside the house and pushed the wire gate open. On the *stoep,* a plump woman lazed on a striped swing enjoying the cool breeze. Her shoes and an empty glass lay on the floor next to her. Every few seconds she would poke the swing sharply to keep it in motion.

'Sorry to disturb you, Mrs. Senele,' Arnie said.

'Just come home and the police want something again. I told you people … I've heard nothing… not a bloody word from Kenny. When his dad is back from work he'll tell you the same thing.' Mrs Senele twirled her necklace made of tiny coloured beads.

It was not until I noticed the tribal pattern in the necklace, that I realised that the Senele's were Zulus. So, Kosigo a Tswana, had a Zulu boyfriend. Most of the time the tribes cooperated and socialized without incident, but marriage - the union of two families was occasionally bumpy.

There was not enough room for us all on the *stoep*. I stood and Arnie sat to the side of Mrs Senele on a plastic barstool. He greased her reluctance with a dose of his charm, until grudgingly she agreed to talk to us. The topic of her eldest son was one dear to her and it hardly took any time for her to talk about him with enthusiasm.

'Do you know what time Kenneth left?' Arnie asked.

'Na. I was working. He was already gone when I came home. Kenny is only twenty-three but he is just like his Pa. He takes off work for a day or maybe even a week, if he likes or decides to leave the house, and he doesn't phone home. He always does what he wants.'

'That's young people today. Tell us more about him,' Arnie said, his stool scraping the brick floor as he moved closer.

'Since he started university, he thinks he's better than us... and he's not respectful. He shouts bad words at me just like his Pa.' She gave the swing an extra shove and slipped her shoes back on her feet.

'And Kosigo? I heard he wanted to marry her?' Arnie said, watching Mrs Senele's reaction closely.

Mrs Senele replied that she had known for months about her son's intention of marrying a Tswana girl. 'It's better he keeps away from those people. They've got plenty money, those *Bafokeng* Tswanas, but they're no good. They're not like us.' Sweat poured down her face and she mopped it up it with a man's large handkerchief. She was adamant that Kosigo was an unsuitable bride and far too young for her son.

'People say Kenneth and Kosigo were arguing the day before she died,' Arnie reminded her.

'There was always shouting when she visited. I heard them and the people next door also heard them.' Her mouth crimped closed and her eyes were on the floor.

Arnie prodded skilfully, until Mrs Senele divulged what he was after. She admitted that Kosigo's interest in the spirits initiated the arguments. Kenny insisted that Kosigo cease her healing and divining work once they were married. He wanted her to follow the family pattern of starting a family early and staying at home to look after the children. Kosigo argued that since she was born with her special spiritual talents, it was a waste not to use them. Mrs Senele said she heard Kosigo yelling that the spirits would be like a grumbling volcano inside her that would erupt if she did not let them out.

Mrs Senele crinkled her nose in disdain. 'My Kenny, he's a big, strong living man, not a dead spirit. He wants a home and babies. With her it was always the spirits,' she snorted.

Arnie nodded understandingly.

'Where do you think Kenneth went, Mrs Senele?' I asked my first question.

She nodded in my direction. 'Some times he goes up the mountain. He's got friends up there.'

'Can you give me the name of his friends?' I persisted.

She shrugged. 'I only know one friend, Old Man Tobias. He's very good to my Kenny. You ask around, everybody knows him.'

Arnie scribbled the name down and then tapped his pen on the back of his hand.

'Sorry to ask you this, but do you think Kenneth could've murdered Kosigo?'

I could not help glaring at him. It was a ridiculous question to ask a mother. What did he expect her to say?

'No never, never. My Kenny is soft inside like the juice of the aloe. He couldn't kill anybody. You finished with questions now.' Mrs Senele wiped her eyes and placed her handkerchief between her full breasts.

Then Arnie asked to see the room Kenneth shared with his younger brother. After a brief search, he found nothing of note in the room apart from two large wall posters of elephants. Arnie pointed to the elephants.

'Kenny's crazy for elephants,' his mother said.

He thanked Mrs Senele for her cooperation and asked her to notify the police if she received any messages from Kenneth.

'The couple's arguments and the way he ran away makes me suspicious,' Arnie said, as we walked to the car. 'We'll have to find Kenneth. He could be our man.'

I was not as certain that we were on the right track. The link to Kenneth was weak and it did not feel right.

'Whether we find Kenneth or not, we'll have to wrap up this case soon.' He flicked a few stray hairs from his forehead.

Twelve

My friend Rosie's blue VW was parked outside the house. Asleep and curled into the seat, she looked like the little girl who was once my playmate. Regularly, she was called out for one medical crisis or another. Her way of coping was to snatch naps as energizers. I tapped softly on the window but she did not wake. She was in the realm of deep sleep and I decided not to wake her yet. I changed into shorts and a tee, put away my shopping and placed food in the oven to warm. After turning on the kettle, I went to wake her.

Rosie shook her head as if shaking the sleep from it. 'I'll get my act together in a moment.' In her haste, she battled clumsily with the car's security lock until she opened the door.

'Rosie, Rosie.' We hugged each other tightly and kissed.

'How are you?' I asked, standing back to look at her.

Rosie was indelibly stamped on my past. I had learnt so much from her. When we were children she and her two sisters lived a primitive life on Pa's farm. They shared a mud and thatch hut with her mother Tansie, who was my nanny. But that was a long time ago.

'Let's find something to eat and drink, then we can talk,' I said, steering her into the kitchen. We carried heaped plates through to the sitting room. We joked that we were like two sides of a coin – one in the light and the other the in shadow. Our understanding and care for each other during those early days continued through adolescence and into adulthood. When I left for Australia, we were parted, but it made no difference to our love for each other. Though we were almost the same age, as children Rosie was taller and broader and much to her displeasure, did not fit into my unwanted clothes. She owned no material possessions other than the dolls and teddy bears I gave her. What she did have in abundance was love – from her mother, aunts and uncles who lived and worked on the farm. We played together, made toys from coke cans, bottles and coat hangers, and played games throwing stones. When we pretended we were doctors and nurses, our injection needles came from the thorn trees and we pricked each other until we drew blood. We tore old sheets into bandages and practiced winding them around our limbs. Neither of us could have guessed then, that she would become a doctor and I would be a nurse.

While I was away, we kept in touch by phone and email, but now that we were face to face there was so much to say. Talking over each other, through mouthfuls of cake and laughing, we asked and answered questions about our families, mutual friends and work. Since we last saw each other, Rosie had moved on from her position as a paediatrician at the Children's Hospital, to senior consultant at a private clinic.

She could no longer stand working with the mass of abused, starving and AIDS infected children, many of whom were orphans that poured into casualty daily. They were patched up only to return in a few weeks. And then there were all the teenage rapes. She explained that it was impossible to shift the irrational beliefs held by some Black men with AIDS, that sex with a virgin would provide them with a miracle recovery. At least now, the government was making antiretrovirals available and the symptoms of AIDS would be controlled, if not cured.

I put an arm around Rosie's shoulder and gave her a squeeze. She was looking weary and plumper. Always so well groomed, her hair dye was fading at the roots and bits of frizz crept in where she had not straightened it.

'I'm exhausted. I was on duty late last night and then back again early this morning.' Rosie rarely complained and was grateful to be able to help those she could. She had struggled more than most to achieve her position. Like all the other Black children on Pa's farm, she attended a church school run by nuns and when the extent of her ability was realised, she was encouraged to apply for a rare scholarship. Winning the scholarship, gave Rosie the opportunity to attend high school at a convent. With extraordinarily high marks in her final year, she was one of the few Blacks accepted into medical school at the anti-apartheid University of the Witwatersrand in Johannesburg. While studying, she worked to support herself as a maid or nanny.

She rubbed her tired eyes. 'Some strong coffee will do the trick. I used to handle strange hours easily but I'm getting older.'

We ate and drank without talking. I waited patiently to ask about Tansie.

'How's your Mother?'

She shook her head and looked away. 'The TB is overwhelming her, but her amazing will keeps her going. I hate to say it … but she probably won't last more than a month.'

'Can I see her?'

'I think it would better for you to remember her as she was,' Rosie said, wiping away her tears with a crumpled tissue.

I did not argue with her, but I would visit Tansie no matter how difficult it was for me. Goodbyes had to be said or I would not forgive myself. An image of Tansie flitted through my mind. I was about three years old, my head lay against her brown satiny breast. She was warm and smelled of *mielie meal*, the staple diet. I was determined to see her. I loved her as much as my parents and my love for her had continued into adult life.

'Let's wait and see what she wants,' I suggested.

Rosie finished the last of her cake. 'Actually I came to talk to you today about Kosigo. I heard you were working with the police on the case.'

'Amazing how quickly the drums beat with the latest news.' I laughed and then filled her in with my meeting with

Arnie Swart at the National Park.

'Kosigo wasn't only intelligent and sensitive, but she possessed a rare caring quality. She spent time with young people who suffered from sickness of the soul, and somehow she helped them to find those first steps along a better path. Apart from her rainmaking gifts, people talked of her psychic powers – call it what you will. All the Moeketsi girls have that special quality that fills the gaps that Western medicine doesn't cover.'

'I'm glad you told me that, I don't know much about her.'

'I brought these photos for you. I took them at Kosigo's last rain ritual... three or four months ago.'

The first photo was of a slim, young woman in a white kaftan and headscarf suffused in light. Her hands reached towards the sky. The next, was a portrait. I couldn't help gasping. 'Oh Rosie, Oh, no,' was all I could say, as a chill seized me. This was a clearer image of Kosigo than the mug shot I saw on television. The shape of her golden brown face and full mouth were hardly different from other Tswana women of her age. It was her eyes - large, fawn and staring intensely – drinking me in.

'I felt I had to show you the photos, so you'd know.'

In minutes my involvement with the body in the veld shifted. Where previously I was interested in finding the killer, I now felt a need festering inside me.

Rosie must've seen the expression on my face change. 'You've seen her haven't you?'

'I've been to the crime scene and looked at the pictures.'

I felt my eyes close as I tried to expunge the images. There was nothing left to say. We didn't have to talk, our bond from early childhood, ignored her early poverty, the cramped mud hut that was her home, her torn but clean clothing and in comparison, my life of a princess. Rosie took both my hands, held them in hers and gave me one of her brilliant smiles.

'It's wonderful having you back here again – close enough to pop in. I wish you'd stay longer this time.' Her eyes had that little girl's beseeching look.

'I would like to stay…but I'm not sure about it yet.'

She squeezed my hand. 'Now I must visit my mother.' She gathered her bag and cardigan from the sofa and slowly walked to the car. She turned towards me. 'If you persevere and put in the effort, I know you'll find Kosigo's killer. I know it.'

I put my hand on the car door. 'Before you leave, I want to ask you two things.'

'Quickly, then.'

'Firstly, do you know anything about Galani, Kosigo's sister?'

'I've met her a few times. She's shorter and plumper than Kosigo but tough and ambitious. She likes to dress ostentatiously, while Kosigo was always in white cotton. Galani gives the impression of being less powerful spiritually than Kosigo and doesn't have the following Kosigo did, but now her sister's gone, she could come into her own.'

'Mmmm.'

'She hasn't Kosigo's natural sweetness and charm.'

'Do you think she could've killed Kosigo?'

'One never knows what happens in close relationships,' she shrugged.

'Just another quick question. Have you heard of someone called Tobias?'

'Oh yes, he's very old, a part-San recluse, who lives up on the mountain. A wonderful man! Meet him if you have the opportunity.'

'Mmmm. Thanks.'

'Right, I'll be off. See you between shifts.' She turned on the ignition and waved.

Stevie curled up next to me on the still warm sofa. I stroked the velvet fur just above his trusting eyes. Dropping my sandals to the floor, I spread out and burrowed into the cushions. Escape was what I longed for. I imagined sunning myself lazily on the beach, back home in Melbourne but thoughts of Tansie kept intervening. She was leaving us and though that saddened me, my concern was that she should have a pain free death.

The first time I met Tansie I liked her. Over the years, I grew to love her like a mother. She listened patiently to my babbles, played with me or sang lullabies. Gradually she taught me her language, Tswana, and we spoke it together. I was not certain if she had loved me in return but the way she kissed my hands and feet and carefully prepared my food should have answered that question.

Thirteen

Checking my email messages over morning coffee was a daily ritual. Friends from Melbourne had written and I had an invitation from Ivan to meet with his colleagues over lunch at a Chinese restaurant in the town.

I dressed carefully, choosing a skirt and top. Josh was in the kitchen baking biscuits. I could not resist a hot one from the rack. 'Mmmm delish, almonds.'

He looked at me and sniffed the air. 'Dressed up and with enough sweet scent to catch something?'

I laughed. Sometimes Josh's remarks were too personal and nosey but his well-meaning kindness overrode all of that.

'Chanel No 5?' He sniffed again. 'Definitely.'

I pretended I did not hear him and walked away.

By the time I left, the sky shimmered with heat. After several circuits, I found parking in the shade. Ivan sat towards the back of the restaurant with three men and two women. They stopped talking and stared at me as I approached. Ivan drew back his chair to greet me and introductions followed. George an archaeology colleague, had been at university with Ivan in Cape Town. Maryanne, Mannie and Carol were archaeology students from the Pretoria University. An older man with a wild grey beard, who studied me for some time without blinking, was Professor Falcon, head of the archaeology department at the University in Johannesburg. From the corner of the restaurant, a larger than life sized golden Buddha gazed down on us all.

The food took so long to arrive that by the time we ate, the restaurant was packed and noisy. One question after another about my life and work was tossed at me until everyone except the professor was satisfied. 'After living in Melbourne all those years, you have inherited your father's house. Are you spending your holidays here or moving here?' he asked.

I laughed. 'The house is comfortable and has a spectacular view of the mountains. It's my first holiday I'm spending there but it's much too early for such serious decisions.'

'You're very lucky to have those choices,' he replied earnestly.

'She's an amateur sleuth, Prof – not so amateur really, a private investigator. I've heard on the grapevine that she's working with the police on a murder in the National Park,' Ivan said with a touch of pride. 'The gossip is correct, isn't it?' he asked turning towards me.

'Yes, a young woman was murdered in the Park and I have a minor role in assisting the police.'

'Very interesting,' George said, leaning forward to be heard above the din.

My mouth was too full to answer.

'I overheard the bunch of Tswanas helping me out with my rock art grumbling that so far no one has been charged for a young woman's murder, but I didn't catch all of it,' he said.

'The police are useless, bogged down with crime and their forensic investigations take ages. I wish you luck in working with them,' the professor said with an emphatic tap on the table.

I observed George eat a plate of chicken and corn soup with relish and scoop up the dregs with a crusty bread roll. There were crumbs all over the tablecloth but he was too involved in the conversation to notice. He was a striking man with a short, coarse beard and a full head of unruly, flecked hair wanting a cut. Was it the tone of his voice, the tilt of his head as he listened to my comments or his interested green - grey eyes that drew me to him?

'Let's hope you help them to catch the killer,' he said.

'Are you the person who discovered the new San art

sites?' I asked, changing the topic.

'Now you've got me on my favourite topic,' he said with a grin. He explained that his work was slow, and that some would call it tedious, but every day or two he was lucky enough to add to our knowledge of San civilization. So far he had uncovered some new rock art, mainly the San depiction of animals.

'Are you going to join us at the dig, Linda?' Ivan asked, raising his voice above the talk.

'Yes, I'd like that.'

'I'll show you how to find us,' George said quickly. 'I'm on the hill just above the area where Ivan and his crew are working.' He rolled up the sleeves of his shirt, pushed his plate to the side and bent to retrieve his napkin from the floor. He felt in his pockets.

'Looking for a pen?' The professor handed him a ballpoint.

'That's where we are and that's the dig. It's easy to find.' He sketched a map. 'Now you'll have no excuses,' he said, handing me the napkin.

My gaze shifted to the easy movements of his tanned body, his eyes engaged elsewhere. I recognised his absorption.

After the meal, Ivan caught up to me. 'Hope you enjoyed meeting the gang and I look forward to seeing you at the dig. I'll email you directions.'

'I'll be there, George drew a map for me.'

'Oh!' His forehead lifted in surprise. 'See you then.'

I took the long route home. Instead of undulating hills as far as the horizon, pillars of smoke greeted me. Fire trucks had cordoned off the road. I reversed quickly and left the burning veld, though a charred smell clung to the car's upholstery. Travelling in an opposite direction, the dark mountains towered behind me. George was an attractive man in his early fifties, though he looked younger. I sensed his interest in me and would have followed my impulse to visit the dig the next day, if not for my cautious side.

Fourteen

The orange farm was my beginning, the cradle of my childhood memories and secrets. Each time I returned I felt the same delight. I stopped the car near the gate and crossed the road to the grassy strip, where a tall boulder commemorated the spot where my fourteen-year-old brother Hannes had died. I stood before it, aware of the link between us that would endure like the limestone.

My eldest brother, Connie owned the farm now, but many of the original workers had left him, to work alongside Nathaniel at *Mosego*. Those who recognised me waved. The kitchen was empty, the house quiet. My sister-in-law Raelene was out. The tangy aromas of citrus peel and fresh baking recaptured memories of Ma's orange puddings and fluffy cakes with orange icing. I placed my overnight case on the *stoep* near the front door. The house stood on the highest point of the land and from there, the orange farm fanned out before me. I wandered down the steps and along the path past the jacarandas, to the dam. As a child, I'd called the jacarandas the blue ladies and imagined them showing off their frilly spring dresses. That day there were no blooms and some of the trees were dead or wilting.

Connie was in the orange groves, where the trees were starting to bud. Within a few months they would be heavy and fragrant. When he spotted me, he rubbed the soil from his hands and rushed towards me. He walked with a bounce, had lost weight and looked healthier than on my previous visit. His abundant crop of export quality oranges and new varieties of popular mandarins, gave him every reason to look pleased with himself.

We kissed stiffly. Little else than our history and blood links connected us.

'Let's sit outdoors for a while and I'll take a break,' he suggested.

We walked towards the house, then up the steps together and sat facing the garden. He looked up at the gathering clouds and pulled at his goatee. 'The weather's changing. Who knows, it may even rain…but meanwhile let's have coffee.'

Emily placed a platter of biscuits on the table and poured the coffee.

'You must be the master's sister. I've heard a lot about you.'

She was shortish, in her late thirties with a round, brown face broken by heavy black rimmed glasses and on her head, she wore a white scarf knotted at the nape of her neck. Her stiffly ironed uniform and apron was the only firmness about her.

Connie moved his chair closer. 'So, tell your brother what you've been up to.'

I filled him in with details of my stay at Pilanesberg and my visit to Nathaniel at *Mosego,* but left out the bits concerning Arnie Swart and the viewing of the crime scene.

He fingered his goatee again. 'I expected that you'd want to rent out the house and stay here with us at the farm for your holidays. That house of yours would fetch a pretty price.'

'I love the farm, always will, but I want a place of my own now and seeing Pa left me the house…'

'Ja, Ja I understand.' He held up his hand. 'Well then… you know that if you have any problems you can count on me for help … day or night.'

'Thanks, Con.'

Having Connie on my side bolstered me up, made me feel tougher than I was. Though it was too late for love between us, he could offer me help and security. We talked on about the running of the house and he seemed satisfied that the electricity and water were functioning.

A dive in temperature accompanied by charged air arrived suddenly and interrupted our conversation. Dark clouds obscured the blue and turned the mountains purple. Luminous streaks shot across the sky followed by claps of thunder and cries of *pula* or rain, boomed through the farm. We waited, hoping. A sprinkle was a teaser but no raindrops followed.

'The bloody drought! I don't know how much longer we can go on.'

We watched the workers down their rakes and hoes; their voices rising in anger.

Connie sighed loudly and felt for his cigarettes. 'They can't take much more of it, either.'

'How long since the last good rain?'

With another sigh, he looked up to calculate the months. 'Since this time last year.'

He stood slowly. 'I'd better go back to work... sort things out. See you over lunch.' He walked a few steps, glanced at the overcast sky and with shoulders stooped, continued in the direction of the orange groves.

I thought how Connie had ensured that in spite of the drought, he had bought sufficient water for his neat garden, with its bordered flowerbeds and landscaped shrubs and trees. But the worker's families who owned small strips of land were forced to rely on the elements to fill rivers and streams.

From the garden, I picked a variety of roses and followed the path to the family cemetery. Just inside the gate, I glanced up at the sky and at the sun now glinting through clouds. All around a high frequency hum pulsed louder and faster than cicadas on a summer's day. I plucked red roses from the bunch, inhaled their perfume and kissed them. They were for Pa. *Red is for life,* Pa had said. Was it my imagination, I asked myself, as I sniffed the breeze? Was I detecting Pa's favourite aromatic blend of tobacco competing with the rose perfume? The vibrant pink roses were for Ma. She would appreciate the hue and scent of the flowers. As the sun slipped behind the clouds once more, my brother Hannes' headstone was dramatically stark. I chose brilliant yellow roses for his vitality and sense of fun. But before I could place the roses on his grave, one petal and then another, fell on the marble.

I did not linger at the cemetery. A fierce wind rippled through the thirsty veld. I passed a huddle of workers and though I greeted them they were too immersed in conversation to notice me. From my knowledge of Setswana, I understood that they were concerned that the death of Modjaji, the Rain Queen and Kosigo's murder, had caused the inexplicable changes in the elements. The wild sky that day and the sharp wind, they said, was due to the rampant evil around us. They insisted that it was evil that had prevented rain from falling for months. Why were the *badimo* allowing such havoc in the sky? And what had *they* done to anger their forefathers, they wailed. The group broke up when they heard Connie bellowing.

I spotted Samuel, Connie's right hand man. '*Dumela* Samuel,' I greeted him. He was digging a trench around an orange tree. 'If you have a minute, I'd like to talk to you,' I called. As he walked towards me, his glance took in the farm. 'The land is very dry. Today the sky say rain …but no rain come.' He threw up his hands in confusion.

Talk about the weather was becoming boring.

He wiped his hands on his khaki trousers. I stood silently.

'Questions you want ask me?' he said tersely.

'Have you heard anything about Kosigo's murder?' I asked tentatively.

'Aaaah.' He wiped his brow. 'The bad spirits bring the heat but no rain. And they take away the life of Kosigo.'

'Apart from bad spirits do you know anything about her murder?' I persisted.

He sighed deeply. 'The police, they don't look underneath … for the reason of the killing.'

I nodded.

'Lots of people say the boyfriend Kenneth killed her. Other people say the sister, Galani is the killer.'

'Why would Kenneth kill her?'

He gave me a sidelong glance. 'Is Missie working for police again?'

'Yes, I'm trying to help them to find out who killed Kosigo.'

'They need plenty help. They too busy to find the murderer.'

'You're not wrong.' I laughed. 'Well, do you really think Kenneth killed her?'

He shrugged. 'Kenneth stays many times with his uncle Tobias on the mountain.'

'Do you know Tobias?'

'For a very long time. He is old, half San …and very clever.'

'Could you take me to speak to Tobias?'

'*Hai!* I much too old. You ask Joshua to take you.'

'Good idea. I'll speak to him about it.'

'And what about Galani? Do you think she could have killed Kosigo?'

'Maybe. She's in a big hurry to be rich.' Samuel tapped his foot restlessly and stared at the orange plantation.

'If it isn't Galani or Kenneth, can you think of anyone else who could've killed her?'

The closed expression on Samuel's face told me that there would be no more answers from him that day. He returned his attention to the dry earth and I slipped away. Raelene had returned from the shops with parcels. Once I washed and unpacked my case, I caught up with her in the kitchen.

I was sampling her baking when a touch on my shoulder startled me. 'Starting your holiday in the kitchen, eh?' It was a familiar voice - my younger brother Vince. He had managed to leave work earlier than expected.

'Dinner's going to be late tonight but Connie will set up the braai. Why don't the two of you catch up,' Raelene suggested.

'Good idea, let's sit in the garden before the light disappears.' Vince tugged my hand. We carried glasses and a bottle of red wine through the back door. Vince found two plastic lounging chairs and we made ourselves comfortable. He pointed to a wavering light on the left. 'Remember, Derek du Toit? He lived over there.'

I followed the direction of his finger. 'What about him?'

At that point my phone buzzed. My hand was raised to turn it off but I answered. Arnie was on the line. He wanted to let me know that his boss had insisted on setting up a police caravan in the town. In only two days, several people had come forward with information about the murder. 'Most of the information will be useless but once we've sifted through it we might find something.'

Arnie could have waited until the morning to phone. One minute he was over keen, the next he was rigid and uncommunicative.

Vince handed me a glass of wine. 'As I was saying, Phil, Derek's son inherited the farm when Derek died, but his heart wasn't in farming. He sold up the place within two years. A bloke called Nel bought it.' He filled his glass. 'People round here say that Nel was one of the senior police called to testify at the TRC for unspeakable acts of torture and murder.'

'Hold it. The TRC?'

'Sorry, the Truth and Reconciliation Commission. I'll slow down. When Nelson Mandela's democratic government came into power, the crimes committed during the apartheid era were investigated. That's the basis of it.'

'Right, tell me more.'

'The commission was established in 1995 and anyone who considered themselves a victim of violence during the apartheid years could come forward and tell their story to the TRC panel. It wasn't one sided. The perpetrators – police, politicians and business people had their say as well. If those found responsible for crimes, *told it as it was from the heart* and could claim to *being part of a regime, acting according to orders*, there was a good chance they would be granted amnesty.'

'I don't know a thing about it.'

'It hasn't really ended, debate is continuing about the wisdom of the whole thing. Even though many victims were compensated, some remain unsatisfied, adamant that those who committed the worst crimes were let off too lightly and that justice wasn't served. I've followed it from the start. It was like the lancing of a boil, with pus oozing out before healing could take place.'

'If one thinks about it, the Blacks are amazingly generous considering what they went through during those terrible years. They could have easily struck back in revenge.'

'True. The Commission was meant to be a balanced approach with people on the panel like Archbishop Tutu, who talked of closing the door on the past. There are those who believe the violence we're experiencing now could be the result of pain that wasn't healed. We'll all be wise when we look back in twenty years. Now we're living through it.'

'You're very clued up about all this.'

'I've followed it carefully. Some very positive things have happened here. We have a vibrant Black middle class now and many more young Blacks are being educated. Scholarships are being provided to talented students studying at universities and when they've completed their degrees they'll contribute to the society. Houses are being built, more clinics set up but it's slow … a teardrop for the have-nots.'

Right then the sky looked like black suede dotted with shiny studs. Our hands touched. Vince and Connie were brothers who couldn't have been more different. Vince took after Ma, with her gentle and caring qualities, but Connie was not like either of my parents.

'Let's stop talking politics.'

'Good idea.'

'Tell me, how are things working out for you, Lindie?'

I mentioned Kosigo's murder and my role in the investigation. Vince told me that years ago, Kosigo had been a patient of his. She was about thirteen when she fell in a school race, injured her Achilles tendon and needed physiotherapy.

'There was a special quality about her, even then. I can't put my finger on it. She noticed I looked tired and kindly said I needed to care for myself as well as others. That sticks in my mind … after all she didn't know me. She was concerned and interested in everything, asked so many questions – not about her injury but about physio as a therapy.'

When Raelene called us, we picked up the glasses and the empty bottle, and joined the others for the braai. Connie had excelled himself by preparing a traditional South African braai with *boerewors* and the spicy lamb kebabs known as *sosaties*.

'I made the *boerewors* myself. Any good?'

'Delicious,' came the united reply. 'What did you put in it?'

'Just a bit of this and that – spices and a mix of beef and pork. I added a bit of lamb too. That may have added flavour.'

When we were drinking coffee, Vince asked about Tansie. He was almost as fond her as I was and from time to time visited her.

'She's critically ill. Rosie doesn't give her long, it's very sad.'

'I'm sorry.' He put his arm around my shoulder. 'If you want to see her before … I'll take you to see her. You shouldn't go alone.'

The rest of the evening passed pleasantly and I was able to catch up on family news and gossip. Later, when I climbed the stairs of the old house, I noticed that the old red carpet had been replaced by a thick green one. I smiled at the squeaks in the wood in their original places. Even though the home of my childhood held rich memories, I was certain that my choice to move to my own house was a sound one.

In the bedroom I'd slept in as a child, hardly a thing had changed. I stood at the open window, watching the wind stirring up fine particles of dust on the brittle veld. Bits stuck to my face and nightgown. Animals rumbled in the distance and I was certain I could distinguish shrieks of baboons creeping closer than usual in search of food.

The portraits of Ma and Pa in their silver frames were reassuringly at both sides of the single bed where I once slept. As I turned off the light, the moonlight slipping through the uneven curtain fell on Ma, illuminating enough to make her recognisable. I turned towards her. With Ma gazing down on me, Pa close in the inky dark and the sounds of animals outdoors, I fell asleep.

Fifteen

'Ma had another very bad turn last night. Aunt Nandi has been looking after her. I've taken leave and I'll go there too.' Rosie paused before speaking again. 'Ma's asked to see you.'

The awful news from Rosie was not unexpected, but I had not faced up to the idea of Tansie's death. I drove into Rustenburg, hoping that the activity of the town would distract me. In a café, I ordered sandwiches and tea but I cannot recall whether I ate cheese and tomato or beef and pickles. Aimlessly, I wondered past shop windows without focusing on the merchandise. Outside a photographic shop I heard my name called. I turned about. It was George.

'Hello there, nice to bump into you. I was looking at some powerful lenses for my camera …and there you are. What a lovely surprise!'

I was glad to see him and my coat of sadness slipped off my shoulders.

'I've been hoping to see you at the dig.'

'I meant to come this week. There are a couple of things I have to attend to first and then I'll be there.'

He walked with me to my car and left with a wave. By the time I was on the road home, my thoughts were once more of Tansie.

❧

A balloon of orange dust followed us as Vince drove me to Nandi's house. The small house was only distinguishable from others in the street by its colourful flowerpots and the fleshy yellow creeper trained to follow the curve of the front door. Rosie and her aunt, Nandi stood in the doorway.

'Thanks for coming, Lindie.' We embraced and Rosie ushered me indoors. Rosie put her hand up to stop me mid-sentence when I asked after Tansie. 'She's been asking for you ...you can see her now.'

My eyes were already moist but I blotted them with a tissue and tried to keep a tight control of my emotions. These were my last precious moments with Tansie and I was not going to spoil them. The room was cold in spite of the warm day. Lavender was sprinkled liberally in an attempt to mask the odour of decaying flesh. Tansie's face was gaunt and mottled and the rich brown of her skin had vanished. Clinging to her dignity, she struggled to pull a lacy bed jacket around her bony chest. After breaking into a spasm of coughing she lay exhausted against her pillow.

She patted the quilt next to her. 'Sit Missie. I am going to rest now ... to sleep... with my family.' Her voice was a husky whisper as she stared at me, as if she was drinking in every part of me. Then like the wing of a dying bird, her finger touched my hand. 'Missie ...is like my child'

'Tansie is like my mother,' I replied. The tears I could no longer stem, streamed down my face.

'You got big work ...to find the killer of Kosigo.'

'I know. I will try my best,' I whispered.

'*Modimo* ...look after you.' She pushed out each word. I realised her effort in giving me the Tswana's supreme god's blessing.

'*Modimo* be with you too.' I kissed her hand and left the room.

Nandi stood outside the door. 'Now we wait. She will be going soon... today late or maybe tomorrow.'

I looked away.

'Last night she told me it is my job now to look after you.' Nandi said, touching my arm.

'That's very kind but I'll be fine. Don't worry about me.'

She stared at me. 'Spirits of mother and father … they stay very close by you. They know trouble is looking for Missie.'

'Trouble … what kind of trouble?'

'Evil is watching you.'

'Do you see the Evil spirits?' I threw my question at her.

Dodging the question, she delved into her pocket. Out came a vial filled with a lilac concoction. As a midwife, Nandi collected all sorts of strange and often revolting bits of anatomy in bottles. At least this was not one of her pink bloody bits of afterbirth that was supposed to have magical properties. She shook the vial until it frothed, opened the stopper and let its acrid smell escape. I coughed and though I would've liked to run from her, I continued to stand beside her.

When I was a child, I guessed that Nandi was a secret *ngaka*. Muti in bottles and swatches of herbs lay around the house and she did a lot of murmuring to herself. Tansie often complained about Nandi and her spells. Once, when I asked Tansie if her sister was an *ngaka*, she laughed loudly but did not deny it. As female *ngakas* were once feared in Tswana society, Nandi disclosed her insights into the supernatural to only a few trusted people.

Nandi held the vial of lilac froth at arm's length, frowning as its contents turned a deep purple. 'Yes, I see that Missie must be very, very careful.'

When I was a child I laughed at Nandi and her prophesies and put any of her positive predictions down to chance. Most of her warnings were of calamities that rarely occurred in the powerful form she envisaged them. Like her warning to me that night, they could apply to almost any situation.

'I'll be careful Nandi. Thank you for worrying about me and warning me,' I replied, as she joined her family in the front room. It was time to leave.

Vince was waiting for me. 'You'll have rich memories of Tansie,' he said kindly.

Sixteen

'You're looking very sad. Waiting for a person to die is a terrible thing,' Josh said in his gentlest voice. Before speaking again, he gave the kettle an extra shine. 'Samuel told me you want to visit Tobias. We should go today. Mountain climbing is good medicine for the sad heart or the mind that thinks too much.'

He did not have to wait for my answer. 'Good idea, Josh.'

'We can leave after I've washed up the breakfast plates and cleaned the kitchen.'

'Thank you ...' My words were choked.

Luck was an inadequate description of my feelings of gratitude for finding Josh. After all, I was nothing to him - an employer and a White one at that. Many Blacks had suffered during the apartheid years and became bitter but he showed me only respect and kindness and acted as if he carried no grudges.

He delighted in being my mountain guide. Tobias was his distant cousin and one of the few relatives to support him during his recent crisis. When Josh was discharged from hospital, Karel and a friend carried him up the mountain to Tobias' shack, where he stayed until he was healed.

The morning was cool and mist clung to the mountains. Josh pulled down his knitted cap and rubbed his hands. I tucked my scarf into my buttoned jacket. Patiently he helped me up the steep, slippery path over rocks, and past sudden dips. I was not as sure footed as I imagined.

Tobias was old and highly respected but I knew nothing

about him. When we reached more stable ground, I asked about Tobias. Josh looked at me out the corner of his eye and smiled. 'When you want answers you're like a hungry lioness hunting buck.'

He was being personal again but I smiled back. He explained that Tobias and his brother Jack, younger by a year, were both half San on his father's side, a father they never knew. He ran off as soon as he found that their mother was pregnant. Born on the mountain, they grew up unsupervised until they went to school. Their mother worked full-time as a housekeeper for a farmer, who was a widower. Jack was five and Tobias six when they started school, attending only on those days when the weather was fine enough for them to climb down the mountain unaided. Once they were in their teens, they worked for the farmer who employed their mother. Both boys inherited the San slight build and agility, which made them useful. They climbed to the tallest boughs to pick oranges, squeezed into small places to retrieve things and lent a delicate hand to tasks like grafting orange varieties.

Tobias' affinity with animals was tested with sheep and by the time he was fifteen he was training horses. Soon he gained a reputation for taming the most unruly horses. The brothers were ignored by the other workers. The San were almost as unpopular amongst farm workers as Whites, but acceptance came after they had lived and worked on the farm for three years.

They were settled into the farm community when Jack had an accident. While he was riding his horse, it reared in fright. He slipped off and was so badly injured, that he lasted only a day. Without Jack for company, Tobias was unbearably lonely and once again became sensitive to the difference between himself and the others. He felt he had no option but to leave the farm. He headed for the mountain and from then on, he rarely descended. Fortunately he had frequent visitors who sought his wise counsel and did not visit empty handed.

Out of breath and slightly dizzy, I tried not to look down the sheer cliff and kept my eyes on bits of rock or plants directly in front of me.

'Eagles, jackals, bucks and leopards once lived here,' Josh said. 'Now they've gone to the dam, looking for water.'

'There were lots of stories about leopards on the mountain when I was a child, but no one ever spotted one.'

'Many people have seen the tracks and they're sure leopards live here.' Josh looked at me with half a smile.

'Who are these people that you talk about?' I laughed.

'We all have to believe in leopards. My people believe in leopards on the mountain. Fathers tell small children that leopards are always here, that through floods, frost and hot summer they never die.'

'All right then, maybe there *are* leopards up here.' Josh chuckled.

At a stark drop, he put out an arm to protect me. I could tell that my breathing was laboured. 'We'll take little rest now,' he said pointing to a group of flat rocks.

'It's a good idea that we visit Tobias. Maybe he can help… start to find Kosigo's murderer. The police are too slow and they don't care,' he said with a snigger. 'When you think of how many of us are murdered and raped in a day, a week, you know it will never stop. Never ever!'

The higher we climbed the more the mist clung like a wet suit. Through lacy breaks in the mist, I glimpsed tall ferns and creepers hugging the trees. That side of the mountain thrived in the hazy film. I almost slipped on a loose stone but shock alerted me and made my steps more cautious. At last, we reached a plateau and Josh pointed to Tobias' shack. It was tightly constructed from corrugated iron, stones and bricks – an eye sore but sturdy. A small, bent man, well past eighty and draped in a blanket, stood in the doorway. His smile was toothy, his nose a squat button and his face a crushed brown paper bag with two slits for eyes. He happily accepted the two bottles of brandy that Josh suggested I bring him as a gift. Much of what Tobias said was difficult to grasp - a salad of San dialect, mixed with Tswana and Afrikaans.

Tobias refused to look in my direction, giving all his attention to Josh. It was not the time to fight for women's rights. Tobias was master of his patch on the mountain, dealing with the wind and rain. I could tell that he was advising me of my lowly place as a female interloper.

The inside of his shack was well insulated with plastic of odd shapes and sizes and surprisingly warm. It was comfortable too. He had carved a bed, a stool and a narrow table from the tough *boekenhout* or wild beech. A fire blazed in a dented petrol can, blackened frying pans and pots, a soup ladle and two wooden spoons hung from the roof. Empty bottles and a pile of biscuit tins were stored at the back of the hut.

Tea was brewing and he offered us each a grubby chipped mug. A dollop of brandy went into our tea and he stirred it vigorously. He sat on his stool and we stretched out in front of the fire on animal skins. I pretended to sip the hot brew as Josh and Tobias talked. Though I understood snippets of the conversation, Tobias ignored my comments. I gave up and observed the two males talking and adding brandy to their tea. After what must have been at least an hour, Tobias grew more accustomed to me and glanced fleetingly in my direction, but still did not include me in the conversation. The more brandy they poured into the tea the more the two of them cackled as they gossiped. At last, Tobias banged two of his metal pots together, a signal that they had talked enough.

He stood unsteadily at first and turning towards me, beckoned. I followed him past the hut to a well-organised vegetable patch. He grinned proudly pointing to the full heads of cabbage and lettuce, healthy carrots, beans and pumpkin. Food gathering was traditionally a woman's work so perhaps that was the reason he showed me his vegetables.

Back at the hut Josh jested, 'If he shows you his vegetables, you're okay.'

Tobias delved into his pocket and produced a flat tin. He opened it with one hand and withdrew cigarette paper. The operation of placing the tobacco on the paper, rolling it, placing it in his mouth and lighting it was achieved with the same hand. A long, satisfied draw and he stood and beckoned to us both. There was something else he wanted to show us. The mist had cleared and we trailed behind him along a narrow path, curving between high boulders. With amazing strength for a man his age, he freed a piece of corrugated iron wedged between two boulders. Standing back and puffing, he leant against a rock until he regained his breath. He stood as tall as his bent frame would allow and plucked at a torn blanket, until he had pulled it back far enough to reveal a slab of rock. On the rock was a painting of a proud eland, the largest of the spiral horned antelopes that often appeared in San rock art. I gasped at the powerful and sensual image.

The artistic quality of the painting was extraordinary. The overlay of paint was delicate, a rich brown with rosy glowing washes. It was hard to believe that this work of art had been painted so many years ago by an ancient, San painter. Josh stood back to appreciate the painting. 'The eland is the most important animal in the San culture.' He moved in closer. 'Wow, and this eland's got power!'

I sensed too that the eland, suffused in light, emitted potent energy. After admiring it for a while, my eyelids flickered. I could imagine its hoofs raised ready to run, its nose quivering and its ears twitching.

Josh helped Tobias to replace the rock painting, and shift the cover in front of the treasure. Once Tobias had recovered his strength, he talked animatedly about how as a young man he had discovered the painting while climbing the mountain. It was a sign, he said pointing to the sky, that he was meant to live on the mountain, to remember that part of him was San.

Tobias was including me in the conversation by then and I was able to ask how old he thought the painting was. Using his fingers to count, he pulled back each finger in his right hand, started on the left hand and then shrugged.

Back at the shack, I asked Tobias if he had heard about Kosigo's murder. He wiped his eyes as he talked. Josh acted as interpreter. 'He says that he is very sad about Kosigo … and that Kenneth must also be very sad.'

Through Josh, Tobias told me that Kenneth had spent the weekend during which Kosigo was killed, and the following week with him on the mountain. 'Kenneth stayed with him before he went to *the big spirit in sky* Josh interpreted with a wry smile. 'After Kenneth left, an old friend visited to tell him about Kosigo's death.'

My cell phone was out of range but as soon as we were home, I would phone Arnie. He could scratch Kenneth off his list of suspects.

Josh looked at his watch and caught my eye. We left with Tobias smoking in his hut. Our descent was uncomplicated compared to the morning's battle in the mist. As we climbed, my memories were of being four or five. Pa was holding my hand as we followed a similar path down a mountain. His tanned hands held me securely and his voice was reassuring. I was not afraid of stumbling but of nettles that stung or creepy lizards. Mice darting across the track frightened me. About halfway down, Pa hoisted me onto his shoulders and we plunged into the bush. With nothing else to hold onto, I grabbed his dark hair. How could I forget the resounding laugh originating from his gut. At a group of rocks he stopped, lifted me onto one of the tallest rocks and said, *my little one you have the whole world in front of you, and isn't it beautiful?* Together we looked down on the vast dam, the rolling countryside and farms, the outline of the buildings and the smoke of Johannesburg on one side and the tree lined city of Pretoria on the other. If only I could find that spot again, have another look, I thought wistfully.

Seventeen

Rosie's voice was thin and strained. 'Ma died late last night. I thought you'd want to know.'

'Oh Rosie! I'm so sorry.' Pain gripped my chest.

'I have to organise things over the next few hours. Then I'll stay at the house for four days until the funeral.'

I expected relatives from throughout the country to congregate at Nandi's house over the days before the funeral. They would be sitting on the floor recalling precious shared moments or praying to the ancestors to bless Tansie's travels in the next phase of her journey. All the windows in the house would be smeared with ash, photographs and pictures framed in reflective glass turned to the wall. The door of Tansie's room would be closed and no one allowed in her bed for at least a month. Before sunset, on the day before the funeral, the undertakers would return Tansie's body to the house for the night vigil. Several sheep or more likely an ox would be slaughtered, to appease the *badimo* and feed the guests.

Only males could ascend to the rank of ancestor. For a woman, the prescribed death rites had to be followed if the *badimo* was to intercede with *modimo,* the highest authority. The *badimo* were believed to be all knowing and an integral part of the daily life of individuals and the tribe. Observing the correct procedure was equally important to the living members of the tribe. Observance was a means of ensuring the ancestors' benevolence and protection against misfortune or illness. An untethered spirit could wreak misfortune on tribe members.

As I sat at the kitchen table with my head supporting my hands, the intensity of loss was overwhelming. My sobs persisted until Josh insisted I drink honeyed tea. The heat and sweetness calmed me sufficiently to stumble back up the stairs and creep into bed. I had known Tansie was dying for weeks, but the knowledge did not prepare me.

She shaped my early years, taught me that if the group was to survive, its needs were more important than the wants of the individual. From her I learnt about the rhythm of nature and all I understood about plants and creatures of the veld. Ma attended to my physical needs but had been hasty with me. It was Tansie who showed me how to care through gentle words and touch. Together Ma and Tansie gave me the finest mothering a child could hope for.

⁂

A haze fell over the days before the funeral and I put the investigation into Kosigo's murder aside.

Early one morning Arnie knocked on the door. 'Sorry to disturb you, I was passing and needed a friendly place to stop over and… a cup of coffee. I hope that's okay with you.'

I looked up at the kitchen clock. 'It's not like you to be on the job so early,' I said. Josh was late, I thought, as I peered out of the kitchen window. Arnie and I had developed a strange friendship. We were not true partners working on the crime, and I was making hardly any contribution to the investigation into Kosigo's death. I saw myself as a shoulder for him to cry on, or share his frustrations. But, there must have been more to his request that I join his team. Though there was no attraction on my part, three years earlier, during my first visit, he had sent me red roses to woo me to bed. My cool response then, must have disappointed him and there were no further advances. Surely, he wasn't still hoping I would have a change of heart.

As I boiled the water and placed instant coffee granules in a cup, I looked at him. Though he had deep circles under his eyes, his smile was as jaunty as usual.

'A call from the chief woke me at dawn. A Black man from the Cameroons who came here for the soccer was attacked overnight and taken to hospital. He's a visitor and the Chief asked me to look into it personally. I'm on my way to the hospital now … but a cup of coffee won't hurt.'

Before I could answer him, Josh arrived looking rushed. He appologised for his lateness and tied his apron around his middle. 'Some toast with the coffee?'

'I wouldn't mind two slices with butter and jam,' Arnie replied.

By the time Arnie had finished his toast and coffee, I dragged bits of information from him piece by piece. The victim was Raymond, a popular witchdoctor in the Cameroons who had set up a tent in the Elephant Sanctuary.

'Naturally we're expected to make a show of police protection for all the foreigners here for the soccer. But I have no idea what this guy was up to or why he was attacked.'

'Elephants again. It sounds interesting. I wouldn't mind joining you, if that's okay. I'll dress quickly.'

'Fine ... I'll phone Phineas Phefo meanwhile and tell him to meet us at the hospital.

When we arrived at the hospital, Phineas was pacing outside the emergency department. He filled us in quickly. Raymond was employed by the Cameroon soccer team as their personal witchdoctor. As was the custom, each team had their own protector. The Cameroons team had won the preliminary finals and so Raymond arrived in Rustenburg well ahead of time to ensure a win.

I giggled. 'A witchdoctor working for a soccer team to guarantee a win.'

'Oh yes, every African team needs some special help from the spirits.' Phineas smiled.

'You're talking about voodoo?'

'The story goes that the witchdoctors sometimes kill a goat and bury parts of it under the match turf to please the ancestors. Before the match they fix the goalposts by smearing pig fat on them. They grease players' arms with the fat, wash their uniforms in magic water and make cuts on their bodies – anything to win.'

I couldn't help it, I winked and we all laughed.

Meanwhile, Arnie pushed through the throng in the Emergency Department in search of information about Raymond. While we waited, Phineas told me that Raymond was a mad soccer fan. When there were matches he watched the soccer at the stadium and between games, he set himself up as a witchdoctor for the locals in a tent he erected. Queues of people lined up to see him. Phineas made disparaging remarks about foreigners taking locals for a ride. He added. 'I don't know if they realised he's a witchdoctor in with the evil spirits and not a healer, a *ngaka*.'

The casualty department was busy but Arnie spoke to one of the doctors treating Raymond behind the curtains of a cubicle. When Arnie returned he said with a snigger, 'Raymond's unconscious now… been stabbed in the abdomen but he'll live to make more of that muti of his. We'll have to wait to hear what he has to say when he comes round.'

Though I was surprised Arnie didn't investigate further right then, I said nothing. There might have been some clues, if he or Phineas had taken the trouble to search Raymond's tent and speak to the workers at the Elephant Sanctuary. Arnie was merely going through the motions to please the boss.

We left the antiseptic smell behind us. As we walked through the hospital garden to the car park, Arnie stopped in his tracks. 'There's something I forgot to tell you. Remember the information caravan we set up in Rustenburg? People told us all sorts of stories that were dead ends… except for one.'

Arnie went into a lengthy explanation. Early on Sunday morning, the day after Kosigo's death, a doctor was called to attend a patient in one of the lodges at the Pilanesberg National Park. The doctor said he saw a black Land Rover on the side of the road with no one in it. He remembered it because it was against the Park rules to leave a parked car unattended or to wander into the bush alone. If one had car trouble one called the ranger for assistance. The doctor wondered why the Land Rover had been left there and where the driver was. At the time, he thought it may have been connected to the murder but did not report it and let his doubts simmer. When two days later, he noticed that the police had taped off the area close to where the car had been parked, he approached the police with his story.

'Unfortunately the doctor couldn't remember more of the license plate than the first three letters and that the vehicle looked new. The tour guide who found the body didn't report seeing a Land Rover and neither did the police or rangers. We followed it up and found one thousand Land Rovers that fitted the doctor's description.'

'One thousand!'

'Now it's a matter of finding the staff and the time to go through them all. An enormous task!'

What could I say? With the number of car jackings that took place daily, Arnie and his team would not find the time to tackle the mammoth task. With the burgeoning business for stolen cars overseas, the Land Rover could already have been in a container on the water.

❦

I pulled the curtain cord and stared into the dark. The half-moon hung in the starless sky. Tansie's funeral was to take place before sunrise. Many Blacks believed that *baloi* or evil witches were asleep until sunrise and therefore could not interfere with the corpse before burial. She was to be buried on Connie's farm, the farm where she had lived and worked and where many of her family now lay.

It was well before dawn when I joined the mass of mourners dressed in black. There were more White faces present than I expected - two of Rosie's, neighbours, the pharmacist's assistant, a bank teller and some of Rosie's medical friends .

The priest's incantations in Tswana and the soloists from the Church of Zion's choir singing with passion, were momentary distractions from the burial. Rosie, Nandi and the other women in the family, distinguishable by headscarves and sashes of mourning, formed a bank of wailing mourners at the open grave. Two of Tansie's older male cousins and her brother, whom many called John, rather than struggle with his given name, followed the traditional death ritual of shaving their heads.

Before the elaborate casket was lowered, family and close friends dressed it with a thick blanket and added gifts for its journey. First her brother, then relatives and friends filled the grave. With each shovelful, I shuddered. At last, her coffin was covered with a mound of sand. After the handshakes, hugs and kisses of love and support, everyone attending the funeral was invited to Nandi's house. I had attended Black burials before but had never been invited to the mourners' home. Follow the others, I told myself uncertainly as I joined the line of black silhouetted against the claret sky.

At the gate of the house, we began the cleansing ritual by brushing the graveyard dust from our clothes and washing our hands and faces in the buckets of water provided. Then the women washed down the path to the house. That done, the priest sprinkled holy water over the gateway and path.

Inside the house, animated chatter was interspersed by low, sad sounds. Male relatives carved the sacrificial ox and children carried platters of the beef around amongst the guests. The undercooked beef bubbling with fat did not appeal to me and I refused politely. In the centre of the room was a food table. Much earlier the women had prepared bowls of maize porridge or *pap* and green vegetables, to eat with shredded beef. A large platter of *vetkoek* much like doughnuts filled with meat, had been refilled twice and was almost empty.

'Time to relax,' John said turning towards me. 'You want a beer?'

'Please.'

'Let's take it outside. Come, we'll find a place to sit.' Carrying two of the packing crates Nandi used for chairs, John beckoned me to join him in the tiny back garden. He found a spot on the pathway between the vegetable garden and the flowers Tansie had planted in her healthy days. He took a deep breath and then a swig of beer.

'It's much quieter here,' I said.

'So, you're working with the police to find the person who killed Kosigo?' he said, without pausing for me to comment. 'The story that it's an elephant has to be nonsense. I know elephants.' He took another sip of beer.

'Ah hah.'

'You've found the person already?'

'No. Not yet.' I wondered why he wanted to discuss the murder at such an inappropriate time.

'Some people say Kosigo's sister, Galani is the murderer but I don't think it can be true.'

'Why do you say that?'

He removed his tie. 'A tie's a stupid thing,' he said taking another swig of beer. 'Plenty of people talk about the Moeketsi family... say Jeremiah Moeketsi is too happy with himself. He's rich and doesn't care enough for poor or sick people ... holds his money inside the family. They say Galani is like her father. Maybe she is, but I don't think she killed Kosigo.'

'Well, who do you think did it, then?' My voice had an edge to it. It was hot, I was upset and discussing the murder was the last thing I wanted to do.

'Ay, ay, don't get cross. We must not forget Emmanuel Tagoe from the farm next door to Moeketsi. He's a little bit crazy,' John said, pointing his finger at his forehead. 'And he hates the Moeketsis.'

Tagoe. This was a new name to me. 'Right I'll tell them to look into Mr.Tagoe as a possible suspect,' I replied snappily, ending the conversation. I did not consider his suggestion or ponder on why he had made it. I joined the others indoors, where alcohol had created an ambiance of artificial jollity. From my rusty Setswana, I understood that Tansie was being toasted and admired. Above all, she was respected for the way she had single-handedly raised her family.

Rosie left the group of relatives and came to talk to me. 'Had to get away from them and all that tribal stuff for a breather. I've grown away from it.' She took my hand. 'A brandy, please – neat,' she whispered, closing her eyes as she leant against the wall. I found the drink table and after a wait, secured a glass of brandy. In the jostling, crowded room I protected the glass from spilling with both hands. Finally, I handed Rosie the brandy. She swallowed it with long gulps. 'I suppose I'd better get back to the family.'

It was time to leave and I was making my way to the door when a burly man with an elongated, sweaty face stopped me.

'Excuse me, you're Linda Van Wyk, aren't you? I heard you were here and I've been looking for you.'

'Yes, I'm Linda.'

'I'm Jack Nkotsoe,' he said, extending his hand.

I glanced at his expensive shoes and silk tie, yanked open at the neck. 'So how can I help you?' My response was sharp and tired.'

'I've heard that you're working with the police on Kosigo's murder.'

I looked at the floor as I counted to ten.

'I'm a cousin of Kosigo's... absolutely adored her. All I want is to see her murderer caught and locked up for life. All the police are interested in at the moment in giving a shiny image of the country to foreigners... and to hell with our safety. That's why they need your help.' He waited, sizing up my reaction.

'They do have a heavy load, you know.'

He eyed me as he took a swig of beer. 'Look, I'm prepared to pay. That is if you put in that extra work to find her killer … and soon. Call it a bonus, I'm offering for...'

I stopped him mid-sentence. 'Look Mr... this isn't the time or place for a discussion like this. And I don't want a bonus or whatever you're suggesting.'

'Oh, I'm sorry.'

I pushed past him and breathed the cool, fresh air outside. I had been rude to both men but I was too wrung out to care. Family members and friends were in tight clusters, others who had drunk too much, had degenerated into bawdiness. I joined a straggly group heading for the makeshift car park.

Eighteen

When I lived in Melbourne, I forgot how hot Rustenburg could be in summer. I left early for the suburban shopping mall while it was still cool. Once I had parked in a shady spot, I chose a coffee shop and treated myself to cappuccino with a slice of luscious cheese cake. After indulging, I peered into the windows of the variety of stores that stocked almost everything I could need. I passed the stalls selling fruit, vegetables and food items. Some traders competed for the tourist dollar by selling scarves, caps and brightly coloured ornaments stamped with football logos. All I bought was a bag of fruit, a sun hat and some protective sun lotion.

'The policeman is back…again.' Josh said hovering at the door. 'Do you want me to bring him inside?' Josh wore his quizzical expression.

'Please.' I didn't mind Arnie popping in, but wondered why he had not invited me to a briefing at the station. Surely everyone involved in the case sat in front of one of those large whiteboards with photos on it and other bits of information, I had seen on television. I placed my half-eaten chicken mayo sandwich on the plate and stood to greet him.

'At last, I have some news for you. I had to deliver it personally.'

'Good, you are in time for a snack. Please join me.'

He placed his briefcase on one of the chairs and sat at the table. I pushed the plate of sandwiches towards him.

'Thanks, I'm starving.'

'More sandwiches please, Josh.' I called out. A tail flicked my leg.

'Stevie leave the sandwiches!' Josh shouted. 'Sorry, I'll get him out of here.'

'Cut a bit of chicken for him first,' I said.

Arnie ate hungrily. After his second cup of coffee, he stretched for his briefcase and extracted a manila folder. He seemed to take forever fiddling with papers. I yawned as I waited for Arnie to speak.

Inexplicably, the light in the room brightened for a moment and my body tensed as a pair of unseen hands seemed to push me against the back of the chair. The chair shifted and its legs grated on the floor. It was Pa. I could smell his tobacco.

'Everything all right?' Arnie stared at me questioningly.

'Fine. Just moving my chair.'

I straightened up as I wondered why Pa was visiting.

Arnie placed the papers on the table. 'These are the autopsy findings,' he said, patting the papers. He read parts of the document aloud. 'An initial deep thrust to the heart was made with a long sharp tipped object, probably a knife. It caused her death immediately.' He looked up from his notes and then continued reading. 'Apparently after death, deep rips were made to the flesh in the breast and pelvic areas. A knife could've done that,' he said scanning the document. 'But it seems that the killer wanted to create the impression that tusks of a rampaging elephant made those wounds. And … most important, it was a stabbing, at close quarters and there were no signs of a struggle. No defensive scratches or skin under the nails. So, she either knew or trusted her attacker and she didn't fight back.' He scanned the sheet of paper again. 'Oh, and there was also discolouration on the lips and mouth.'

'Are you saying it was definitely made to look like an elephant attack?'

'It seems like it. He was smart but not smart enough, eh?'

'The murderer must've calculated he'd get away with it. I suppose he knew how stretched the police are these days, that there are too many suspicious deaths for the pathologists to perform autopsies on each one. He reckoned that this murder would slip through the system like so many others.'

'Exactly.' He fidgeted with the papers.

'That powerful thrust to her chest. I guess it had to be a man.'

'Most likely, but you never know the way some women are built.'

'And what about that discoloration around Kosigo's mouth?' I asked.

He looked down at the report. 'Caused by poison but forensics haven't got a fix on the type yet. Apparently the poison made her sick but didn't kill her.'

'So, when will we know?' I heard the frustration in my voice.

'I'm pushing pathology for answers.' His left foot stamped the floor so lightly that if I had not been watching closely I would have missed it.

'Now that Kenneth is off the list, any other suspects?'

'Only feelers so far,' he said, looking worried. 'It's not a random killing but there's no obvious motive for her death.' He thumbed through one of his files.

'Yes, that is strange.'

'Black girls die here by the dozens every month but the public will be up in arms if we don't find Kosigo's killer. The Blacks worshipped her almost like Modjaji, the original Rain Queen.'

I waited for the punch line. There had to be more to Arnie's enthusiasm to solve the murder than the Black woman's popularity.

'Did you know that Kosigo is a Moeketsi?'

I nodded.

He went on talking. 'The Moeketsi family belong to the *Bafokeng* Tswana clan. With all that platinum found on their land, they received massive settlements from the mining companies. They're filthy rich and very influential!' He rubbed his eyes. 'I try but I'll never understand the things that go on with the Black tribes.'

I ignored his comment and continued with my questions. 'Have you spoken to Kosigo's family yet?'

'They've been in deep mourning and we were advised not to question them until later. But we'll be paying them a visit later this week. You're welcome to come along if you like. We'll have to firm up the time later, though.'

How slowly the investigation machine moved. On the one hand Arnie complained of being under pressure from the big boys and on the other he was hamstrung by tribal niceties that made the investigation crawl. I could not imagine a criminal investigation moving as slowly in Australia.

'Some of the boys in homicide have reverted to an earlier suggestion … that followers of Modjaji, the Rain Queen could have something to do with the murder. With so many people outspoken about Kosigo muscling in on the space created by Modjadji's death, it may be an idea to pay her group a visit.'

A tenuous connection, I thought, especially with the Rain Queen's base hours away. But Arnie wouldn't make a suggestion like that without a reason.

'I'd better get a move on. Back to chaos at the station. Our soccer team, Bafana- Bafana have a practice match at the Stadium today and that spells big trouble with the crowds … and the boys at the station.'

'Oh?'

'The women officers are working as usual but the men have gone berserk about the soccer. They talk of nothing else and it's a definite distraction. More than half of them watch their team on their fancy cell phones and refuse to work while a match is in progress.'

I shook my head in disbelief. Arnie was an irritating man but right then I couldn't help feeling for him. He carried an unbearable load, even if a lot of it was due to his own inefficiency.

※

A loud grinding sound woke me. In the dawn light a glass lightshade spun on the ceiling. Luckily, I was off the bed and onto the carpet before it came crashing down. The shade fell on the dent in the pillow where my head had been. In fright, I ran from the room, down the stairs and into the kitchen. Once I had made tea and toast with a warm drink, my fear receded. Perhaps the lamp was old and badly wired. Though that explanation didn't satisfy me fully, I could think of no other right then.

Nineteen

The road along the freeway took me beyond the town and towards the mountains. I followed George's crumpled map and turned onto a dirt road pitted with potholes. I was in the heart of the Magaliesberg ranges where approximately two million years earlier hominids once lived. Fossils discovered revealed that they fished in the clear mountain streams and hunted to survive. Much later, the San and then the Tswanas occupied the territory.

The precious land was scarred by war. I remembered learning how in 1822 the Zulu king, Shaka, ordered his armies led by Mzilikazi, to attack the tribes of that region. He scorched the land and decimated the tribes living there. Peace for the surviving tribes lasted only fifteen years, when the Voortrekkers in search of arable land, subdued the indigenous Tswana and established farms on their land. The Boer farms flourished briefly until the area became the scene of war once more. Then the Boers fought the British for sovereignty of their land in the Anglo-Boer war. Though fewer in number than the British, the Boers' familiarity with the rocky mountain pathways and their canny battle strategies, led to many of their victories.

As I followed the map, the windscreen wipers worked furiously to clear the dust. At the spot marked with a cross, I spotted a row of dirty Land Rovers. I turned into the bumpy area and parked next to them. A well-trodden path took me to a gaping wound in the mountainside, the archaeological excavation site. I stood at a distance watching the procedure.

Stakes and cords divided a wide but shallow pit into a grid of squares. Ivan, with map in one hand and notebook under his other arm, shouted instructions to a group of volunteers. They prodded the earth with spoons and trowels and then carefully passed it through a sieve. Any material left on the sieve was put aside for analysis. Ivan paced between grids noting details of any discoveries. When he saw me he waved, too busy to talk. I knew I would be in the way, unless I was prepared to join the others sifting earth. I waved back and walked on.

'Where's George?' I asked one of the young helpers.

'He's up on that ridge,' the man said, pointing.

The climb was not taxing. I reached the ridge, manoeuvred my way along it and found George examining a group of rocks.

'I wondered when you'd come up here,' he said with a broad smile. 'Have you snared the murderer yet?'

I grimaced and shook my head.

He produced a hard hat from under a pile of clothing. 'You'll need to put this on,' he said, before I had time to answer. 'Careful as you go through the cave. Lots of rocks and rubble lying about.'

I followed him and his bobbing torch beam under a rock shelf and into a shallow cave, where only slithers of light filtered into the darkness. He stopped suddenly. If not for the light we would have collided and we laughed at our clumsiness. As he shone the light on the sandstone rock face, the beam illuminated a large, graceful eland painted in ochre, brown and shades of red. I sucked in my breath. 'Magnificent,' was the only word I could find. 'So... so aristocratic and powerful ... and those big horns.' I said at last. After a while, I realised that the eland was not as brightly coloured as the one on Tobias' rock.

'It's probably dated around the late Iron Age but we're still testing.'

'Tell me all about it,' I asked, edging closer to the stone.

'The San's art is based on their belief in the spirit world. The eland was a sacred animal for the San, painted by the medicine men in the tribe to harness its supernatural power.'

George's eyes flashed in the torch light. 'Just think what occurred in this cave all those years ago, before a medicine man painted this eland on the rock wall. To connect with the spirits, he danced and danced while the women clapped around him … until he went into a trance. To put it roughly, the San believed that in a trance state the medicine man was able to tap the eland's power and with that power, he could make the rain and heal the sick.'

While George continued talking enthusiastically about the San, I was distracted by shards of light forming a halo about his head, emphasizing spikes of his unruly hair and stubbly beard.

George dipped the torch. 'Sorry, San cave art is my passion and I get carried away. Tell me to stop if I go on and on.'

We left the eland and scrambled through the cave to its opening and the light. By then he must have noticed that I was no longer listening to him and he stopped mid-sentence. Our eyes met and taking a few steps forward he pinned me against the rock wall, his hands exploring my neck, hair and face as gently and expertly as if caressing a rock painting. My eyes closed. As our lips almost touched, I raced with desire and uncertainty but I bent my legs and I slid free. If he was taken aback or disappointed, he did not show it.

'I'm hungry, it must be time for lunch,' I said clumsily. 'Let's join the others.'

He took my hand and all the way downhill we did not speak. We had lunch in the tent the archaeologists used for shade and refreshment. It was comfortable with a tall battery operated fan and gas cooker that they had cleverly connected. Though most of the food was already eaten, we found bread and cheese and heated leftover coffee.

We left the tent and played at being tourists, examining the rusted artillery and war relics from the Anglo Boer war that were scattered about. George's hand helping me over rocks and past dips was cool and there was a sturdiness about him.

'I was here with my wife Evelyn, a year or two before she died. She was born in the Cape and wanted to see this part of the country, make up for lost time and see as much as she could before ….'

'Oh, I'm sorry,' I said touching his arm. 'How long is it since …?'

'It's three years since she died and it hasn't been easy. One doesn't forget but as everyone says, time does heal.'

We discussed our children. I told him about my son Davie in the U S A. George had two daughters, one at university and the other in high school. His son was older and working. We talked about the difficulties of parenting and laughed.

'I'd better get back to the eland,' George said, with a glance at his watch and a smile. 'See you soon, I hope.'

'Yes, you definitely will.'

On my way to the car I passed the excavation site. Ivan was supervising the brushing of a delicate vase. I did not disturb him. In the car, I touched my lips. They burned even though we had not kissed. I was not ready to head for home and followed the road up the mountain, stopping at a point renowned for its view of undulating plains strewn with volcanic boulders. It had been Wil's favourite cuddling spot when we were young lovers. As I looked out, the view blurred and I felt unsteady. I took deep breaths but it did not help. Though I had accepted the finality of my relationship with Wil, my first and only lover, on a rational level, such a powerful emotional link would take its time to shift. The sudden strong feelings I had for George were delicious but new and unnerving. I was looking for signs, the subtext to his words and actions as I wondered if he cared for me or if I was just another discovery.

Twenty

'I've had some interesting news from Pietersburg … Polokwane, as it's called now,' Arnie's voice was indistinct.

'I can hardly hear you. Speak up!'

'One of the cops there heard about Kosigo's murder and remembered that a female *ngaka*, was attacked a few months ago in one of those touristy places in the bush, half an hour's drive from Polokwane.'

'That's very interesting.'

'He said the woman was stabbed in the breast and pelvis and died later in hospital. She was sliced with big cuts similar to the ones found on Kosigo's body… and this is the weird part … an elephant footprint was found close to the body.'

'Yes, that is strange. Did they follow it up?'

'Unfortunately not. With elephants roaming the area and no other leads, they assumed the woman was attacked by a rogue elephant and let the investigation go at that.'

Arnie decided to go to Polokwane on the Friday with Phineas to discuss the possible link in the two cases. While in Polokwane, he intended to combine the visit with a chat to Queen Modjadji's followers in nearby Tzaneen.

'You're welcome to join us. It'll be a great way of getting away from the madness at the station… breathe some mountain air.' I noticed the lighter tone to his voice.

'I'm sure.'

'About Kosigo's family, the Moeketsis … we're visiting them again on Wednesday. Are you in for that too?'

'Yes, count me in for both.'

'We'll be keeping you busy all week.' I heard him laugh heartily for the first time.

※

The phone call from Arnie drew me back to thoughts of Kosigo's body lying in the veld. There was no rational explanation for my niggling concern that I had missed something important. *Check, check, check*, my inner voice echoed. The open veld was no place for a woman alone. Josh had the day off and a long-standing date with Karel, but I had to go. With no other option, I contacted Amita. She was not pleased with my request to view the crime scene again but grudgingly agreed to drive me there. Though she said she was far too busy, she admitted that the idea of a break from work appealed to her.

The day was warm, the atmosphere in the car cool and tense. During our drive to the crime scene, she made her disapproval of my demands obvious by raising the volume on the radio's rock station instead of talking to me. At the spot where a piece of torn police ribbon still fluttered from a tree, she pulled up with a jerk. We clambered out and as I predicted, she slammed the car door. Hands on her hips and staring at me, she said, 'I don't know what you expect to find here. It isn't as if we haven't combed the whole area thoroughly.'

I ignored her and began my search. For some inexplicable reason my urge to examine the area increased. I needed to inspect the elephant footprint unheeded. Neither of us noticed a group of Black men in the veld until they were almost in front of us. Amita squared her hat, put on her official face and drew herself up to her full height. Using her most authoritative tone, she questioned them in Setswana. The men took a few steps back but sniggered amongst themselves. The tallest, maintained that he and his friends had every right to be there, as they were guarding the sacred site of Kosigo's death, protecting it from vandals.

'More likely they're charging people to have a look at the sacred site, she muttered. With a wave of her arm she yelled, 'you lot, get going! This is a restricted area'.

Cursing loudly, they disappeared into the veld.

When I last visited the site, the day was cloudy and vision limited but now rays of light pierced the gaps between branches. When I bent to examine the footprint for a second time, I spotted a blue-green feather pressed into the ground. I beckoned to Amita.

'Ah ha,' was all she said as she prized it from the earth with a scalpel and scooped it carefully into a plastic bag. She said she thought it looked like a peacock feather but identification was impossible, due to dirt and dark stains. As far as I knew there were no peacocks in the district unless they were strays from a farm.

'Glad we came, after all,' she smiled. 'I'll have the feather analysed. The murderer could've dropped it.'

'Or made a point of leaving it behind … his calling card or signature?' I had read that murderers often left something personal at a crime scene. It was possible, but less likely, that one of the many visitors had dropped it. I was beginning to like Amita a little more in spite of her officious exterior.

Amita looked puzzled. 'I've never come across a murder anything like this one before. There's something very odd about it,' she said. By the time she dropped me off at home, we agreed that the more we tried to make sense of the crime the less we understood.

※

During the night, I woke with my chest pounding. I had been dreaming of a peacock feather, its blue-green eye glinting as it grew in size. Eventually it was so large that I was small in comparison. Like a huge broom, the feather swept me into the footprint. I managed to climb out but the broom swept me onto the road in the path of an oncoming car. I woke terrified.

I interpreted the dream as a warning that I was in danger.

Why had I involved myself in Kosigo's murder, I berated myself. When her face appeared in my thoughts, her large eyes with that beseeching expression, I knew the answer.

※

Determined to have a lazy morning, I left instructions for Josh not to wake me until 10.00 A.M. My only appointment was with Vince for lunch at a bistro in the centre of the town. Gentle and amenable, he had always been my favourite brother. Happily, I dressed in bright clothing and tried a new hairstyle.

Vince was waiting for me at a seat near the window. We talked fast, catching up on news. After the meal, we walked a block and a half to an ice creamery that made rich and delicious ice cream. Lost in the delights of licking the cold, creamy chocolate, we strolled through a lunchtime crowd. From a side street we heard screams. Within minutes, just metres from us, a large group of chanting men carrying sticks and knives began chasing a group of terrified people. We threw our ice creams to the ground and ran.

'Let's get the hell out of here! To the car, it's nearer than the practice! The car, quickly!' Vince shouted to be heard above the din. I clung to his hand as he dived down alleys and around corners. From behind a column a man lurched in my direction and tried to grab me. Vince acted fast and gave him a shove. 'Come on … run.' He fumbled with the car keys. In seconds we were in the car.

'What's going on?' I screeched. 'Why did he try to grab me?'

'Shush...shush.' He put his hand on my shoulder to still me. When we were out of the town's centre, he turned on the air conditioning. I noticed how fast my heart was beating and the sweat beads collecting on my face and between my breasts.

'Shit, I'm a mess.'

'Look in the glove compartment. There's a towel in there.'

He pulled up on the roadside. 'Wait a sec before we drive

on.' His voice was hoarse as he bent over the steering wheel.

'Who are they?'

'Illegals from Zimbabwe who've been through hell since the upheaval due to Mugabe, and other Blacks refugees. There's no shortage of trouble in Africa.'

'But that guy who tried …?'

'Let's not talk about it now. It's not worth worrying about.' He looked at the clock on the dashboard. 'I'll drive you home, then ring the practice and tell them to expect me a bit later,' he said, delving into his coat pocket for his cell phone.

I said nothing more but I could not wipe the image of the man from my mind. I recalled my dream and shivered.

Josh was vacuuming when I entered the house. I told him about the violence on the city street.

'*Ag* well, we've just got to get on with the way things are here.'

'What about the police – can't they do anything to stop it?'

'Na. That sort of thing is springing up all over the place.'

'As bad as that?'

He nodded, put the vacuum cleaner away and returned. 'Wow, it'll be fun watching the soccer with Karl this afternoon. We've got all our nibbles ready.'

'Enjoy!' I walked towards the *stoep*.

We were lucky in Australia. Life was relatively peaceful. There were demonstrations and at times, things went wrong, but at least we did not have to pretend that it did not matter.

Twenty-One

A rnie's voice was tired and flat. 'An urgent departmental meeting has been called, so I won't be able to make it to the Moeketsi farm with you this morning. I'm sending Phineas Phefo along instead. In a way it'll be better for a Black policeman to conduct interviews with the Moeketsis. He'll be more aware of their customs. And anyway, he's a fan of yours.'

The air was still cool when I left for the Moeketsi farm at the foot of the mountain. I passed dry veld dotted with only Aloes and Euphorbia, and turned into a newly developed area with its recently tarred roads, small holdings and elaborate farmhouses. The *Bafokeng* Tswana's horizontally striped flag adorned with its crocodile tribal logo, waved proudly from most gateposts. But sadly, one farm after another was blanketed in the dust of the drought and rows of frazzled crops lay forgotten.

A life size *Bafokeng* crocodile dominated the strip outside Lot 42, the Moeketsi property. The farm's thriving crops and paddocks of fat cattle made it stand out from all the other farms I had passed. Could the Moeketsis have discovered a secret means of watering the property? There were no outward signs of hoses or water sprays and it was difficult to believe that Kosigo's magic had brought rain to her father's farm alone. The driveway edged with daffodils and hyacinths, at their peak of flowering, led to a large Spanish styled house.

I pulled up in the paved courtyard. Josh had told me that

Kosigo's rain rituals drew crowds so large, that they spilled from the courtyard onto the lawns.

A young woman dressed in a black dress, with white apron and cap opened the front door. When I asked to see Miss Galani Moeketsi, she asked me to follow her to the sitting room. 'You wait please.' She pointed to a chair.

Phineas beamed and jumped up from the sofa to greet me. Tall and lean, he moved awkwardly. 'Good to see you. And even better that you're working with us again.'

'It's nice to be working with you, too.'

Phineas hadn't changed much. Apart from a minor hair loss, he carried none of Arnie's dissatisfaction lines on his face.

'Look at all the stuff in this room.' He pointed to the replica antiques with gold trim, the velvet and satin. The ornaments were exotic, mainly Indian and individually lovely, but clumped together they made the room look like a junk shop. 'Typical of the *Royal Bafokeng*,' he said, emphasizing the royal so strongly that I looked around quickly, hoping that no one had heard him.

'I take it you're *not* from the *Bafokeng*, crocodile clan and *not* exactly keen on the tribe. They're smart though, have invested their money well and have built that enormous sport complex.' I had heard only good things about the *Bafokeng*. Several of the workers on Connie's farm belonged to the clan and he had not said a negative thing about them.

'While we waited for Galani, Phineas summarised the little he knew about Kosigo's murder. I recalled that he was meticulous about detail and had a photographic memory.

The maid stood at the doorway and coughed. 'Miss Galani says she's sorry to keep you, please wait.'

Phineas sighed and drummed his fingers on his thigh. We must have waited for another ten minutes for Galani to make her entrance, with two black oriental cats flanking her on either side. Her ankle length emerald kaftan could not hide her dumpy plumpness. Josh had told me that Galani only wore shades of green and that she owned several black cats.

Galani's oval face surrounded by a halo of black hair

was dominated by wide, dark eyes that flashed with dislike. 'You police ... you should leave us alone at our time of mourning. Detective Inspector Swart was here the other day with questions and now you two are here.' Her glare was stony. When two of the cats broke from their position under Galani's gown and made straight for me, tails high and noses twitching, she called them sharply. 'Orion, Pluto, come back to Mama right now!'

Cats do their own thing and though they may have heard the command, they were drawn to me and allowed me to stroke their sleek fur.

'They can tell I own a cat I love,' I said to placate her.

Phineas chose his words carefully. 'I'm sorry, but if we're going to find Kosigo's murderer we have to ask you and your family questions. After all, you're Kosigo's closest relatives ... but of course we do respect your grief at this sad time.' He then explained Arnie Swart's absence and my presence.

'Do you know that Detective Inspector Swart had the nerve to imply that we have sprinklers hidden underground to keep our property green?' She rubbed her forehead.

'He's a policeman who understands only what he sees, so forgive him,' Phineas replied, but avoided asking the obvious question about the water source.

Galani sat on the edge of the couch and sighed. 'Kosigo was very sick, so sick that she cancelled all her appointments with clients for psychic readings, but I can't believe she was murdered.' She wiped her tears with a bunch of tissues. Sniffling as she spoke, Galani told us that before Kosigo died she was weak and tired, barely ate and looked dreadful. When none of the *ngakas* she had consulted could diagnose what was ailing her, she saw a white doctor in Rustenburg. He thought she had an unusual virus, and that good food and rest would cure her. She refused to take his advice and instead wandered about.'

'Before her death, did she arrange any meetings?' Phineas asked.

'I don't think so.' Galani looked up remembering. 'She went out briefly on the day before she died but I don't know where she went. I begged her to stay in bed but she wouldn't listen.' Galani began to cry. 'I should've stopped her. I should've... she could've been meeting her killer.'

'You couldn't have known.' Phineas said attempting to reassure her.

She nodded and wiped her eyes. I did not warm to Galani in spite of her sorrow.

'Our only comfort is that Kosigo's spirit is still with us. It will leave us to rest later and enter the ethos, but for now it is here,' she said, smoothing the material of her kaftan.

Phineas looked at me out the corner of his eye and suppressed a smile.

'Kosigo was so talented. She had the gift of clairvoyance. I have it too of course... but I can't tell you how accurate she was, and at such a young age too. People came from Jo'burg and Pretoria and further to consult her. In a few years she would've built her reputation.'

'I heard that you will be holding a rain ritual soon,' Phineas cut in.

'True but I haven't fixed a date yet.'

'Do you think it's possible that a dissatisfied client could have killed her?' he asked.

'As far as I know, everyone loved her and as I said, she was very accurate in her readings. I can't imagine a client murdering her. She didn't mention anyone who was dissatisfied.'

'What about the servants? One of them could've had a grudge against her?'

'Oh no! She treated the servants like friends.'

Phineas tapped his knee impatiently. 'I have to ask you this... police procedure. Where were you on the day Kosigo died?'

Galani looked flustered and took several seconds to answer. She explained that she was at home all day, working in the kitchen making potions. 'That's one of my skills. I get lots of orders for my healing medicines from Europe, Asia and Australia. I make remedies for insomnia, gout, coughs, constipation, colds, love potions, aromatherapy essences and lots more.' She was adamant that the servants had seen her working and even cleaned up after she had finished.

'I will have to talk to them but meanwhile you could tell us something about the rest of your family,' Phineas said, opening his notebook. Speaking gently he teased out the information we were after. She told us about her sister Thabang, who worked on the property as a herbalist. And that her father was elderly but still ran the farm, with the help of her cousin Baba.

'Kosigo's death almost killed my father. He hasn't come out of his bedroom for days.'

'I see,' Phineas said, as he walked to the corner of the room and examined the items on the table. He turned to her. 'You have some very attractive things … and that box on the coffee table. Chocolates?'

'Oh yes, sent by one of my admirers.' She smiled at us in turn. 'Have one, we've all been eating them. They're handmade, some with liqueur or unusual centres.'

I went over to the table and lifted the heart shaped box with its gold quilted lid. 'This looks interesting.' The chocolates were decorated with swirls and twirls and nut clusters.

'Absolutely delicious. Please, go ahead and have one,' she repeated. 'Nothing on the shelves can beat them. So many different flavours that you won't believe the inventiveness. I'm hooked.'

'No thanks.' I replied. It was too early in the day and I had not developed a taste for such rich chocolate.

Phineas scratched his head with his pen. 'I'm sure I've seen a box of chocolates just like this before… in that sorcerer Raymond's tent,' he said to me softly. Then facing Galani he asked,' you're absolutely certain that they're handmade?'

'Yes, I'm certain and before you ask, no, I don't know who made them.' She scowled and shifted her position on the couch. 'But what have the chocolates to do with the murder of my sister?'

Phineas dismissed her question with a wave of his hand. 'We'd like to talk to your cousin Baba if he's available.'

Galani called the maid, who was hovering in the doorway.

'Keneuoe take them to *Baas Baba,* I'm too tired.'

We followed Keneuoe through the herb garden and past the small but thriving tobacco crop. She disappeared into the foliage and we waited while she looked for Baba. A brawny young man as tall as Nathaniel ambled towards us. He greeted us grumpily, adamant that he had been working on the land at the time of the murder and had not left the farm. His team of workers verified his alibi immediately. When I asked him if any of the workers had a grudge against Kosigo or the family, he laughed. 'A jewel, that girl, who wouldn't like her... and murder her. *Aikona!*'

I smiled at the word he'd used. There wasn't an English word like *aikona* to describe that adamant *no.*

'I believe the oldest sister, Thabang, a herbalist, works here too.' Phineas said, tapping the ground impatiently.

'All three girls have blessings from the spirits. Poor Thabang has taken her sister's death so badly. She is working again but her heart isn't in it. She says that at least work keeps her mind off Kosigo's horrible death.'

Baba escorted us to Thabang's small consulting room in a corner of the garden. Three patients sat on a bench waiting to see her. Rather than disturb her, we explored the property. The land behind her room dipped, revealing a partially filled dam. An idyllic picture with families of ducks gliding and birds swooping to wet their feathers. On the dam's tree lined side, fat cattle vied for drinking places and sheep rested under hanging branches. The Moeketsi's were fortunate, a mountain stream at the high end of the property trickled into the dam.

'I'm having a quick look at this stream,' Phineas called out.

I sat on the grass while Phineas pushed back reeds and clumps of weeds and made his way along the bank. He was puffed when he returned and sat next to me. Excitedly he talked about the mechanics of the dam's sluice gates, but he lost me with his wealth of technical information.

'Do you think it's the water from the dam that has kept the whole farm so green?'

'Not lately.' He shook his head. 'There's not enough of it.'

It was midday when we returned to Thabang's room to find the door still closed. While we waited, I asked Phineas what was important about the box of chocolates.'

'I noticed an identical half eaten box in Raymond's tent. It stuck in my mind but probably means nothing.'

The door opened as the last patient left and a petite woman behind the desk looked unhappy when she saw us. 'I'm finished consulting for today. You'll have to come back tomorrow.'

Phineas explained our presence.

'My apologies, I took you for patients. Please come inside and sit down. Anything I can do to assist, tell me. I want to see Kosigo's killer caught and charged as soon as possible.'

I could not help staring at her. She resembled Kosigo physically but was slimmer and older. Phineas did not have to ask Thabang to account for her movements on the day Kosigo died. She placed her diary on the desk. On that day, the page was crammed with appointments. It would have been extremely difficult for her to slip out, kill Kosigo, cover up the murder and be back in time for her sessions.

We left her room together and talked as we walked through the garden.

'It's hard to imagine Kosigo's gone. She was such a vibrant person. Everybody I know loved her, apart from a few of Modjaji, the Rain Queen's groupies, who saw her as imposter,' Thabang said in her matter of fact manner. 'I'm the one who uses the computer most, keeping up to date with herbal trends on the net, so I saw the emails from the Modjaji followers first. The emails started arriving months before Kosigo died, accusing her of attempting to undermine the power of the Rain Queen, ordering her to stop her rain making rituals.'

'Ordering her to stop?' Phineas eyes flickered with interest.

Thabang shrugged. 'No doubt about it, Modjaji was the true Rain Queen. Kosigo was still in her teens, a sardine in the pool.'

'Well, did you take the messages seriously?'

'Not really, I thought the Modjaji folks were just making noises. But I suppose they saw Kosigo maturing into a diviner whose popularity could eventually steer people away from the Queen and preferred her out of the way early.'

'Did you keep any of the messages?' I asked.

'I deleted them, but they must still be on the computer.'

'We'd appreciate you recovering them and printing them out for us.' Phineas said.

We walked in silence across the daisy-speckled lawn in need of mowing. Her step was energetic and in spite of her sadness she talked freely, proudly telling us that all her female relatives she knew of as far back as their great, great grandmother, had been talented in the art of psychic healing and rain making. I could not help wondering why it was Galani and not the less ostentatious Thabang, who was pursuing a career as a clairvoyant and rainmaker.

Phineas looked at his watch. 'I wanted to interview the servants but it will have to wait. I must make a few quick notes and then I'll be going.'

Twenty-Two

'I'll stay on a bit,' I said. 'I'd like to see the garden if that's okay with you, Thabang?'

'I'm always pleased to show off our garden, even at such a sad time,' she said with an attempt at a smile. Rows of pansies, violets and marigolds were flourishing and straw baskets of impatiens swayed under the trees. We left Phineas making his notes and passed under an umbrellas of branches to a wide area of lawn. There seven life size crocodiles stood in circular formation around a charred, stone altar. It was an imposing sight.

'Seven because of the ancient African belief in the seven powers of the spirit ...and the crocodile is our totem,' Thabang began to explain, but I held up my hand to stop her. Tansie had taught me that each Tswana clan could be identified through a sacred animal or totem, the group's protector. An animal chosen as a totem was never hunted, killed or eaten and even its fur or skin remained untouched. The clan that Tansie and Nathaniel belonged to, the *Bahuruthes*, had a baboon as a totem. I remembered her saying, *baboon is very clever like a person. He is in the trees and on the land and if someone attacks he can bite very hard.*

'No ordinary crocodile,' I said moving up close to one of the statues. 'The closed jaws and short tail make it look like a peaceful non-aggressive croc and the two legs give an almost human appearance.'

She gave me her first full smile. 'That's the idea.' She stopped and stared at me. 'I'm picking up strong vibes about you - another intuitive, I think?'

I shrugged.

She smiled again and pointed to the altar. 'That's where Kosigo performed sacrifices to make the rain gods happy.' She watched me for a reaction and seemed surprised that I was not shocked. Sacrifices went back to Solomon's Temple, the Druids, the San, and many others who burnt animals to appease their gods.

'Chickens, wild ducks and rabbits mostly... but at special times she burnt a buck, sheep or even an ox to ask for blessings from the ancestors.'

'Who is going to perform the rain rituals now?' I asked.

'I suppose Galani will be making the sacrifices for rain now. She enjoys the theatrical side of healing and prayer.'

'Uh huh.'

I followed her across the lawn and down a slope to the herb garden. There luscious plants were laid out in squares outlined with bricks. Thabang pointed out culinary herbs and showed me the area where medicinal herbs like Golden Seal and Feverfew grew beside Chamomile, St John's Wort and Burdock. The cats like mini panthers, moved through the herbs, nibbling as they fancied. As I bent to stroke a sinuous oriental in front of me, I slipped on one of the retaining bricks and fell.

'Oh! My ankle!' I called out in pain. I tried to scramble up, but I couldn't.

Thabang rushed over to me and felt my foot. 'Nothing broken but you've sprained your ankle. We'll get you back to the house and then decide what to do.' A shrill whistle through her teeth and a gardener appeared. 'Please call some of the men, we'll have to carry Mrs Van Wyk back to the house.'

'Help me up and I'll make it, I don't want a fuss,' I said in a brave voice. She ignored my protestations and four men arrived with a folded sheet tied onto four branches. They lifted me and then carried me to a downstairs bedroom and placed me on the bed. An embarrassing experience!

Thabang tended to my foot. Her hands were cool as she

expertly felt for the painful spot. Certain I had sprained the ankle, she applied a herbal compress and held it in place with a crepe bandage. Initially I refused to drink a foul smelling concoction she recommended to ease the pain, but finally I bolted it down. She insisted I rest and as I could not stand on my foot let alone drive, I was forced to acquiesce.

I fell asleep and woke in the dark. Thabang heard me moving about and was at my side immediately. 'How does your foot feel now?'

'Much better,' I mumbled sleepily.

'Have something to eat and I'll dress it again. You can't drive tonight, so sleep over and you should be fine tomorrow.'

I could have phoned Josh, Connie, Vince or my friends to fetch me and collect my car the next day but the sleuth in me told me to stay. This was a perfect opportunity to find out what went on in the murdered woman's family home.

During the night I woke shivering. The window was open and the room chilly. I hobbled out of bed supporting myself by clutching the furniture. Before closing the window, I looked out at a moonless sky. Something urged me to put my hand through the window. I felt the finest of drizzles like angels pee, a mist that could not have come from a sprinkler or from any artificial form of watering. Puzzled and cold, I went back to bed. Restlessly I slipped between dreams and semi wakefulness. At one stage, a wild storm swept the room. All I could do was to put my hands to my ears to wait out the thunderclaps. Then an icy wind ruffled the sheets and the blankets slipped off the bed.

Later, all was calm as I dreamt I sensed Pa's protective presence. I was a child again, waiting on the *stoep* for him to take notice of me. He placed his paper on the side table next to the chair, ready for me to hop into his lap and turned down his radio to give me his full attention. No one would care about me enough again to listen to the events of my day so attentively and lovingly.

I woke to the repetitive crow of a cock. My sheet had become a serpent bunched across my middle. I straightened the bed and lay back, thinking of Pa. In my hazy sleep-wakefulness, a collage of our long talks mingled with my shrieks of laughter as he piggy - backed me about the garden. The unpleasant thing; his wild temper when he'd had too much beer melted away.

The sun turned the unlined calico curtains golden by the time Thabang came in with a tray of light breakfast. She placed the tray down and gave the room a quick look. 'Bad spirits have been here overnight haven't they?'

'I thought I was dreaming it.'

'No my friend, I doubt it. I'm sorry if they disturbed your sleep,' she said without offering any explanation.

'But....the drizzle over night?'

'Kosigo used to ensure we had fine rain but now it is Galani's job,' she answered coolly.

I wanted to ask how the mist fell on their farm and not the others in the vicinity but I thought better of it. My eye caught patches of embedded mould in the corners of the ceiling and on the windowsills. I sensed she did not want to discuss the mystical moisture any longer and we turned our attention to my foot. She felt it and pronounced me almost healed. I stood and found my foot was only slightly tender.

I had swallowed the dregs of my coffee when one of the cats hopped onto the bed, a black, sleek beauty with a Siamese profile and knowing eyes. He rubbed his head on my arm begging to be petted. Disappointed when the stroking stopped, he sat on the bed watching me dress.

'You know everything that goes on in this house, don't you?' I whispered. He gave my hand a lick and jumped off the bed. I walked downstairs slowly, testing the pressure on my foot. Galani was in the kitchen, still the priestess, even in her green silk dressing gown.

'Hello, you're looking better.'

'I am thanks. Thabang did wonders with my foot.'

'She's a marvel. She should've studied medicine.' She gave the marble bench top a tap. 'Last night we printed out the emails sent to Kosigo, you wanted. They're in the study. I'll give them to you in a minute, but first I have to organize a few things in the kitchen.' She went to the refrigerator, placed a tub of meat and vegetables on the bench top and beckoned to the maid. 'Keneuoe, chop up these vegetables nice and fine and mix them with the cat meat inside this box,' she said in a strong voice, as she pointed at the item of Tupperware. 'No messing about, I want it done by the time I get back.'

Keneuoe swallowed, dropped her head and muttered. 'Yes madam.'

I hadn't seen a Black employer speak to her Black servant in such a harsh manner. Was Galani upset over her sister's death or did she always order her employees about?

As I followed Galani to the study, I realized that I had not seen or heard Mr. Moeketsi. 'Where's your father?' I asked tentatively.'

'He's still in his bedroom. We've been taking his meals in to him.' She looked at the floor. 'Kosigo was his favourite and he's still in mourning.'

I almost felt sorry for her.

The large and imposing study was lined with wood from floor to ceiling and the tall shelves filled with books. Galani handed me a sheaf of emails held together with a paper clip.

'Take your time with the emails. When you're through with them you'll find me in the kitchen.'

Galani left and I glanced through the emails. As I had expected, most of them criticised Kosigo for attempting to usurp the Rain Queen's position. Some pointed out Kosigo's low breeding, an ordinary Tswana with no royal lineage, while Modjaji belonged to a line of ancient kings and queens. In four of the messages, the threat was in the last paragraph, warning Kosigo to watch herself and her family carefully, in case something awful happened to her or them. She was advised to stop her rain rituals if she cared about her sisters and the rest of her family. Though I looked for a signature, other than the email address, the messages were anonymous.

Yelling interrupted my thoughts and I followed the sounds to the kitchen. 'Oh no! Not again!' Galani shouted.

'What's going on?' I asked.

'It's our next door neighbour. If it's not his cattle straying onto our property, then it's his insecticide killing our crops.

This time he emptied a whole lot of filthy water over our fence.'

Before I could question her about her neighbour, she opened the kitchen door. 'I'll have to go and sort this out. Keneuoe will show you out.'

In the car, I took a deep breath and turned my radio on high volume to blast the Moeketsis from my thoughts. Instead of heading for home, I drove towards a spot with a panoramic view and parked on the shoulder of the road. Even ravaged by drought, the mountain range in the distance was majestic.

I had hoped to relax and empty my thoughts of Galani and the strange house but my attempts failed. I turned her alibi around again and again. If Keneuoe's fear of her bossy mistress was anything to go by, it was possible that the servants who had all vouched for Galani's day spent in the kitchen, were so afraid of her, that they lied to Phineas. Unfortunately, I had no evidence at all to support this theory. Then there was Mr Moeketsi. Galani had created a cover for her father but during the period I spent at the house, I had not heard Mr Moeketsi's voice in the background or seen anyone take him food. I wondered if he was still there. Why wasn't he showing himself? After all, he was the head of the family.

There were no answers. Before driving off, I checked my cell phone and found a message from Phineas. When I told him about my bizarre night spent at the Moeketsis, he wanted to know more and insisted on stopping at my home after work.

He arrived tired and hungry, grateful that Josh insisted on making him a snack. After he had wiped his chin with a napkin, he was ready to discuss the case. I placed the copies of the computer printouts sent to Kosigo in front of him. He read each one and disappointedly threw them onto the table. Then he fired questions at me about my stay in the house. He was a rational person and could not accept my account of my unpleasant night. He was however, taken aback that my ankle had healed overnight. Recovery of his similar injury had taken weeks. Phineas left frustrated that he had learned nothing further about the killer's motivation.

⅗

I could tell that Josh was entertaining Karel from the strong whiff of curry in the yard. He made curry or something as pungent, when he cooked for Karel. The house was quiet, apart from the scratch of creepers against the glass windows and the tap of the trees on the eaves. A glass of red wine, a traditional Cape pinotage, was what I thirsted for. I uncorked the bottle and sniffed the bouquet. I filled my glass and sank into the couch, turned on the television and restlessly flicked through the stations.

An aching aloneness since the break with Wil still lingered. Was it our connection after years spent together that I missed, or the routine drawing together of the threads of our daily lives that I yearned for? Trust was shattered, respect for him gone, and yet the finality of divorce distressed me.

Would it matter if George and I spent time together? There was no need to risk a long-term attachment, I told myself. I could not deny being attracted to him and not only on a sexual level; I sensed his depth and sensitivity. Perhaps there was more to our relationship, if I dared to allow myself to feel it. My glass was empty and though I cautioned myself against more wine, I polished off the bottle. A little later, I succumbed to the tempting chocolates I kept in a dish on the coffee table. Indulging in the sweetness of chocolate was always soothing.

It was almost midnight when I laid out my clothes, in preparation for an early start the next day. I was to join Arnie on a trip to Polokwane and Rain Queen country.

131

Twenty-Three

'Wake up,' Arnie's voice roused me from my nap. 'We're near Polokwane. Time for a coffee break.' The car quivered and then stopped. I rubbed my eyes and looked out of the window. We were in the parking area of a roadhouse.

'I can't handle all the new names of places. Pietersberg was named after one of the Voortrekkers, but now its name has been changed to Polokwane. It means a place of safety in Sotho,' he said, as he stretched and yawned. 'I hope it lives up to its name.'

'Have I been asleep all this way?'

'You were snoring softly.'

'Come on.' I laughed.

'I'll go in and order. What'll you have?' he said, climbing out of the car.

'Coffee and chips with tomato sauce for me.' My childish love of chips had continued into adult life. I dug into my purse.

'Don't worry. Let the force pay for it.'

I dozed again until the car door creaked open. My punnet of hot fluffy chips emptied fast. Arnie complained about the weak coffee.

'Right, if you've finished eating, we'll make for the police station. I sent Phineas on ahead, so he'll be waiting for us. Enough of this time wasting.'

Polokwane had changed more than its name, since I had visited it as a teenager, when it was an agricultural town. Now it was a thriving modern city with a police station that looked like every other rural station. We found Phineas far from public scrutiny in the staff room joking with the other cops on a lunch break. He gave us a mock salute and buttoned up his uniform.

'Right boss, let's get moving upstairs.'

The police rabbit warren was a huge open planned office and cramped men and women sat behind small desks dominated by computers. Some computers were turned on to a soccer match. Phineas scanned the area and approached a plump policeman with a goatee, who was hunkered behind his computer. Phineas talked to him while pointing to us. Unhurriedly, the cop disengaged himself and slowly made his way in our direction.

'Des Terreblanche,' he said just as slowly. He shook hands with Arnie and gave me a cursory nod.

'Looks quite busy in here. No big dramas, though,' Arnie said, surveying the office.

'You people have got it much tougher down there in the crime belt. I don't know how you do it.'

Arnie's smile was closer to a grimace.

Des pulled up three chairs and dusted them off with his handkerchief. 'Take a seat and I'll find Chris.' Some minutes later an equally rotund but taller policeman walked unhurriedly towards us. 'Let me introduce Chris van Loggenberg.'

Chris and Arnie shook hands. Arnie introduced Phineas Phefo, explained my presence and described my role in the investigation. The Polokwane cops eyed me suspiciously – a woman who was not even a regular member of the clerical staff. Des coughed and shuffled his feet, Chris stared at the linoleum floor.

Tired of talking about the crime rate, the cops went on to dissect a recent rugby match and then the topic turned to soccer. I asked myself what I was doing in this poorly designed, over-lit building with a bunch of cops who ignored me, and had not even discussed the case yet. At last Arnie lifted his briefcase – a sign to resume work.

'We'll go into the conference room. It's quieter in there,'

Chris said.

It was a windowless room, barely large enough for the long wooden table, about fifteen chairs, a white board up front and the obligatory television turned on to the soccer. Thankfully, it was on mute. Chris went off to organise coffee while Des placed his case notes and a large brown envelope on the table. He waited for Chris to return before telling us about the attack on a woman he described as a witchdoctor. Her name was Rethabile Lesebo.

'Let's see now. From the case notes, on 20th September 2009, Rethabile Lesebo was stabbed in the chest and pelvis, but the attack didn't kill her. Maybe she frightened off the attacker,' Des quipped and then chuckled. 'She was found by kids playing in the veld, then taken to hospital and died there a few hours later.' He coughed and continued. 'As we informed you on the phone, she worked in one of those touristy places about twenty kilometres from Polokwane that had regular tribal dancing shows. Her bone-throwing act was an added attraction. Very popular with visitors, I'm told.'

Arnie moved around in his chair. 'Get on with it.'

'The whole point is that her injury, with deep cuts on her torso, was consistent with an attack by a raging elephant. On the ground next to her, our boys found an elephant's footprint. Naturally, they came to the conclusion that an elephant had killed her. And let's face it, lots of elephants do frequent the area.' He hesitated before adding, 'And so, it didn't seem necessary to take the matter further.'

Arnie coughed. Phineas peered at a stain in the linoleum.

'Thank you for that information. It may link to our case in the National Park but it's too early to say,' Arnie said. 'Before we continue, let me say that finding Kosigo's murderer is still priority number one, according to the top brass. They're pressuring me about it and when they hear about your findings in this case, I assure you they'll be breathing down your neck too.'

The two Polokwane detectives looked at each other.

A young police woman brought in our coffee and a

platter of biscuits on a tray. Nervously she offered us milk and sugar.

Phineas spoke for the first time. 'Any idea what tribe and clan this woman belonged to?'

Des scowled and scanned the report. 'She was a Tswana but I don't know the clan.'

'A huh.'

'Is it that important?' Des asked with a snigger.

'The other victim was a Tswana too … of the *Bafokeng* clan.' Phineas replied.

Chris picked up a slim folder and glared at Phineas. 'There was no further investigation. There are too many attacks and murders here these days to investigate every case to the fullest, to find out small details like names of clans. You should know what it's like.'

Arnie interjected quickly to stem the discussion that had aggressive overtones. 'Just as well you have some photos from the crime scene. Let's see them.'

Des opened the brown paper envelope, scattering the photos on the table like autumn leaves on a footpath.

'Right then, take us through your reasons for making the connection with the murder at the Pilanesberg Park?'

'I'll hand you back to Chris,' Des said. 'He's the one who spotted the connection.'

'Thanks, Des,' Chris said. 'The recent report of the death of the young rain maker at your end came through on line … and something clicked, 'he said, knocking his curly head with his knuckle. 'I remembered this case with the witchdoctor and her similar injuries. Can you believe it two witchdoctors?' His laugh came from his belly.

Phineas and I glared at him.

Chris straightened his shoulders, shuffled the photos and then pointed to blown up pictures of the long, deep chest wounds and lesser wounds in the pelvic area. 'As we said, at the time we thought that an elephant had attacked and killed her with its tusks. But last week we had another look at enlarged photos and a chat with the coroner. He cleared things up for us. From the photo's alone, he's pretty certain that the wounds were not caused by an elephant's tusks but by deep stabbing at close range with a long bladed knife.'

'Do you think the wounds were made to look like she was attacked by a crazed elephant?' Phineas asked impatiently.

'That could be the case,' Chris replied.

Arnie picked out a few of the photos and passed them on to Phineas. While I leant over Phineas shoulder to view them, Arnie lifted his briefcase. Within seconds, he had withdrawn his folder of photographs, pushed those already on the table to one side, and selected a handful of pictures from the scene of Kosigo's death. Deftly he matched the two sets of pictures.

'That's amazing. The wounds are similar and the footprint is almost identical. Weird sister crimes,' Des said excitedly. 'Looks like we've got a serial killer here.'

'If so, he's a smart one,' Chris added.

Phineas and Arnie gave each other knowing looks.

'What do you think Linda?' I hadn't said a word and yet Arnie made a point of addressing me.

'Early days to call it a serial killing but there could be a connection. What about motive?' I heard the strain in my voice.

'What about motive?' Phineas tapped the table and waited for an answer. I noticed the lines of tiredness on his face.

No one answered his question.

Arnie sighed loudly. 'We'll come to that one. Chris, did you speak to friends or relatives - anyone who knew the deceased?'

'At the time, I spoke to the victim's daughter who saw her mother just before she died.'

'Could she think of anyone with a reason to kill her mother?' Arnie asked pointedly.

'She told us that her mother was a healer, an *ngaka* but you know what it's like, there are always people who are unhappy with advice and bear grudges'.

'Anything more specific?' Phineas raised his voice.

Chris shook his head. 'Sorry no.'

'What a waste of time. They didn't even do an autopsy on the woman,' Phineas muttered under his breath.

'Well it's too late for that now,' Chris said. 'We're not exhuming her body.'

'Perhaps you should visit the victim's daughter again and have a longer talk to her. There's certainly more to this. You need to do some digging,' Arnie said in a raised voice.

'Right,' Chris' face was red. 'We'll get on to it.'

Arnie looked at his watch and gathered up his photos and files. I lifted my hand to gain his attention. 'One moment Chief Detective Inspector, there's something I need to clear up before we leave. Did Amita tell you about the peacock feather we found lodged in the footprint near Kosigo's body?'

'Peacock feather?' Arnie's stare was blank.

I realised I should have mentioned it earlier. I was taking communication amongst Arnie's team for granted. I explained how during a second visit to the crime scene, and in far sharper light, I had noticed something deep blue pressed into the muddy indentation of the footprint, and that it turned out to be a peacock feather. I added that Amita had put into a plastic bag for testing.

'Now that you mention it, I think she did say something about handing a new piece of evidence from the crime scene into forensics,' he said vaguely. 'I've had a lot on my plate and been involved with other cases…'

'A peacock feather is not the sort of thing you'd forget easily. It's far too big and too brightly coloured,' Phineas said sarcastically.

'The feather is important because there aren't any peacocks in the area. The killer could've dropped it or perhaps it was his calling card,' I insisted.

Immediately Arnie dialled the Rustenburg station. After the call his reply to my question was to the point. 'I've spoken to our forensics department and I can tell you that the feather was definitely from a peacock, an older male bird, an uncommon breed in our area. It was partially covered in Kosigo's blood and no prints were distinguishable.' He leant on the table. 'Did you find any feathers here, boys?'

'I'll phone for the evidence box to be brought up. We'll have a look. Rethabile Letsebo's bits and pieces are in there,'

Chris said.

Arnie moved to the back of the room to make phone calls, Phineas leant against the wall and I stared out of the window onto the lush grass and regimented flowerbeds in the park over the road. A couple strolled arm in arm. He was White and she Black. I thought of the shadow of apartheid over the country's history. Those two would not have been walking about openly twenty years ago. They sat on a bench and pointed at the flowers. The same bench would've had a *Whites Only* sign on it. Phineas tapped my shoulder. A young constable carrying the evidence box placed it on the table.

'Phew, it stinks,' Des said, pulling out a blood soaked floral skirt. Stuck to one of the folds was a feather dulled by blood.

'It's the size of a peacock feather but it will have to be tested. If it is a peacock feather the implications would be very interesting. Confirms the serial murderer theory,' Chris said.

Chris was about to close the box when I noticed a bit of red material about the size of a baby's fist. 'Can you take a pencil and lift out that red bit,' I asked.

Chris glared at me but did as I asked. It was part of a larger piece of blood soaked red velvet with torn edges.

I spoke to Arnie in a near whisper. 'It's likely that there were traces of this red stuff at both Raymond and Kosigo's sites. There isn't time for explanations now but trust me.'

'I'll ask him to send it to pathology along with the rest,' Arnie replied.

Chris and Des talked quietly. Arnie issued his final instructions as he and Phineas stood ready to leave. 'You two run your tests, talk to the victim's relative and get back to us as soon as you can, please. As you know we're battling against time.'

'I've made a copy of our photos and our notes for you,' Chris said, handing a folder to Arnie. This time we all shook hands.

Twenty-Four

The inside of the car was like a cooker and the air conditioning turned on high, did not even bite into the heat. We were in a moist, tropical zone. As we climbed, circling the mountain, we caught glimpses of clumped ferns, wayward creepers and water gushing between tall pines. The valley was as I remembered it, green and lusciously fertile.

At the mountain peak, Arnie stopped at the hotel for a pee and returned with more coffee and a brown paper bag stuffed with assorted doughnuts. As he climbed into the car, I noticed a peppermint smell again - an attempt to disguise alcohol, I thought.

'This coffee is just what we need! We'll take a break and then get back on the road,' Arnie said, biting into his doughnut with a gulp of coffee.

Phineas wore a peeved expression. 'No doughnuts for me. I'm taking a stroll,' he said, opening the door.

Arnie leaned back. 'Magnificent view. I wouldn't mind retiring somewhere in this neck of the woods.'

'Retiring?'

'Another year, at the most, then I'll take my pension and get the hell out of the force,' he said, rubbing his eyes. 'I've had enough!'

'But you're too young to retire.'

'I'm 58 but I won't get older if I stay around here,' his voice was choked with emotion. 'Its days like this that keep me sane.'

We discussed the pressures of his job, the high crime

rate, the insufficiency of staff and their inadequate training. He gave me statistics of the cops who had burned out and left voluntarily, or had been sacked for poor performance. 'I've bent your ear far too long with my troubles. I'll let you admire the magnificent view now.'

I was lost in the past. On Ma's annual painting weekend, she stayed with her artist cousin, Deena who lived on a farm only a short drive from the gorge. In the early days of apartheid, this short break suited Pa, though he would not have admitted it. Each year at that time the pro government Afrikaans secret society, the Broederbond, met to choose their office bearers. Pa was heavily committed to the organization then. For Bond members the precious time away from their wives and families, also allowed them to drink as much as they liked and listen to sport on the radio.

I was five then and old enough to go away with Ma. 'I'll be very, very quiet Ma, I promise.' Ma was mine for the weekend and that was all that mattered.

'Nice memories, eh.' Arnie's voice was unusually gentle.

'Um beautiful.'

'You're amazing...thought so when I first met you ... all those years ago.'

I wriggled uncomfortably at the direction our conversation was taking.

'Oh?'

'I wonder if you realise...there was a time when I could've killed to spend a night with you?'

I coughed and then mumbled incoherently.

Phineas returned from his walk just in time. During our descent, Phineas sat at the back of the car, making notes of our discussion with the police in Polokwane, while Arnie listened to a review of the week's sport on the radio.

Though the terrain was still hilly, the mountain pass was behind us and we headed for the domain of the Rain Queen.

'Do either of you know much about the Rain Queen?' Phineas asked.

'I don't, tell us all about her,' Arnie replied.

'First of all, I must make it clear that all the Rain Queens through history have belonged to the Lovedu tribe. The Lovedus believe that she has the magic to regulate the seasons and to bring rain. Every October, deep in these forests you can hear the drums beating as the people call the Queen to bring rain.'

'Bloody spooky, if you ask me,' Arnie said with a sneer.

'Tell us about Modjaji, the Rain Queen who died recently.'

'She was young, attractive and educated, only 27 when she died,' Phineas said. 'What a stir she caused - too modern in her jeans and tee shirt. She liked TV soap operas, used a computer and was never without her cell phone. Lovedu tradition doesn't allow a Rain Queen to marry but the members of the tribe expect her to pass on her rain bringing gifts by having the children of relatives or those with royal blood.'

'That is weird ... and not a good idea,' I said.

'Modjaji had one daughter, who must be about four years old by now and she is likely to become the new Rain Queen.'

With Phineas navigating, we drove along the river and then towards the pine covered hills. When we arrived at the Rain Queen's residence, I was disappointed. I expected her to live in a palace or at least a grand mansion. The remnants of a burnt, ranch style, mud brick house, some huts and an office was all we saw.

Phineas told us that the buildings were destroyed in a fire an hour or so before Modjaji's funeral. Nothing was known about the motive for the fire or about the culprits.

Arnie parked behind a row of huts where children were playing. A group of older women stood outside the huts gaping at us. One of the women stepped forward and faced us. Phineas knew enough Lovedu to walk up to her and greet her.

He returned to the car minutes later, wiping his forehead and looking rattled. He repeated his conversation with her. Once he had identified himself as a policeman, he asked her if she knew of the Moekesti sisters in Rustenburg and Kosigo, in particular. From her abusive answer, he assumed she had not heard of them. She showed no reaction when he told her that Kosigo had been murdered and that we were investigating her death. But, when he mentioned threatening emails sent to Kosigo by followers of Modjaji she was furious. Phineas was sure her anger was due to her lack of understanding. She had never heard of an email and though she knew computers existed she had never seen one and did not understand their function.

Phineas threw his hands in the air and allowed them to drop slowly into his lap. 'Now what?'

Arnie tapped the car door, 'Ask her if there are any younger people living here who use computers.'

The woman's sneer was followed by another outburst. 'She says can't we see that nobody is here. All the younger people have left to work in the towns.'

'Explain to her that we are not accusing her people of making threats or of murder, but we are asking for help,' Arnie said. 'Tell her again that Kosigo was murdered.'

The woman nodded and motioned to two of the others. They chatted amongst themselves for what seemed ages and then the spokeswoman motioned to Phineas.

'She says that some of their men who work in offices in Polokwane use computers. She can tell us who they are,' Phineas said, repeating the context of his conversation.

'It looks like you'll have to sleep over and check this one out. We'll keep an eye open for some accommodation for the night. Come up here tomorrow, get a list of those men who work with computers or anything else that could point us in the right direction. Then you can liaise with the cops at the Polokwane station if you need help.'

'Before we leave tell the woman … thank you.'

As Arnie turned on the engine, one of the women called out loudly.

'She says we must remember that there is only one Rain Queen and that Modjaji was the youngest Rain Queen in 200 years. That God gave her, and only her, special powers to make rain. That the royal line goes back thousands of years to Zimbabwe so we should have respect. All the chiefs know her power.'

The woman spat on the ground as if to emphasise her point.

Arnie turned to Phineas. 'Do you think it's worth taking the road back via the cycad forest? I've heard it's something special.'

'Sure. The Lobedu think the fern-like palms have magic and they use them in their ceremonies. The story is that these cycads originated in times when dinosaurs snacked on them.'

We all laughed.

The cycad forest made me dizzy. I picked up uncomfortable buzzing sensations and after a kilometre or two amongst the high palms, I urged Arnie to take the first turn back to turn off to the highway.

'Seen one, seen them all,' Arnie said disdainfully.

We were driving through flatter land, when Arnie swerved in the direction of a small motel advertising special overnight prices. 'Phineas, you'll need a place to sleep so we'll drop you off here. It looks as good as any, but if you strike problems, ring the blokes in Polokwane and they'll find something else for you.'

Phineas scowled.

'And I'll hear from you close of the day tomorrow, eh,' Arnie said as Phineas reluctantly climbed out of the car and strode towards the motel entrance. We were both too tired and caught up in our own thoughts to talk. Arnie turned the radio back on to listen to sport and I dozed off.

We returned to Rustenburg in the dark. I went straight to bed and did not eat the dinner Josh had left for me. That night Ma sat on the end of my bed. I could feel her light pressure near my thigh though I could not see her. I was not imagining it, I could not be, I told myself. After all, I was fully awake. When I felt her fingers gently move strands of my hair behind my ears, I was certain of her presence. Ma had liked my hair off my face when I was in my teens. She said it showed off my bone structure. I fell asleep with her near.

❦

Phineas returned with a list of Lobedu men who operated computers in Polokwane. Disgruntled about the search, he deemed a useless waste of time, he handed the job of interviewing to the two policemen in Polokwane.

The journey to Queen Modjaji's residence had not provided Arnie with the answers he hoped would put an end to the case, and he turned to the only other possible suspects, Galani and the servants. Though Phineas had already made comprehensive notes virtually denying Galani and Thabang's involvement in the murder, under pressure to find a suspect as soon as possible, Arnie's stubbornness asserted itself. He insisted that something important must have been overlooked at the Moeketsi household.

Twenty-Five

The morning did not start well. As usual, Josh collected the post. Amongst the bills and letters was a cardboard box addressed to me. When I opened it, a small bone broken in two lay inside.

Trembling, I shut the box.

'*Hau*, someone is wishing you very bad things, throw it away quickly.' Josh took a few steps back and touched the back of his neck.

'No, I'll wrap it up and show it to the police.'

'A sheep's neck bones?'

'Or a goat's.'

Neither of us mentioned what was on our minds – that the broken neck bone was a curse, warning me of my vulnerability. Small animal bones similar to this one, were frequently used by *ngakas* when they *threw the bones* as part of ritual divination. Yet I doubted that a healer would use such a prized spiritual tool for evil means such as witchcraft.

Arnie was waiting outside my gate before I had finished breakfast. 'Morning,' he said, tapping the steering wheel. 'You're late.' He glanced in his rear view mirror and then at his watch. 'I don't see Phineas. We won't wait for him, he can meet us at the Moeketsis,' he said impatiently. Arnie's usually florid complexion was sallow, his eyes tired.

'I had another early morning phone call – more orders

from the top brass to pull finger with this case.'

'It's understandable, Kosigo was an important person in the community and belonged to an influential and wealthy family.'

'I'd be happy to oblige and find her killer but it doesn't make sense spending so much time concentrating on this case with the morgue stacked with murdered bodies.'

I couldn't help wondering if Arnie had retained any remnants of a policeman's soul, the bloodhound mentality that dug its teeth in and chased a murderer to the ends of the earth?

During the brief journey I told him about the bone sent to me. To avoid contaminating prints, I had carefully placed it and the small box in a plastic bag. He took the bag from me with a promise to hand it to forensics for testing.

'I don't like it one bit, looks like a sorcerer's curse!' were the only comments he made.

As finding the bone had disturbed me and had sinister implications, I had expected him to be alarmed, ask appropriate questions and make an effort to ascertain who sent it and why. Arnie needed me, or at least he thought he did, but I knew that I could not look to him for help. There was someone out there trying to frighten me and doing a good job of it. Arnie complained he was overworked but the truth of it...he was concerned about himself, too concerned, when he ought to have been more concerned about protecting others. That was his job as Chief Inspector, I thought angrily.

'Well then, let's get on with it.' He grabbed his briefcase from the back seat.

We were on the doorstep when Phineas turned sharply into the brick courtyard. 'Sorry I'm late boss, a neighbour's burst pipe blocked my driveway and I couldn't get the car out of my house.'

'With our power failures, water and sewage problems this is like a third world country.'

'Oh, well.'

Keneuoe opened the door to us and scowled.

'I will tell Miss Galani you are here, meantime, you'd

better wait in the clean kitchen. Sitting room stinks from cigarettes.' She pulled up her nose. We sat on wooden chairs around an oak table. The smell of a pine cleaning agent dominated.

Arnie tapped the table. 'Where's that damn maid?'

'Yes sir, you calling me?' Keneuoe rushed forward adjusting her white frilly cap.

'How long will Miss Galani be?'

'I'm here, sorry to keep you waiting.' Galani rushed in, still in her dressing gown and sat holding her middle. She complained of having been ill with a stomach bug. 'Snake in the belly,' we call it.

'Not very pleasant,' Phineas said.

'I think I've got something similar to what Kosigo came down with. Of course she was far sicker for days before she died. Thabang's got a touch of it, too.'

'Sorry to hear that,' Arnie said, not very convincingly.

'As if Kosigo's death wasn't enough, the police from Polokwane phoned late yesterday asking me questions about a sorcerer in their area…Rethabile Letsebo. I've never heard of her. Apparently, she died in similar circumstances to poor Kosigo. I haven't been to Polokwane for at least ten years, but they asked me to account for my movements at the time of her death. I was here as usual, everybody knows that. How can they think I had anything to do with that woman's death?' She wiped her eyes with the sleeve of her silky dressing gown.

Phineas whispered something to Arnie who shrugged him away. Using his authoritative voice, Arnie asked, 'So then, what were you doing the day Kosigo died?'

Phineas tapped his notebook and glared at Arnie.

'Now I'm being accused of my sister's death, too. I've already told him,' she said indignantly, nodding in Phineas' direction, 'I was in the kitchen the whole day making my potions. If you don't believe me, I'll take you down to the kitchen right away and you can speak to the servants.'

'That would be helpful,' Arnie said. 'We need to talk to them.'

Phineas' body stiffened and his natural frown deepened as we followed Galani to the yard. Three servants were talking animatedly over jam and tea. With a flounce of her dressing gown, Galani walked away and left us. We introduced ourselves to the women and explained our presence. Keneuoe was adamant that she had helped her mistress to make potions the day Kosigo died. 'Miss Galani is a very cross lady, but she did not kill anybody. She likes to make plenty money from plants.' Keneuoe screwed up her face in distaste. 'She worked in the kitchen from after breakfast … all day. She not take a lunch break. I was eating outside but I see her working through the window.'

'Are you absolutely certain she didn't leave the kitchen at any time?'

'Only to go to the toilet,' Keneuoe laughed.

The other servants backed up Keneuoe's story. They had also seen their employer working in the kitchen all day. Arnie went on to assess each one's feelings about Kosigo. As cynical a cop as he was, he could not dispute their love for her.

While Arnie and Phefo left to examine Kosigo's bedroom, I joined Galani in the study. Her expression changed to one of annoyance. 'That policeman Swart … to my face he puts on an act of being polite but underneath I know he's laughing at me, and doesn't believe in my powers.' She looked up and took a deep breath. 'His aura is muddy, while yours is bright and clear.'

'That's good to know,' I answered flippantly, with little belief in Galani's visions.

'And your aura tells me some of your family has already gone to the other side. But they're around you, loving and protective.'

'You're correct. I sense them too.' I changed the subject. 'Any news about the rain ritual?'

'Next week, all going well,' she said, as she looked around for her cats. Her shrill whistle was followed by pounding paws in our direction. Five black cats answered her call. She stroked a cat that had crept onto her lap and gave the others a pat on their heads. 'They have the best life, spoiled rotten.'

She smiled at me. 'And I like to spoil myself with chocolates. Come on, have one.' She pointed to the heart shaped box on the coffee table. 'Mouth-watering! My stomach aches but I can't get enough of them. I know I shouldn't.'

I shook my head. I preferred plain chocolate in the block. Heavy footsteps announcing Arnie and Phineas' return gave us both a jolt. I could tell by the disappointment on their faces that the morning's visit had not been fruitful.

Galani accompanied us along a tiled path flanked with blooming potted plants. A few metres from the path, an elderly man lay in the sun on a plastic lounge chair. 'There's my father. It must be the first time I've seen him outdoors in the last week.'

Mr. Moeketsi looked so crumpled and sick that not even Arnie suggested interviewing him.

⚜

George invited me for dinner that night. I had met Carol at the luncheon with the group and talked to her again at the dig. We met at a bistro on the outskirts of the town. I chatted with Carol, catching up on local gossip while George drew Ivan out, listening to his academic talk. I doubted whether Carol or Ivan could've guessed how powerfully we were attracted to each other. Just a look, a touch, ignited my desire.

Carol and Ivan laughed at George's English accent, mimicking his anglicised manner of pronouncing Afrikaans words. I recalled how Ma had battled with colloquial pronunciations. No matter how hard she'd tried, when she spoke Afrikaans she was instantly stamped as English. I had to admit to myself that I found George's manner of speaking endearing and I felt at ease with him. What was it about him that attracted me? I did not have to question myself for long. I knew the answers. He was as quiet and forceful as Pa. As a partner Wil was nothing like Pa, and we had nothing in common, other than our early farming background and our physical relationship and that had waned by our thirties. It

149

was ages since we'd made love with passion. George seemed more gentle and considerate. I would find out soon enough.

I wound my pasta around a spoon, dipped it into tangy sauce and was about to put it in my mouth, when the restaurant lights failed. The total blackout was a shock to me but everyone else in the room seemed at ease with its suddenness. Immediately lit candles were placed on each table. The manager appologised. He had ordered a backup generator but was still waiting for it.

Carol giggled. 'You look so surprised? We have regular power cuts here and you're lucky not to have been caught out before.'

Ivan explained that the country had major power problems. Demand outstripped supply, and the government had not made provision for that. There had been enormous economic growth in the country and unfortunately power insufficiency has slowed things down.

George walked me to my car. My mind told me to hurry inside, but I lingered. He placed an arm around my shoulders and for a moment or two his grip on my shoulders firmed. He kissed me gently and released his hold. I wanted to move in, feel him closer to me but I straightened up.

'Let's take it slowly,' he said softly.

I swallowed hard. 'Thanks for a lovely evening, I enjoyed it. I'll see you at the dig in a few days.'

'I look forward to seeing you.' He waved and was gone.

George tasted of earth and stone. I had forgotten how delectable and enticing a kiss could be.

Twenty-Six

A scatter of clouds partially obscured the sun. Since my arrival, the drought had bitten even deeper and the farm I once knew was almost unrecognizable. On the path to the orange groves sunburnt grass scratched the back of my legs and twigs snapped underfoot. The lack of rain was bound to be the topic of conversation.

Connie was in the orange groves, supervising the watering. Pa had once said that watering deep and long was the way to keep orange trees alive in a drought. Connie was too busy to be interrupted with idle chatter and Raelene was in the kitchen baking. I left them and took a familiar path to the dam. Greenery along the edge of the water was now a limp tangle, and brackish water barely skimmed the pebbles at the dam's base.

I heard the crunch of footsteps. 'Missie Lindie, Missie Lindie.' It was Samuel. 'Baas Connie says to tell you he is busy now with the orange trees, but he will come soon. You must please wait for him.'

Raelene's ample body was spread across on the sofa. She barely lifted her head to suck the straw in her bottle of lemonade. 'I'm getting older and baking is getting tough on my feet, but I do love being in the kitchen.' She took another sip of lemonade. 'Sorry I'm full of complaints... but I am pleased to see you.'

Once we had discussed her grandchildren, my house, the drought, her weight increase and the rise in violence against farmers, we returned to our favourite topic, food. When I mentioned Connie's name, her expression soured. 'We hardly talk these days, and our separate lives are much like the ones one reads about in agony columns. If I had somewhere else to go, I'd leave.'

'But you've made a life for yourself here.'

'It's a common story. One day I'll be sorry that I didn't go when I was still able to. We'll hate each other when we are old.'

I gave her a hug. There was nothing I could say and I reached for the platter of her newly baked *melk terts,* just within my grasp.

Connie stomped in carrying his mud caked work boots. His face was dark with worry. 'It's hell out there, just trying to keep the oranges going and the animals alive ... takes all I've got.'

Raelene pulled herself up and searched absentmindedly for her sandals. 'In his time Pa got through terrible droughts. You'll do it too.'

'I'm not Pa. I don't know if I can tough it out,' he muttered, pushing a lock of sweaty hair from his brow.

'I hear Galani is going to hold a rain ceremony soon,' Raelene said.

'Anything. Just let it rain,' he said, on his way to the shower.

I sat on the *stoep* sipping a beer. When Connie joined me, his cheeks and hands were pink from hot water and the family favourite aftershave, Old Spice, was a halo around him.

'I'm fit to drink with a lady now,' he said, nibbling the froth off his beer.

My attention drifted to the forest and the sounds in the distance. 'Listen!' I thumped the arm of the chair. 'It's the elephants!' Their orchestrated trumpeting buffeted against the mountainside.

'They feed up there every day, but their supply is running out. I don't know what will become of us all once the sun is through burning up our land.' he said, staring at the mountain. 'It's not only the drought that's worrying me.' His arms formed an arc. 'All this work... and the farm won't be left for my children.'

I stroked his arm. 'Come on Con, the drought is making you pessimistic.'

I didn't want to use the word depressed. My brother's eyes were dull stones, and his shoulders drooped. The animosity between him and Raelene did not help.

He talked about his fears that the government was aiming to take back about a third of white owned land in the next ten years. So far, they had expropriated four per cent, paying the farmers a price he considered well below the value. 'They're returning the land to the Blacks for next to nothing. The Blacks claim that they were driven out and that our families seized their tribal ground all those years ago. Believe me, there's always some story or other... and it's not always true.'

'Have the Tswanas who work for you ever complained that this farm was snatched from them by our forefathers?' I asked.

'Not yet, but in the end they will.'

'I doubt it, the family has treated them well.'

'It's easy for you to talk!' He was on the verge of yelling. 'You only know the nice romantic side of life in this country. I see it in your eyes, the multi-racial society, the growing middle class and the rise in black opinion makers.'

'Not true – what about the unbelievable poverty, AIDS, TB and unemployment.'

He ignored my comment. 'We need pricey generators, power can't be relied on. And there are all the other costs like security, water and God knows what else, just to scrape a living'

I could not placate him; the drought had every farmer in the vice of panic. It was dusk by then, the mountains a broody purple, signalled it was time to leave. A kiss on the cheek and I left him drinking on the *stoep*.

On my way home, I drove through the flower-lined streets of Rustenburg. Somehow, proud gardeners had managed to keep their gardens alive. I stopped outside the once Afrikaans only girls' school, I had attended. It was empty at that late time of day, but I imagined the rows of cars parked as mothers of all races waited for their children. When the bell rang, Black, White, and Asian children running, holding hands or giggling, pouring through the elaborate wrought iron gates. Perhaps the next generation would have a chance at living in a prejudice free society.

⚜

Josh enjoyed cooking and he had prepared grilled steak and a salad, with a creamy dessert for my dinner. Fattening of course, but I told myself I was on holiday and ate it all. After the meal, I looked for something healthy to fill an empty spot. I was gnawing an apple when the phone rang.

It was Arnie. 'The pathology report came in this morning. There was a substantial amount of poison in Kosigo's blood … some sort of plant poison, but they can't get a fix on it yet. The lab will do more tests to narrow it down, but I don't know when we'll have the report. With the soccer, productivity in the department is even slower than usual.'

'I suppose the poison could've made her weak and unable to defend herself.'

'We'll know more when we find out the sort of poison used. No good guessing.'

'You're right.'

'Another thing, the boys from Polokwane found no link to the threatening emails. So it looks like Modjaji's followers at the camp are not implicated in the murder.'

There was silence from Arnie though I heard papers being shuffled and pens clicking on his desk. It was Arnie's way of telling me that he had nothing further to say. If he could not charge a key suspect within a day or two, he was likely to ditch the case.

The bulldog in me drove me on. If I was left to work on the case alone, I knew I would give it my all to establish the identity of the murderer. How could I help myself? Kosigo's picture was etched in my mind and I had made a commitment to try to find her murderer.

⁂

The next morning Rosie was waiting for me downstairs. She tapped her foot impatiently. 'Come on, you're late. I only have a few hours off work.'

'Where are we off to today?' I said. She had been the leader during our early days and I fell back into that pattern.

'I'm in the mood for a nostalgia trip to the farm, if that's okay with you? I haven't been there since your last visit.'

We left for the farm after I had phoned Connie to tell him to expect us. Walking along a little used path, we came across survivors in the browned veld – proteas with proud pink crowns, two fiery kaffirbooms and a resilient syringa tree crowned in lilac. The land was our shared foundation. Holding hands as we had when we were children, we continued in the direction of the farm worker's mud huts. At the hut that was once home to Rosie, she squeezed my hand and wiped her eyes. Tansie was in our thoughts. Rosie could not resist a peep through the window.

'Look, an untidy person lives here now. Breakfast dishes in a basin, cup on the floor. Not like we used to keep it.'

On the shady side of the huts, passion fruit still climbed the bank and pumpkin and squashes clutching the earth competed with watermelons for precious moisture. From their plump stems and fleshy leaves it was obvious that someone was watering them.

I giggled. 'Remember how the men used those bushes. Nothing grew there... and it still doesn't.'

Rosie tapped the watermelons with an expert's touch. 'This one's perfect. It has a sweet smell,' she said tearing the green ball from its base. It was smallish, the zigzag stripes silvery green. She carried the watermelon to a patch of veld and I followed her. In seconds she plunged a pocketknife into the melon's flesh until it bled pink juice. We ate the pink flesh fast gulping down the sugariness, pips and all. I licked the sticky juice from my lips, using my tee shirt to mop up dribbles. We rubbed our hands on our thighs, looked at each other and grinned. Our joy blended into a moment of childlike bliss.

'Tell me, what's happening with the investigation?'

I sighed. 'It's moving at a snail's pace.'

'Everything here moves slowly but you'll crack it... eventually. You'll see. Keep at it!'

I felt another load of responsibility dumped on my shoulders and did not reply.

'Any news about your new boyfriend?' Rosie asked as we walked back to the car.

'Boyfriend, at my age,' I spluttered.

'Lover then.?'

'We're taking things slowly.'

'You're blushing.'

"Alright then, I'm falling for him and I think my feelings are reciprocated but...'

'You're scared.'

I nodded, feeling like a little girl.

'I wish you'd learn to take it all less seriously and enjoy men like I do.'

Her statement about her sex life was bravado. The letters she had written to me while we were parted were crammed with longings for a stable partner. There had been lovers. Several. They were men from another tribe or white doctors from the hospital, all unions she knew would not last. A Tswana man was her match, but the Tswanas she had dated were afraid of her and cowered before her qualifications. Her work was far too important to take second place, and so she aged alone.

We talked on but Rosie's thoughts were elsewhere. Her smile had disappeared and her eyes looked weary.

'What's up Rosie?'

'I don't know if I can handle my work much longer.' She told me that even though she worked now at a relatively small clinic, every day orphaned children from parents who had died from AIDS and other diseases, poured in for treatment. For some it was too late, in spite of the new medications available.

'I'm thinking of doing hands-on work.' She explained she had visited an orphanage in the mountains with a fully equipped medical clinic, schools and the therapy required to assist recovery from the devastating ordeals the children had experienced. 'The children look well fed and contented and I'd like to work in a place like that.'

With a start, she looked at her watch. 'Sorry, I have to go, I'm running late.'

We walked back to the car and hugged. After she left I sat on the stone wall along the driveway, enjoying the late morning sun.

❧

Arnie phoned with news from the coroner that Raymond had died in hospital. Apparently an infection and not stab wounds had finally killed him. The coroner's finding concurred with Arnie's view that the pattern and depth of the wounds were similar to those found on Kosigo's body.

'They found poison in Raymond's system, identical to the one found in Kosigo's blood but they'll take a while to identify it. We have a serial murderer … and they can't see how important it is to hurry.'

I recognised one of Arnie's deep, long sighs. 'I don't know how we'll manage to investigate all of this. I suppose the Cameroons government will be asking questions soon and I haven't got answers.'

'Yes, they will want to know.'

'We'll talk tomorrow, work out a plan.'

A plan? I knew he would do nothing, or virtually nothing. I thought about the inefficient post, the electricity failures and the potholes in the roads. It was all part of the disease that had infected my homeland!

I replaced the receiver aware of the desperation in Arnie's voice. His zeal had been sucked up by his need to keep afloat. As it was, Phineas was handling most of his work. If Arnie had been thinking clearly, he would've realised that people in the area would soon hear about the serial murder and fear would spread like a virus.

I made an instant decision, Josh and I would visit the elephant sanctuary again the following day. Snooping and questioning might elicit some answers. I left a message telling Arnie about my intention.

Twenty-Seven

Josh grinned and rubbed his hands with delight at the prospect of another visit to the Elephant Sanctuary. I hurried through breakfast and he stacked the few dishes instead of drying them. He disappeared briefly and then emerged wearing his black, leather detective's cap.

'You're looking smart.'

'I like simple, plain colours. No checks or flowers for me,' he said, as he opened the car door. He appeared to be reasonably up to date with our progress, or lack of it, and I realised that he could easily have been listening to my conversations with Arnie on the extension phone. It was too late to worry about it, but I would be more careful in future.

When we reached the sanctuary, the smell of grass and elephant dung was in the air. We found Johan, the manager, feeding the elephants with compacted foliage. Each pile disappeared as fast as his fork dumped it. It was a comical sight and I did my best to suppress a giggle, while Josh covered his mouth to staunch his guffaws.

We waited outside the elephant enclosure for Johan to put down his pitchfork. He did this slowly and reluctantly. 'You two back again!' he said gruffly. Before I had time to answer, he added, 'I suppose you're here again about Raymond?'

'He died in hospital and the police are looking for his murderer.'

'I thought it was just an attack and he was recovering.

Murder now, eh? One less voodoo doctor in the world is fine by me.'

I looked away. 'How come he set up his tent here in the Sanctuary?'

'He tried to find cheap accommodation and a place for his tent. I guess our offer was the best. We have the space here and any visitors he brought to the place would be our visitors too.'

I reminded him that I was working with the police, that I needed to talk to his staff again and have another look at the crime scene.

He pointed his angled chin in Josh's direction. 'And what about him?' he said, rolling his eyes.

'My assistant,' I said sharply.

He muttered something inaudible. 'I suppose you two can go and look at Raymond's tent, but I've packed up all his stuff and put it in boxes in the shed over there.' He pointed to a structure at the side of one of the enclosures. 'You can open it and have a look.'

After feeling in his pockets, he extracted a key and threw it in our direction. Josh stretched for it and had it in his clasped hand. We made our way through the dry veld. Part of the tent had broken away from its pegs and was fluttering in the wind. At its entrance, I shivered. The icy drop in temperature was sudden. As we entered the tent, an acacia branch broke free and flew at us, but we ducked in time and it hit the ground with a thud.

'Phew! What's going on?' Josh spun round looking worried.

I tried to speak but high-pitched buzzing drowned my answer. Minutes later the warmth returned and the buzzing stopped.

Josh gave me a long look. 'Spirits! Definitely spirits!'

My eyes met his, but I said nothing.

Our search in the tent revealed little more than scraps of rubbish and stale food. When we unlocked the corrugated iron shed, we found four cardboard boxes shoved on top of machinery. Josh lifted the boxes and placed them on the ground. After spending time with the professionals, I had come equipped with two pairs of gloves and several plastic bags. We picked our way through the boxes. They contained collections of amulets, voodoo dolls of all sizes, bunches of herbs and grasses, and bottles of strange looking roots. In the last box, amongst a pile of papers, was a sticky brown mess that smelled of chocolate. Josh had the patience to prise the papers apart. Immediately I recognised a soiled and battered version of the heart-shaped box I had seen on Galani's table. It could have been the one Phineas remembered seeing in the tent. I tore at some of the melted chocolate and squished it into an evidence bag. The rest we packed into the boxes and carried them to the car. I would hand the material over to Arnie for testing. I was going through the motions, adhering to a procedure that most likely, would never be followed up.

The elephants were chomping away when we returned to the enclosure. I questioned each one of the four young men who worked with them, but none could remember having heard or seen anything unusual during Raymond's attack. When I asked if they had noticed any differences in Raymond's behaviour before the attack, Hal, the youngest worker, told us that during the week before his death, Raymond had been ill and vomited daily. He had talked about calling a doctor, but had not done so. Though I sensed that the others knew more than they were prepared to say, I could not break through their silence.

'Strange that this attack also has a link to elephants?' I said to Josh as we turned onto the freeway.

'Weird! Maybe the attacker wanted us to blame the elephants again.'

Back home, I placed the chocolate in the fridge and left a message for Arnie about the morning's activities and the boxes.

※

Arnie had lost the rudder and we were about to sink. I was obsessed with fulfilling promises and completing tasks, but this one was becoming too much for me. I needed a more rational approach. If I wrote down all I knew about the murders and then reviewed it, I expected to be able to draw some logical conclusions. I took large sheets of paper and pens from the study cupboard and drew up an analysis sheet. I assigned Kosigo, Raymond and Rethabile a column each and noted the meagre facts gathered about each murder. My efforts drew nothing new. I left the analysis sheet on the desk and decided to visit Nathaniel at *Mosego*. Nathaniel still made *Skokiaan* for the men on the farm, a strong homemade brew from sugar, yeast, hot water and secret additives, to give it a kick. It smelled dreadful. During the apartheid years, brewing *Skokiaan* was considered a crime. Pa once said that if drinking it on Friday and Saturday nights kept his workers happy and did not interfere with their work, he would turn a blind eye to it. On a Wednesday or Thursday at the latest, to be ready for consumption on the weekend, the brew was mixed to ferment. Probably Pa did not realise the amount of running back and forth, checking, stirring and scooping of froth that went on towards the end of each week, and I did not tell him.

After working for Connie for many years, Nathaniel had developed a taste for Lion Lager, the popular South African bottled beer. He preferred it to *Skokiaan* but continued brewing it for the men on the farm. I went past a bottle shop and bought two slabs of Lager to take to the farm.

Nathaniel was tending to fledgling mandarin trees when he saw me. He wiped his hands on his shorts and walked over. 'I am happy to see you.' His smile turned into a grin. 'Ah, and you also bring beer.' He jumped up to help me carry it. 'I will take a break now and we can talk.'

After assuring me that all members of his family were well and asking after my relatives, he told me about the rows of mandarins and lemons he had planted next to the orange trees. He was concerned about the plants requiring special feeding and extra watering. He became quiet and stared at the mountain until I interrupted him with talk of my overnight stay at the Moeketsi home. My account of the mysterious

162

night drizzle fascinated him. He was particularly interested in the Moeketsi sisters and plied me with questions about their garden and Galani's black cats.

'The *Bafokeng* people have a crocodile totem, not a baboon totem like us *Bahurutshes*. 'Ugh, Crocodiles!' He shuddered. 'Cold, creepy things. They can jump up and bite you like snakes.'

We both laughed.

'The *Bafokeng* people think they are very, very clever. They say they are called *Royal Bafokeng* because they have a king. But everybody has a chief. We have plenty of chiefs.'

'Yes, there are plenty chiefs here in Rustenburg,' I said with a smile. 'Anything else you don't like about the *Bafokeng*?'

He gave me a swift sideways look.

I felt sure that Nathaniel's intense dislike of the *Bafokeng* was fuelled by jealousy. They owned the largest area of farmland and were extremely successful. They had a great deal of money behind them from payouts for their land, from platinum mining companies. Enmity between the two clans was not new and continued to raise its head.

'The Moeketsi family doesn't seem to get along with the people next door.' I said.

'Not talk any more... not one word.'

'Why?'

He threw his hands up in the air and lowered them slowly. 'That's how it is.' His mouth puckered.

We needed a change of subject. I asked if he and Mina were going to attend Galani's rain ceremony.

'Of course we are going! Everybody's going. It will be big entertainment.'

Nathaniel opened one of the cans of beer, gulped down the liquid in a few long and practiced gulps, and threw the empty can into a garbage bin. 'I think of the good days back on Baas Piet's farm – drinking *skokiaan*, dancing after work is finished, no worry with feeding the wife and children... not have to make the workers hurry a lot. Very good days.'

It did not take much to launch me into thoughts of the

past. All those years ago, Saturday night was the night the huts throbbed with music and dance. But memories of my childhood also had the shadow of apartheid leering over them. Blacks and Whites were not allowed to dance with each other, attend the same cinema or concerts. Attending any place that even looked as if it could be a public meeting place was forbidden. How separately our lives had to be lived then. I considered myself lucky. As a child I slipped under the ropes, and unnoticed, visited the black's huts and tasted their passion for dancing. Real dancing, I called it, compared it to the stiff, steps Ma and Pa called ballroom dancing.

By the time I left *Mosego,* the temperature had risen unbearably. Later, a cool shower and iced lemonade barely eased my discomfort.

Twenty-Eight

'Wake up! Wake up quick!' I heard in my sleep. What's going on?

The light was turned on and Josh hovered over my bed. 'Get up!'

'Oh my God!' The smell of smoke registered. 'Is the house on fire?'

'Not yet. The fire's in the veld next door.'

I sat up, holding the sheet against my nakedness. 'I'll throw some clothes on and meet you downstairs.'

With no time to fiddle with undies, I grabbed the crumpled tracksuit I had worn the day before, lying on a chair, and pulled it on. Hurriedly I pushed my feet into my runners, half tying the laces. When I entered the kitchen, Josh had just replaced the telephone. 'Fire department's on the way. Bloody second time I'm phoning.'

Tall columns of smoke rose from the vacant plot next door. Young men and children were already fighting the fire, beating it with sacks but they were not winning. Leaping flames the colour of *kaffirboom* blooms announced that we would be next if the firemen did not hurry. My heart thumped as the crackle of blackening veld and falling trees grew louder. I had been close to fires before, when Pa burned off tracts of land to encourage growth for the next season. He made bonfires of dead leaves and grass. The difference was that Pa's burning was controlled.

I stopped myself from rushing outdoors. Keep your head or you'll be lost, I told myself. I ran to the study to collect my photos and important papers and put them in the boot of the car. I suggested Josh do the same. 'We'll put our things in the car, and if things turn ugly we'll drive to a safer place and park there.'

'Ja, good idea.'

'What about Stevie?'

'He's under the bed shaking,' Josh called to me.

'Tie a lead or rope onto his collar and we'll put him in the car, too.'

Once we had loaded the boot and urged Stevie into the back seat, there was nothing further we could do. We stood helplessly watching the fire rage. Sparks flew, the wind ignited a bush or dried log and spread its flames in the direction of the house. My panic made me unaware of the smoke I was inhaling or the singed hairs on my arms.

At last we heard a welcome siren. Children intrigued by the fire drew closer as the fire engine rolled to a stop, spraying dust and pebbles. In the truck, the men were packed like olives in a jar. Eight of them jumped out and working as one, uncoiled thick hoses. Quickly and efficiently they connected the hoses to the water pump and directed fierce jets of water at the flames. I don't know how long we stood watching the men wrestle with the fire but eventually it was a smoldering heap. More water finally killed it. Taking their time now, the firemen wiped the sweat from their faces and began rolling up their hoses. At last, yawning children and nosey neighbours went home.

I asked for the person in charge. Two men pointed to a tall man yelling orders.

'Gilbert Mmeko, M'aam.'

'You and your men have done a wonderful job. You've saved my house. Thank you.'

He nodded. 'Part of the job, M'aam.'

'How did the fire start?' I asked.

'I don't know right now. We'll take a break and then have a look around. One thing Ma'am, you're very lucky. When we rocked up one hell of a wind was driving the flames from the fence line into your property. Some of the shrubs and trees on your side were already burnt. When it was looking bad for you, suddenly the wind shifted, blowing in the opposite direction, taking the flames away from your place. Very, very lucky.'

The fire fighters polished off the coffee and sandwiches we made them and hung about the fire truck for a bit longer. They rose tiredly and then in groups of twos and threes, used high beamed torches to examine the heart of the smoky ground and its fringes.

One of the men called his boss. 'I don't like the look of this bush.' The arson squad should be called in. I can see two or even three points where the fire was lit and there are some B & H cigarette butts we've picked up along the fence.'

'I'll take one of those if you don't mind,' I said.

Gilbert gazed at the sky. 'The wind's up so watch carefully. Sparks could start it again. Call if you need us.'

The firemen packed into the truck and rumbled back up the road.

Wrung out, I watched them leave, waved, and returned to the house. I fell into my most comfortable chair and closed my eyes. They stung even more closed than open. Some drops would soothe them but I was too tired to fetch them from the medicine chest. I must have nodded off for an hour or so, but woke with a thumping chest and a question in my mind. Was there a connection between the fire and the murder enquiry? Was the fire lit by someone who smoked Benson and Hedges? And had this person attempted to frighten me off?

It was 4.20 A.M. and smoke still clung to the carpets and curtains. Too restless to go back to sleep and apprehensive of what the day might bring, I paced the passage. I turned on the television. One look at the violence in the streets of New York and I switched it off. In the mellow light, I gazed at the photos of Ma and Pa. *You were both beside me today, sending protective power in my direction. If I was protected why did I feel so unsettled and afraid?*

The house stank and outdoors the acacias bent to the wind. As much as I wanted to remain curled up in my chair, difficulty in breathing forced me out. I grabbed the car keys and drove ridiculously fast towards the hills, with only the thought of reaching sweet smelling air. With no particular destination in mind, I swerved onto a mountain path. When I noticed a sign announcing The Kgaswano Nature Park, I pulled up in front of closed gates. It was too early for even the most enthusiastic wildlife fans. When I was a child, the animal reserve was small and not particularly well stocked with game. Now, it had obviously been developed into a commercial venture. After adjusting the car seat, I opened the windows, eased back and waited. Soon a pink sky stained the mountains and the ancient volcanic rocks in the dustbowl began to turn orange.

⚜

Though I felt shaky after the fire, I returned to the pattern of my daily life. With a coffee next to me and a cigarette, I sat at the computer checking my emails. In Melbourne, my calmer existence made it easier to reduce my smoking to one or two a day. Now I stopped counting.

There was one message, from George:

I wish you would join me up on the ridge again. I've broken through to new areas and made some interesting discoveries. There's so much I want to show you. If you come up to the ridge, you'll need to wear overalls and sturdy shoes. Looking forward to seeing you soon, I miss you, George

I felt a wave of excitement. The message had come when I longed for affection and understanding, without lengthy explanations. Intense feelings could be risky but there were no insurance policies for the important aspects of life. I would visit the ridge soon.

I was on the couch reading and Stevie was next to me sharing a chocolate biscuit, when the phone rang. It was Arnie sounding pleased. 'Kosigo's tox report has come in at last and it's given the murder a different twist.'

'Well...?'

'The high concentration of poison in her blood came from the plant Scilla Natalensis, the bulb of the Hyacinth. It took them ages to track it down but now they're certain. Hyacinth grows in lots of gardens here and like a weed on the mountains. From the look of the scars and burns in her gullet and stomach, they think she was poisoned over several weeks.'

'Do you remember Galani complaining that the whole family had some mystery illness that made them feel ill?'

His sigh was audible. 'So we have two attacks on Kosigo – the poison and the stabbing. And apparently Raymond was also sick before he was stabbed.'

'It could be connected.'

'Unfortunately we don't have the resources to follow up the serial murder angle.'

I gasped, but I doubt he heard it. 'If the man we're looking for is a serial killer ... we have to find him...think of the consequences!'

He mumbled a few words as he wound up the conversation. He was in a squeeze but I had run out of excuses for him. I thought of our Boys in Blue in Melbourne and sighed.

I noted the hyacinth poison found in Kosigo's blood and the attempts to frighten me with the broken bone on my analysis sheet. I placed a question mark next to the fire.

That night I fell asleep thinking of Tansie and hyacinths. To decorate her mud hut, Tansie had tall jam or pickle jars full of hyacinths. She'd say, *we need flowers, plenty flowers, Everywhere is sickness, ugly things, bad smells. Flowers make beautiful, like medicine.*

The following day, Josh entered the sitting room looking worried. 'Another policeman is here. Police are everywhere.'

'Ask him in,' I said, reluctantly putting down my book. The murder mystery I had been reading was at a pivotal point.

'Inspector Sarel Cronje, Arson,' the tall man in uniform introduced himself.

He sat awkwardly on a low soft chair and removed his cap. 'Chief Detective Inspector Swart asked me to come by to look at the area that was on fire. I've brought two of my men.'

I put on my shoes and led him out to the fire site. After investigating, he concluded that the fire had been lit with a few basic molotovs thrown on to the dry veld. He stayed a while and chatted about the frequency of fires since the drought and left.

I finished my book before dinner. Josh was disappointed that I had barely eaten the piquant chicken salad and dessert he had prepared. Since the fire, I had lost my appetite. I settled in the sitting room and lit a cigarette.

Stools being moved and cupboard doors closing told me that Josh was coming to the end of his kitchen tidying routine. 'Please check the windows and doors before you leave,' I called out to him.

'Karel is coming over so I'll be home tonight, you can call me any time if you get worried.'

Right then, I missed my sedate, predictable life in Melbourne. I had felt secure there in spite of the occasional burglaries and muggings reported in the news. How did people manage to live with the degree of crime and violence in South Africa? Even with Josh outside, I could not relax.

Twenty-Nine

As I woke, I thought of George. His energy and intellect drew me to him, but his sexual appeal swamped the rest. Perhaps I was being ridiculously cautious but a twinge of uncertainty still lurked. I had tried so hard to keep the investigation in one container, George in another, with no spillage between the two. In my imagination the separation worked and I saw myself keeping my emotions under firm control.

That afternoon I decided to visit the dig. I followed George's suggestions. At the nearest shopping mall, I found a shop that supplied hiking and camping equipment. I purchased denim overalls and tough suede shoes, or *veldskoene,* and changed into my protective gear in the ladies cloakroom. My bundle of civvies went into the car boot.

Ivan was examining recently recovered bits of pottery when he spotted me. Though we had not corresponded for weeks, he greeted me amiably.

'Let's have something cool to drink,' he suggested. I followed him into the tent and we sat around a makeshift table. After a general discussion, he asked with a grin. 'Are you enjoying studying the eland and the spirits?'

'I find it fascinating.'

'Spiritual healers past and present are part of life here, along a continuum, from San medicine men, to the rain makers and *ngakas'*

He placed his glass on the trestle table, grabbed a cushion and handed me one. 'These folding chairs are damn uncomfortable.' After finding the right spot to place his cushion, an expression of comfort spread over his face and he continued to speak in his lecturing voice. 'I'm thinking about the mystical eland and the unique place it holds in the San belief system.' He explained that though the eland was the San's most prized kill, it was revered as a symbol of strength and potency. The powerful, fast moving antelope was difficult to hunt but once killed its sweet meat was a week's food for a clan.

'Sorry I'm talking too much.'

'Not at all. I like listening and learning.'

He smiled.

'Tell me about the eland in rock art.'

His smiled widened. 'When Whites first came across San rock art about 400 years back, they regarded it as a primitive account of the hunting life of the artists. But by the twentieth century the rock art was viewed not only as reference of life in those times but as a pictorial expression of a sacred animal's connection to the spirit world.'

I nodded, hoping he would continue.

'If you haven't noticed yet, George is obsessed with the eland. Not that I blame him. The rock art he's working on is wonderful stuff.' He pulled himself up from the chair and consulted his watch. 'It has been good talking to you, but I must get back to that ancient Tswana village we're excavating. Sometimes I feel as if I've lived there.'

George was on the ridge exploring deeper into the caves. I heard the drill but could not see him through the dust. 'I won't be long,' he shouted over the noise. He had been filing a piece of sandstone and was covered in fine dust.

'Hello there, Good to see you.' George lifted his hard hat and kissed the crown of my head. I smelled his sweat as he tugged my hand. 'Come, have a look at this beauty.'

I followed him behind the rocks and gasped. An eland, raw and rough but magnificent. I stood before it transfixed, until George asked me to help him to clear grass and rubble from the rock area. It was dirty work and took ages. I was pleased I was wearing the right gear. As we worked George told jokes – old but funny ones. His cackle at his own jokes made them funnier and I laughed with him. The sunlight was dying on the mountaintop when we left the ridge.

'Thanks for your help and your company. I haven't enjoyed work so much for ages,' George said with one of his most engaging smiles. 'How about some dinner tonight? Pick you up 7.30?'

❦

Josh was waiting for me in the kitchen. I recognised the excited expression on his face, 'I've got some news.'

I waited expectantly.

'Remember, I promised to find out more about the séances. This you won't believe! Raymond from the Cameroons was also at one of those séances. I found this article about him attending a séance group in a local newspaper, dated two weeks ago. The séance was conducted by Gabriel, who led the group we went to together. You can read about it in this article,' he said handing the newspaper cutting to me. 'It mentions that Raymond was deep in conversation with two local *ngakas* – a young woman who is a rainmaker and an older man. What do you make of that, eh?'

'Thank you, Josh. Very interesting indeed.'

I read the article carefully. Unfortunately without photographs or more detail, it was not the sort of information that stood up in court. However, I realised that the killer may well have known both victims prior to murdering them. That enabled him to get close enough to his victims to take them without a fight. If only we knew the motive for the murders.

❦

George booked a table at a popular nightspot in Rustenburg. He was late but he made up for it with a posy of scented flowers. People of all colours and tongues were out enjoying themselves. Thoughts of poverty, disease and racial prejudice were drowned by chatter, music, food and alcohol. People requested new and old favourites and the musicians played them. George was an excellent dancer and led me across the floor with certainty and style. We danced, sensing the music and each other, the charge between us stirring. When the music stopped we stood connected, waiting for the magic to start up again. Our dancing was so sensual that I quivered, aching for him. His eyes said he wanted me too. I moved closer and our lips touched. A few minutes later we left the restaurant arm in arm.

Thirty

Josh emptied the mailbox and carried a bunch of letters and bills into the house. There was an official looking letter from the solicitor acting for Wil, reminding me to sign the divorce papers. The severing our union, our years spent together, upset me more than I had expected. My emotions dangled back and forth - one minute I felt cast off and unlovable and the next I looked forward to my freedom. In the past I confused love with lust, the passion Wil and I had when we were teenagers making out in the orange groves. Could I trust my judgment this time?

Galani's rain ceremony was due to begin at sunset that evening. With an empty day to fill, a walk was an obvious choice. I was about to leave for my walk on Connie's farm when I heard a car pull up. It was Arnie.

'I hope you've come with some news,' was my greeting.

'Sorry, nothing yet. I was close by and thought I'd stop by to see a friendly face. Just attended the most horrendous murder... blood everywhere.'

I was becoming a refuge for him and it had to stop. But he looked drained and the smell of peppermints clung to him. How could I turn him away?

'Something to eat? A sandwich and coffee?'

'If I'm not holding you up,' he said, looking at my walking shoes.

'Don't worry about it... I'll go for my walk later.'

It did not take Josh long to present a platter of sandwiches and coffee. We ate on the stoep and for once we did not talk about the case. Arnie was a keen supporter of Bafane-Bafane, the country's soccer team and spoke about his hope that they would win the Cup. I did not want to dash his enthusiasm by mentioning the strong competition.

He had polished off most of the sandwiches, when he slumped back into his chair and sighed. I waited for him to speak but he busied himself with the knife-like creases in his trousers before looking up at me. 'I can't wait to be out of this job. It has taken all I've got and for what? Chaos continues.'

'I can see that the machinery works slowly. It must be difficult.'

'Difficult at work. Difficult at home.'

I did not know what to say, or if he wanted me to comment.

'My wife, Dana walked out on me. She'd had enough of my crazy hours...can't say I blame her.'

'It's not easy living with a cop.'

'At work we call the life of a cop a passion killer.'

He gave me a long wistful look and then polished off the last sandwich.

I had once respected Arnie as fine police officer but now I felt sorry for him. The last thing I needed was him knocking at my door at night with a bag of problems to off-load. As it was he was visiting far too frequently. I was relieved when he finished his second cup of coffee and left for the station.

⚜

Well before sunset, crowds jostled for a place closest to the raised altar in the centre of the Moeketsi courtyard. No one complained about paying a small entrance fee, a collection 'for AIDS orphans', the sign said.

The set was impressive with the stage flanked by all seven of the crocodile totems. The stone crocs had been shifted from their garden setting to mark the boundary of the stage. Heady incense mingled with the smell of grilling meat and drums throbbed in the background. It was an atmosphere for making miracles.

I smiled to myself as I imagined what Pa would have

thought about my presence at a pagan ceremony. I could hear his voice. *Why are you attending this ceremony? What's wrong with praying for rain in your own church?*

The impatient crowd whistled and stamped until Galani made her entrance in a glittering emerald kaftan that swept the floor and a white jewelled headscarf covering her head. The crowd clapped so effusively that she held up her hands to halt them. Suddenly a stench filled the courtyard. 'Stink bomb, stink bomb,' people near me shouted, between holding their noses. Thabang hurriedly lit incense sticks and soon the perfumes of neroli, cedar and lavender masked the smell. Galani took a long drink and several deep breaths.

As the sun dipped behind the clouds, a group of teenage girls in white ran on to the stage and surrounded Galani. They symbolised purity and water, someone said over the microphone. Their poses were attractive but choreographed, in a staged Western manner. If Pa had been in the audience, he would have laughed and found this contrived ceremony ridiculous. In his church, the Nederduits Gereformeerde Kerk, prayer services for rain were decorous, institutionalised prayer, nothing like this riotous ritual. Right then I missed him desperately, longed to hear his laugh and feel him next to me.

Galani was trying hard to impress. 'Vestal virgins,' I overheard an elderly Tswana say to his wife.

'Virgins, eh,' she said. 'Not many of them left.'

'How can there be, with those stupid men believing that raping them will be a protection against AIDS,' he snapped.

The important part of the ceremony was about to begin, when a man stood and yelled out, 'imposter! Modjaji the true Rain Queen is dead.'

The hissing crowd watched two well-built men emerge and grapple with the troublemaker. With his hands held behind his back, he was marched off the property. A skinny man next to me with a bush of black hair whispered to his friend in Setswana, that the rude man thrown out had every reason to be upset.

I turned to him. 'Excuse me asking, but what was

upsetting him?'

'What's upset him?' he sniggered, giving his friend a poke in the ribs.

'Quiet please, people,' Galani called out.

'I'll tell you later,' the skinny man whispered.

Dramatically, drummers in animal skins ran onto the stage. The girls in white held their arms up to the sky and cried out beseechingly. Their movements became rhythmical as they gyrated and clapped their hands to the drumbeats. As in most African ceremonies, the crowd joined in, clapping to the beat.

By this time, Galani was in a trance. With eyes glazed she sang, begging the ancestors for rain. She repeated *'Khotso, Pula, Nala'*. I recognised the words from the royal *Bafokeng* flag standard, *'Peace, Rain, Plenty'*.

The crowd responded by calling out, asking why their pleas for rain were not answered. She held herself taut and tall and answered them sternly. 'There is no rain because we the people have committed sins of greed and jealousy against each other. We are selfish and no longer help each other or work together and each one of us is to blame.' She stopped to take a breath and continued. 'We have forgotten our ancestors and they are angry. We have overused the land, drained its food by planting crops every season.' She held up her arms in supplication. 'We must remember our ancestors. Let all wrongs that we have committed be made right, allow all of us, the sinners, to be cleansed and the spirits of the ancestors to be satisfied so that the all-powerful one, *Modimo* brings us rain.'

The drums beat dramatically. Though Galani had a more theatrical presence than I expected, I was disappointed. I saw no spiritual auras in purple or green during her performance. Members of the audience who had previously called Galani an imposter stepped up their flow of insults, accusing her of copying the real Rain Queen's ceremony and of being a fraud. The guards were unable to force all the dissenters out. As I had not witnessed other rain rituals, I was in no position to comment.

She clapped her hands and with a twirl of her skirt entreated the spirits to notice the ox burning on the altar. 'Let the blood flow as we beg for rain!' she called out.

While the ox turned for a final time, I looked for the thin man who had been standing next to me. He had moved closer to the altar, but was easy to identify by his bushy hair and shiny blue shirt. He waved as he saw me approach. 'I don't know who you are, White lady but it looks like you're after answers.'

'That's true. If you have some I'd like to hear them.'

'Jake is the man you asked me about but... I don't know his last name. He's a Lovedu, belongs to same tribe as the dead Rain Queen.' He shuffled closer. 'And guess what? He consulted the other sister, the dead one, Kosigo about his troubles. Can you believe that?' he said, standing close and lowering his voice. 'Weird eh, with Queen Modjaji being the tribe's healer. And she was still alive then.'

'People can do strange and secretive things.'

'Suppose so. I hear Jake has a plot near Pretoria. Keeps a few sheep and cows there. Wants nothing to do with the Modjaji lot in Tzaneen. Cut himself off from them.'

'Interesting.'

'Kosigo was young but she had powers and a big reputation. Such a big reputation, that it was hard to get an appointment with her. I went to see Kosigo myself last year after my father passed on. A perfect description of him and she gave me a message from him. I was very happy.'

'Do you know why Jake consulted her?'

'His wife Leah went cold on him, didn't want to cook or go to bed with him. He was dead sure she had a lover. People say, that one night when his wife told him she was going out with her girlfriends, she came home really late ... two or three o'clock. He sniffed her clothes while she was sleeping and thought that they had another man's smell. He was crazy for her and didn't know what the hell to do, so he went to Kosigo for answers... begged her for help. And boy oh boy, let me tell you that's when the real trouble started.'

'Tell me,' I egged him on.

'Kosigo asked for a picture of the wife. I heard he took a foxy shot of her. She went far away in her head, like mediums do and asked the spirits for guidance. After all of that, she said the spirits showed her a picture of Leah lying on the grass behind the municipal offices kissing some other dude.'

'Really!'

'Sure. Kosigo shouldn't have told him the full story like neat whisky. She should've put water with it. So, poor Jake drove home in a weird mood. He followed that wife of his around the house for days nagging her for the name of her lover. In the end, Leah went down on her knees promising she didn't have a lover, begging him to leave her alone. But, Jake didn't trust her and got hold of a private detective. Shit hit the fan, when Leah found out the detective was spying on her. She was innocent, but fed up with him by now. So, she pushed Jake out of the house and all of his stuff after him. He yelled and swore at her and sure thing; she fell into the arms of the first man who brought her flowers.'

'Goodness.'

'So, Jake went away for a few months. When he came back he found out she had a new man. He cried and begged her to come back to him but she'd had enough of him. He got in a real down mood, didn't eat, couldn't sleep and talked about killing himself. One day a friend found him lying on his bed half gone and the friend called the ambulance. After a week in hospital Jake was released, only one thing was in his mind, to pay Kosigo back for causing his trouble. He couldn't blame himself, so he blamed Kosigo. Crazy eh?'

Cans of beer were opened as I left the courtyard and the brown liquid gushed over the altar. The security men in black doubled as chefs and sliced the cooked meat. They put the heart and liver aside to be offered to the gods. The first slices of meat went to Galani and her family and the remainder to the crowd. I anticipated the crowd's wild surge to grab a bit of the sacrificial ox and as I hurried away, the smell of the beef and the sound of the crowd followed me.

Later I dialled Arnie's cell phone to fill him in with the information I had gathered about Jake.

'Who knows, this character Jake could be our murderer. At least it's another lead, worth following up. There can't be too many Jakes from the Lovedu tribe who own a plot near Pretoria. I'll ask the Pretoria cops to locate him and by tonight we should have his details. All going well, I'll take Phineas and we'll head off to his place tomorrow morning. Unless there are any problems in locating him I'll pick you up if you want to join us.'

'Thanks.'

'Right. See you tomorrow about 10.00 A.M.'

Thirty-One

We left for Pretoria under heavy skies with a whiff of moisture in the air. I turned back to look at the mountain shrouded in gathering clouds. None of us mentioned the word *rain*, as if talking about it would break a spell, but we sneaked glances at the sky now and again.

Jake was sitting on his stoep staring at his withered tobacco crop. His eyes had the emptiness of a man who had drunk and cried too much and his clothes had the stiffness of unwashed cotton. A visit by the police did not seem to bother him - nothing did. We followed his halting step into a filthy house strewn with unwashed plates, beer bottles and empty food tins. None of us sat on the chairs packed with clothing or wanted to touch a thing on the dirt speckled carpet. When Kosigo's name was mentioned, a spark fired his eyes. Talking in half sentences often unconnected, he told us how consulting Kosigo had caused his wife to leave him.

The police had come with a warrant to search Jake's house. While Phineas began the search, Arnie lit a cigarette in Jake's once resplendent garden, that was now a sandpit with a few desert plants.

'Hey everybody,' we heard Arnie yell. '*It's raining*! Galani has gone and done it.'

It began with a drizzle and claps of thunder, and was followed by straight sheets of rain. As the corrugated iron roof of Jake's house tinkled, Phineas turned out drawers, looked under rotting food in burnt frying pans and amongst the piles of clothing. He commented that Jake's study and desk was an oasis of order in the chaotic house. Accounts and payments were tied with rubber bands and pencils and pens had a home in a red plastic organiser. Phineas combed through it all and at last his diligence was rewarded. He found a computer and a file containing copies of emails lay next to it. Copies of the threatening emails sent to Kosigo were amongst them. Enthused with his success in the study, Phineas braved the rain to search the garden shed. He returned with Benson and Hedges cigarettes still packed in cardboard cartons.

Phineas tapped the cigarette cartons. 'You never know, these could be from the same batch as the stubs we found in the veld near Kosigo's body.'

'Take the lot to the station. It looks like we've got our murderer.' Arnie said with a relieved sigh.

I was not convinced of Jake's guilt and though I tried to air my doubts, Arnie waved me away. I could only hope that he would look at the evidence with his former cool eye. He phoned for a police car to take Jake in for questioning, and we left soon after.

Arnie was happier than I had seen him since I had arrived. In the car, he sang the old song about a soldier longing to return to the Transvaal to see his girl. Phineas and I joined in with the chorus:

My Sarie Marais is so ver van my heart.
My Sarie Marais is so far from my heart
Maar'k hoop om haar weer to sien.
But I hope to see her again
Sy het in die wyk van die Mooi Rivier gewoon,
She lived in the Mooi River area
Nog voor die oorlog het begin.
Before the war began

❦

The skies were laden and rain skittered on an earth too hard to absorb it. Even in the morning with the bedside light turned on the room was dull. The thought of leaving the house to face someone either thanking God or Galani for the long awaited change, made staying in bed listening to the patter on the roof preferable. Reports of the ceremony followed by rain in several newspapers, had headings such as *Miracle Maker, Psychic Opens the Heavens* and *Believe it or Not.* Galani must be pleased, I thought. She was now an accepted rainmaker with her name in print.

Kosigo's face continued to taunt me. Had Arnie charged Jake for the murder, I wondered. Arnie's phone was constantly engaged and though I left several messages with the switchboard, he did not return my calls. Finally I phoned Phineas.

'Jake's in the lock up, charged for Kosigo's murder. He's been before the magistrate and the case is closed. The media have been informed of the date of the trial in three months. A big relief for us all.'

'But Phineas, are you sure Jake poisoned Kosigo? That he inflicted those deep stab wounds? And where's the knife? Does he smoke Benson and Hedges or was he hoarding the cigarettes to sell them? And what about the murder in Polokwane and the attack on Raymond...was he involved there too?' The frustration in my voice was reaching a near shriek.

Phineas coughed. 'The boss is determined to move on and he's not waiting for further results or looking into Raymond's murder, or any other incidentals. Jake's been charged for killing Kosigo and that's it.'

'Incidentals! He's sloppy... and unprofessional,' I said, no longer trying to disguise the disgust in my voice. After I put down the phone, my frustration turned to fury. Pity about the promise I had made to Nathaniel! One did not break promises with him or one paid with his sulks for years. I had not been on the receiving end of his moods but had witnessed them. I was far too fond of him to cause a rift. The image of Kosigo was not going to shift either.

I sank back into the comfort of my bed. I had been wasting my time working with the cops, I thought, as I reached for a large block of chocolate in the top drawer of the bedside table. I broke off a chunk and while savouring the richness, the image of homemade chocolates in a quilted, heart shaped box popped up at me. It was time to visit the Moeketsis and have another look at those homemade chocolates. I stretched and eased myself out of bed.

My wait outside the Moeketsi's house in the wet was brief. A new young woman answered the bell promptly. 'Morning. Lovely rain eh?' She smiled pleasantly.

'Morning. Yes, the rain is good. Is Miss Galani in?'

'Ja sure. Come inside.'

'Where's Keneuoe?'

'She is very sick in the stomach. Gone home.'

I followed her into the sitting room. Galani was on the couch in the identical position I had seen her last, her cats cuddled next to her and a box of chocolates lying open on the table in front of her.

'Come in. Nice that you came without the policemen.' Her mood was pleasant and her tone welcoming. She pointed to a chair indicating that I should sit near her. 'What do you think of the rain, eh?' she beamed. 'Kosigo would be proud, don't you think?'

I nodded. 'Yes, I think she would.'

'I feel her with me – her power is here.' She thumped her chest with one hand and with the other she caressed her curvaceous body spread the length of the couch. 'Look, look.' She pointed at her finger. 'A new ring – emerald of course, to celebrate the rain and to always think of Kosigo.'

I was taken aback by the ring's flashy beauty. The stone cut to display prisms of green, lay in a bed of tiny diamonds.

She must've noticed my shocked expression. 'It wasn't bought from the money collected at the ceremony. That money goes to the AIDS charity. Dad bought me the ring.'

'Oh!' was all I could say.

'I wanted to mark this time as special.' She hesitated and then added, 'a remembrance was in order, don't you think?'

I couldn't help thinking that the family could've given the money to the poor in Kosigo's name. Poverty and disease were crying out in the streets.

She pointed a lacquered finger at the chocolates. 'Come on, have one. You're slim and can afford a little richness.'

I picked up the box and ran my fingers over the quilted lid.

'It's an interesting box.'

'The second box sent to me lately. I don't know who makes them.' A lovely note of appreciation came with this box.

'Do you still have the note that came with the chocolates?'

'No sorry, I threw it away'

She stroked one of the cats next to her on the couch. 'I miss my little Chi. The vet had to put the poor darling to sleep. She was a beauty, the sleekest of the cats and she had emerald eyes.'

'What a pity.'

'She was crying out in pain. It was awful. The vet thinks she ate something poisonous. He wants to do a post mortem but I haven't heard yet.'

'Oh!' I said again, remembering the steep cost of vet bills.

'Come on, have a chokkie,' she urged again.

'I'm addicted to chocolate, but I've already had too many today,' I lied. There was something about the chocolates. 'But I'll take two to have later.'

I took two chocolates with different fillings, wrapped them in a napkin first, and then placed them inside one of the plastic bags I kept in my handbag. I would try to have them analysed privately but it would not be easy to find someone with the skills.

A loud voice outside the door interrupted Galani's chatter. 'My father, please excuse me.' She rushed to him, holding his arm and supporting him as he shuffled into the room. 'I'd like you to meet my father.'

The old man carefully folded his embroidered robes around his rounded body before sitting, smoothed the material and adjusted his flat kufi hat perched on his moon face. Then he looked at me. 'I gather you're connected with the police. They come here often but haven't done anything yet about finding my daughter's murderer. I wonder if they'll ever catch him.'

The tilt of his head, demanding tone of voice reminded me of Galani. She had inherited his body shape too. He continued in the same vein admonishing the police force, and Arnie in particular.

I was thinking up an excuse to leave, when Thabang stormed into the room, her eyes wild. 'That idiot next door has just dumped a heap of manure in front of the house again. I can't take any more of it.'

Thabang put her hand to her mouth instinctively, like a child caught saying the wrong thing. 'Oh, I'm sorry, I didn't realize you were here.' She nodded in my direction.

'That's okay,' I said.

'That man next door is incredible. You have no idea the noise we have to put up with from those screeching parrots of his. The sound carries all the way over here.'

'You'd think a Tswana would know better,' Mr Moeketsi said angrily.

'Is your neighbour Emmanuel Tagoe?' I asked.

Thabang nodded. 'Everybody knows about him. If it isn't one thing with him it's another.'

It was time to leave before I involved myself in a tribal feud. 'I'll pop round in a day or two to hear the vet's findings about your cat,' I said to Galani from the doorway. I ran to the car through a hammering burst of rain and almost slipped on slush on the ground.

At home I removed the chocolates from my handbag. In their squishy state they went straight into a separate container in the fridge, next to the sample of melted chocolate I had from Raymond's tent. It would be a waste of time asking Arnie to have toxicology experts analyse either of them. I rang Rosie. As a doctor, perhaps she knew of someone in the forensic field who would be prepared to do the screening, for a small fee. She gave me Phyllis Green's phone number.

❧

Rain fell for five days. Birds were in hiding and the sky was a constant grey. Brown puddles bubbled and mountain streams gushed over rocks. By the fourth day, the paddocks in farms were flooded, streams surged onto the veld and untarred roads became impassable.

Then the orange sun dawned and dried the mud. Slowly the water found an underground home and life went on as before. New growth added green to the veld and all manner of plants sent out their tendrils. Soon the flowers would bloom.

Thirty-Two

I made my way to Phyllis' home via the main freeway. From the peak to the valley, the affluent suburbs stretched for miles and behind them was an endless view of squatter camps. Her modest Edwardian house in a quiet street nestled under overhanging oaks. I banged on the door until an elderly woman opened it. No, I did not have an appointment, I insisted but I had spoken to Mrs Green on the telephone. The woman grudgingly led me to a cluttered front room. From the low couch I was treated to a collection of paintings by well-known South African artists. The shelves were stacked haphazardly with books and a wooden cabinet was jammed with a life's collection of precious finds - beaded miniatures, bits of pottery, spears and wooden sculpture from all over Africa. Papers and periodicals covered tables and some of the chairs.

My initial reaction to Phyllis was surprise. Her fast paced, enthusiastic speech on the phone did not seem to fit the tall bony woman in a white coat, with a single long silver plait that hung most of the way down her back. I had expected a shorter, plumper woman. I handed her the two airtight containers with both samples of chocolate that I had carefully transported in a cool bag filled with ice.

'Come along with me to the lab. These specimens must go straight into my fridge.'

Though Phyllis had retired from her job as a forensic pathologist at the government morgue, she accepted private work referred by barristers and doctors. I followed her down a passage to a heavy door protected with a grill and several locks. The inside of her laboratory had white tiled walls and steel tables dotted with expensive looking equipment.

'You look surprised. This is a fully functioning laboratory with a spectrophotometer. I have government accreditation.'

'Give me the background to these specimens,' she said, perching on a stool.

I told her all I knew of Kosigo's illness prior to her death, Raymond's stomach complaint prior to his attack and that Keneuoe had felt unwell with similar symptoms. I explained that the two specimens were taken from different boxes of chocolate. She promised an answer within a few days. When I asked her fee, she insisted her services were free for a friend of Rosie's.

We returned to the sitting room and over tea and biscuits talked about her past work for the coroner's court. All the while, my eyes were on the exquisite pottery in her cabinet. I left quietly when her mobile phone rang and a lengthy conversation followed.

Before returning home, I stopped at the archaeological dig. At the site, talk amongst the volunteers was frenetic.

Ivan was grinning. 'We've had a major find,' he said, pointing to what looked to me, like dirty bits of bone and stone. 'We can't be sure how old they are yet, but my guess is that they're Iron Age weapons and tools.'

I smiled and nodded but could not manufacture enthusiasm.

'If you're looking for George he's up on the ridge, as usual. Happy eland hunting,' he said as he returned to his discovery.

I found George battling to set up a broad beamed light. I had come at the right moment and helped him to unravel the cord and connect the light without pulling out the plug.

'There's an amazing painting between those rocks and I want to photograph it,' he said excitedly. The light fell on a herd of running eland, each animal looked vital. We took a few steps away from the rock to appreciate the painting. He put his arm around my shoulder and we stood before the painting for some time, sharing the thrill of viewing the herd.

The more exposed I was to images of the eland, the more fascinated I became. Each large antelope on the rock wall radiated colour and movement but was different from the rest. I understood now why George was so involved with the rock images.

We touched hands and moved together, entwined as we kissed. Then with our words tumbling out we talked about the eland. George explained how all the photos he was taking would eventually go onto the Internet and later possibly into a hard covered book to be appreciated by others.

He spent a while chiselling away at a piece of intruding rock, then disconnected the cord and packed his gear into a large bag. 'I'm done for the day. Let's go for a beer.'

The décor of the busy pub was typically African. Thatched straw ceilings, mud walls decorated with assegais and masks stared down at us. The pub attracted tourists and locals.

We took our beers and sandwiches to a corner table that was just vacated. For the first time George talked about himself. He was born in London, the eldest of four boys. At the age of eleven, his father was offered a transfer to Johannesburg. We laughed at his childhood impressions of the new country as backward and insular. The Afrikaners were hostile and anti-British. The entrenched separation between the races upset him and he could not understand why the Blacks were treated so appallingly.

George spent his early years in Cape Town, in an upper middle class suburb and attended a private school. At university, he met Evelyn and they married in their late twenties. 'She was a wonderful wife and gave me two children. She's been gone three years and I still miss her, always will. I guess if I didn't miss her, our marriage wouldn't have been worth a fig.' His children lived in England and he made every effort to see them each year at Christmas.

He rubbed his forehead. 'I'm like the rest of the South Africans now, holding on to what I've got, turned off by crime and corruption. The poverty and disease here amongst the Black population is overwhelming. He explained that he was teaching Black students about the ecological, historical and archaeological importance of the area. 'We must protect this marvellous heritage basin or it'll be lost for the future.'

I asked how long he intended to stay in Rustenburg.

'Until my work is done.' He laughed. 'I hate living in the hotel, but I've been too involved with my work to find time to look for a house or an apartment.'

Later, in bed that night, I realised how much I cared for George. Each time I saw him my feelings for him were confirmed. The guarded look I had noticed in his eyes when we first met, had melted. I felt less vulnerable too, ready to share more with him. But how important was I to him, after his passion, the eland?

Thirty-Three

After placing a cup of coffee and biscuits on the table, Josh hovered.

'How are you today, Josh. Looking smart as usual,' I said, taking in his denim outfit.

He told me he was concerned, about my welfare. He pursed his lips determinedly when I reassured him.

'The bright star, Sirius was more blue than usual last night and I have this feeling inside? He pointed to his gut. 'You must be very careful.'

'It's a perfectly clear, warm day and I'm safe inside the house.' I said, as I waved the newspaper at the myriad black dot-like flying insects that had appeared after the rain.

Later I checked my answering machine. Not a word yet from Phyllis Green.

After reading about the violence of the day and skimming the soccer results, I had an irrational thought. *Look in the cupboards in the garage.*

The Wenning family had lived in the house before Pa bought it and the garage cupboards were crammed with their family's belongings. None of them interested me. I leant against the side of the couch and yawned, but the thought urging me to open the cupboards in the garage continued to pester. Finally I acquiesced

I turned on the garage light. The garage was huge and free of any debris or cobwebs, unlike Pa's - a home for his ancient tool collection and spare bits and pieces. I approached the cupboards in an orderly way, starting with those closest to the door on the right. I found a variety of objects necessary for farm and house maintenance such as nails, screws, globes, wires, all sorted in boxes.

The tall shelves across the back wall were devoted to books. The study had a sizable library but these cupboards contained an overflow of children's books. When I came across a row of Enid Blyton's books, I was thrilled. I pulled out a book from the *Noddy and Big Ears* series, shook it free from dust and placed it on the floor to look at later. Then with delight I found several *Famous Five* novels and higher up *The Secret Garden*. They were added to my pile. I relished the idea of reading these books again. Hundreds of paperback love stories of the Mills and Boon variety filled another shelf, and I gave those a miss.

Down the left wall, shelves reached the ceiling. At the top were diaries. Pa had bought the house from solicitor Hans Wenning's widow in 1999. Sadly, Hans had keeled over during a court case and died in hospital hours later. Pa boasted he was able to by the house cheap as Mrs Wenning was in a hurry to sell and move to her family in Johannesburg. When packing, the solicitor's widow had not concerned herself with the fruits of the attic.

The diaries dating from 1960 to 1995 interested me and to reach them I perched on an old chair I found in the corner. I pulled out nine of the most recent diaries and seated on the floor, I flipped through the pages looking for a familiar name or place. The notes were mainly personal, apart from the occasional details about the solicitor's legal cases.

The entry on August 15, 1990 was worth reading. Hans Wenning had defended Frikkie du Plessis, a farmer of Lot 42 Third Avenue, Rustenburg, charged with assault and battery. Frikkie du Plessis had been sued by his neighbour Manie du Toit of Lot 43 Third Avenue, Rustenburg. I recognized the addresses – the present Moeketsi farm. I placed that diary on the pile to take with me. I decided to ask Connie about the legal case between the neighbours from Third Avenue.

A clattering noise jolted me to attention. It was the roller door winding down and clicking closed. I ran to the door and tried it, but it would not open. I had left the electronic control module in the sitting room. Though there were two high peephole windows on the opposite wall, the door was the only exit. I puzzled over the new sophisticated security system installed in the house. I had locked the house when I went out to the garage and the outside gates were locked as well. The fence was covered with electrified razor wire and the garage door could only lock if the electronic control was activated. How then could the garage door close?

I was in for a long wait until someone noticed my absence. I tried to make myself comfortable by using material I found in one of the cupboards as a pillow. I relaxed and was resting my head, when a cool force swirled around me. I panicked. When the lights flicked on and off, I wondered if someone was playing tricks. The Blacks believed in a mischievous *tokoloshe*. Surely not, I told myself. I could not accept that these strange occurrences were instigated by a mythical pixie-like creature, that the Blacks believed had an extraordinarily long penis, and was at its most dangerous when it performed evil deeds for a sorcerer. After a few minutes, all appeared calm and quiet again and my heartbeat and breathing rate returned to normal.

Rosie and I had arranged to go out for dinner that night and she was to pick me up at 8.00. Would she think I had forgotten our arrangement when she knocked on the door? There was a chance I would spend the night locked in. Three or four hours passed without a human sound. Only baboons chattered in the nearby trees and in the distance I heard the rumble of elephants.

Later, Rosie told me that when no one answered the front door she went around to the back, where she found Josh who had returned from an afternoon outing. Together they searched for me. I heard them calling and I banged and kicked the roller door but they did not hear me. Concerned about my disappearance they phoned Connie.

Even in the garage, the screech of Connie's truck was unmistakable. Apparently, Connie suggested I might be in the attic. Josh explained that the house did not have an attic, but that there was a garage full of spooky stuff. Connie thought it was worth searching the garage since neither of them had looked there for me.

As they battled to open the garage door, they heard me calling. The three of them hunted for the electronic control module. Connie found it wedged between the seats of the couch where I had been reading that afternoon. He pressed the button and the door groaned open. I hugged each of them in turn.

He looked worried. 'How could someone have got in here and closed the door with all the security?' he said to Josh.

Armed with torches they combed the grounds for signs of an intruder but found nothing. Josh promised to check the following day. He hung around until I suggested he join Karel, who was waiting patiently for him. Both Rosie and Connie offered to stay with me overnight, but they looked so weary that I sent them home. I made myself a simple but satisfying meal and listened to soothing music. Soon I fell asleep.

Thirty-Four

The diary lay on the floor next to my bed, together with the children's books I had chosen. After breakfast, I took the diary to my desk and opened it at the page I had marked.

Few of the solicitor's notes were as detailed or as humorous as the case: du Plessis versus du Toit, August 15, 1990. First Wenning described their common history. Both families originated from Voortrekker stock and like many of the trekkers, they moved from the English ruled Cape Colony to settle in the Rustenburg area. Over the years they worked hard and their land yielded profitable tobacco crops. As neighbours, the two families developed a friendship that went beyond good neighbourliness. They visited each other frequently, borrowed anything they needed and their children played together. However, when Manie du Toit decided to build a piggery on his farm everything changed.

The solicitor noted, *Manie's greed obviously exceeded his intellect in even considering such an anti-social step. Manie placed his piggery in a bald spot near the centre of his property where no amount of coaxing the land with nutrients yielded tobacco. Wenning added that Mannie ought to have established his piggery in the valley, where the stench could have been contained. In the area that Manie chose few tall trees grew and almost no bushes, so that the north wind unfortunately carried the stinkeroo straight into the du Plessis' kitchen. At first Frikkie du Toit asked Manie nicely to move the piggery but after several refusals, trading of insults across the fence became a regular event.*

It was then that Frikkie consulted Hans Wenning for legal

advice. Wenning wrote that *the enmity between the two had reached an intensity that made settlement impossible. Each insisted on his day in court. It was an open and shut case and of course du Plessis won. We did not need an ecology expert to prove our point. Du Toit paid costs and a tidy compensatory sum too. To add to it, the judge instructed him to sell his pigs immediately. What a pity, the parties could have settled the matter themselves if they had not been so pigheaded.*

I was mulling over the stupidity of the two men, when Phineas rang to tell me that at last Des, one of the cops from Polokwane had contacted him. Tests performed in Polokwane confirmed that the feather found amongst Rethabile Letsebo's personal effects was indeed from a peacock.

'Of course they didn't speak to the daughter again as we suggested,' Phineas said, sounding irritated.

'I didn't think they would. And is your boss aware of this important development with a peacock feather? I was talking slowly to control my frustration.

He answered softly. 'Jake's been charged and that's it as far as the boss is concerned. He's been overloaded with work... Amita and a few others have been away sick... but she's back now though.'

'Glad to hear that.'

'He's changed since his promotion,'

I heard the strain in his voice. 'You're quite right. He has changed.'

There was silence from Phineas until he added, 'I guess I shouldn't have said that.'

'Don't worry it won't go further. Sometimes one has to let off steam.'

⁂

I knew that a long walk in the orange farm amongst the new growth would lift my mood. Half- running, half-walking, I followed my usual route. The sun was high in the sky and the mountains soft edged, greens of all shades had shot up and the veld wore a bright canopy of new life. I breathed the scented air and sighed with delight.

In the pleasant warmth, I thought of Pa - tanned in his rolled up shirtsleeves and khaki shorts, those black hairs of his crawling like insects over his sinewy legs. My thoughts shifted to George on the ridge. He was like Pa, not physically of course, with that beard of his and his untamed head of hair. It was his manner of speaking, his stance and measured gaze that reminded me of Pa and of course his muscular frame. When absentmindedly I stubbed my runners on a rock, I shocked myself back into the present.

Connie was in the orange groves supervising weeding. The rain seeded weeds stole precious earth juices from the citrus. Connie waved as he walked towards me. The rain brought him the gift of a smile. 'I'll take a break now.'

We sat on a bench Pa made when I was little. Connie mentioned that he had overheard the workers talking about my involvement in the murder investigation. 'Why get yourself involved in one of those impossible cases, enjoy your holiday,' he said stroking his goatee.

I knew he was attempting to deputise for Pa, since he was the eldest male. I patted his arm and changed the topic of conversation.

'Do you know anything about Hans Wenning and the case between the du Plessis and du Toits?' I asked.

Connie had not met Wenning, but he laughed as he told me that Pa enjoyed using the example of the two families as a parable - a warning about what could happen to stupidly uncooperative neighbours.

'Tell me what happened after the court case?'

'Things got so bad between the two of them that they used their lawyers to talk for them. If Manie's cows strayed onto Frikkie's land or a little water from Manie's dam overflowed onto Frikkie's side, there would be a lawyer's letter in the post. Manie would send a counter letter, plus a load of manure on to the front lawn of Frikkie's house, or a load of stones on his porch. Around here we all knew about the two of them. Worse than kids.'

'What happened in the end?' I asked, trying to get to the nub of the story.

'You can imagine that both men's wives were fed up after years of hearing their husbands whining about their neighbours. Their kids hadn't only lost their playmates but endured finger pointing at school. So when the African National Congress came into power in 1994 and made noises about the return of farmland to the original owners, both parties were only too happy to sell their farms. It was a way out of an impossible situation.'

I nodded.

'Not that the government offered them what the land was really worth, but they took it. Neither cared by then and they ran from their farms. Thank God I have a good relationship with Jurgens next door. Gerhardus on the other side isn't quite as easy to deal with, but overall not a bad bloke.'

He stood slowly and stamped clods of muddy earth.

'Does Moeketsi and his neighbour Tagoe have all that land now?' I asked, checking my facts.

'Moeketsi owns both plots … about 1000 hectares in all. He used the government scheme to reclaim the land and to help him to buy it. After a year or so of farming Moeketsi found the area too big and rented part of it out to Tagoe. And you'll never guess what's happened! He and Tagoe have been locked in dispute for ages. It's not lucky land,' he laughed and threw a stone into the dirt.

'Do you know any recent details about their argument?'

He shrugged. 'I don't follow gossip,' he muttered.

Connie returned to work and I walked towards the huts. I would have to speak to Esiekiel, once the head man of the farm in Pa's day. As the oldest person on the farm he knew the local history. Regarded as tight lipped, he was trusted and consequently knew everyone's business.

Esiekiel was outside his hut, carving miniature animals. He had boxes of them and refused to sell them to the tourists, though they could have given him pocket money. I realised I had not greeted Esiekiel since my return. I gave him the respect he deserved and asked ritual questions as he sliced soft wood to form the neck of a giraffe. It was a delicate procedure and he did not look up to greet me until he had achieved a graceful curve.

'That's going to be a lovely giraffe,' I said.

He nodded and pointed to several giraffes he had already completed in different positions.

'This one you're carving looks like he's going to eat new leaves from the trees,' I said, turning one of the giraffes in my hand.

'Very high tree.' He looked at me, cocked his head and waited for me to speak again.

'I'm sorry to bother you with my questions, but you know most of the people in the area from way back.'

'What does Missie want to know?' he asked in a polite tone that eased my embarrassment.

I asked him if he knew Emmanuel Tagoe. He went on carving the giraffe's ears before answering. 'I am very old now …I not remember everybody.'

'Please try your best.'

He frowned and gently placed the carving on his lap before speaking again. He then told me that Tagoe had worked hard to establish his farm but was not as capable as Moeketsi. While his neighbour's farm thrived, his declined. Naturally, Tagoe became jealous of Moeketsi.

'Can you remember anything else about the two neighbours?'

'*Aikona*. Not today, the head's full of clouds like the sky.' He pointed upward.

'If it's okay, I'll ask you about it again another day.'

'Okay Missie.'

I left him fashioning the giraffe's face.

I walked back to the house slowly, digesting what Esiekiel had said and what he had omitted. With Esiekiel, one always had to weigh his words with care.

Perhaps Tagoe had a motive for murder. I was so immersed in analysing what I had learned from Esiekiel that I almost collided with Samuel. He was sitting on a tree stump and smoking. As I greeted him, I recognised the pungent odour of *dagga,* the local marijuana. Everyone connected with the farm knew about the luscious patch of *dagga* flourishing behind the trees in the tiny panhandle of the property. It was too important to the workers relaxation for me to make a fuss about his smoking.

Samuel sat up and held his joint behind his back. 'I am taking a break, Missie. There is too much hard work for my old back today.'

I nodded. As the sister of the farm's owner, I could not condone his action, but I did not comment on it. 'So, apart from the sore back, how are you?'

'Not so good, Missie. The rains come but the land is not the same like before.'

'Why's that?'

'You know, Missie, the day Nelson Mandela come out of jail is one of the best days in my life. When he was president, my next best day. I think everything is going to change, get better... more money for everybody and no more sickness.' He sighed and stubbed the last of his joint on his shoe. 'Look now, crime in the street, killing, rape, everybody is still poor and sick. Aaaih!'

'Unfortunately, what you say is true.'

He stood slowly. 'I'm going back to work now,' he said, putting a finger to his lips to request my silence about his smoking.

In the garden, I cut a bunch of roses large enough for a tribute to the family buried in the farm cemetery. Lately, I visited the farm cemetery more often than I did usually. It was there amongst my ancestors that I felt my protection lay. It certainly would not come from Arnie and the police force. As always, I kissed the bundle of flowers and divided them into bunches, ready to place on the graves. The cemetery was shady and the vibrant flowers glowed on the headstones. After my prayers, I was about to close the cemetery gate, when I heard a sizzling noise. In minutes, the petals of all the flowers withered. They lay frazzled on the headstones, their colours now a dull grey. I hurried away. If the dead flowers were meant to be a message, it was not a pleasant one. The episodes of the shattering lamp and the garage door that trapped me, swept through my mind.

Attempting to ignore my fear, I strode across the veld towards the old mud huts where Tansie and Zacharias once lived. I stopped to pick some new foliage and budding veld flowers. Behind the huts lay both their graves. A wooden cross, once white, but now grey and weathered, marked the mound over Zacharias' grave. The earth covering Tansie was a raw red. I placed the new leaves on Zacharias' grave. The assortment of fragrant buds was for Tansie. My jumbled words of love for her in the simple Setswana we spoke during my childhood poured out. I talked to her, told her how difficult it was to unearth the killer, and how useless I felt. My fears gushed out. Evil had been unleashed, I explained. It was not an irrational fear, I knew I was a target. I wiped my eyes with my hand. When I walked away this time, the flowers remained intact.

As a child, I held Zacharias in awe. Even as a bony 92 year old, the patriarch was revered as a sage by all on Pa's farm. Pa made time for him too. A visit to his hut was an event. I tip-toed into his hut and usually found him asleep in a rocking chair, padded with animal skins. His hearing was still acute and as I entered, his creased eyelids fluttered. He turned towards me and smiled a welcome. When I was four or five, I talked to strange creatures congregating at the pinnacle of his thatched hut.

'They'll be waiting for me, to take me to the other land,' he said with a wink. When my intuitiveness did not lessen with age, Zacharias was convinced that I had a special connection with the spirit world. He would jokingly tell me that if I wanted to, I could become a *ngaka* when I was older. 'For sure, a White *ngaka*,' he said with peals of happy laughter. I had Zacharias to thank for encouraging those early signs of psychic intuition.

I strolled up to the house in search of Raelene, but she was out. I went to the pantry in search of her cookies and found a tray cooling. I ate two with a glass of milk and then another. The sweetness settled my hunger not my anxiety.

I was too dogged, too fixated on sniffing out the murderer to give up. Anyway, my security and my fight against the forces trying to frighten me were linked to the murders. I knew that. I had no option but to continue my search for the killer.

There was one place in my childhood home that had always held the key to secrets, the attic. They were family secrets but for some inexplicable reason, I was drawn there. I found a torch in the entrance hall and climbed the narrow steps. A musty smell greeted me. I fumbled for the light switch and in the pale glow, I negotiated my way past old furniture and piles of bric a brac. Deeper into the attic, the torch flickered in my hand and an arc of light swung in the direction of old clothing piled on a dusty shelf. Edging closer, I noticed felt hats on top of the bundle. The torch beam shone directly on one of the hats. It had a feather in it, a blue- green peacock feather.

I understood the message. *Concentrate on the feather.*

Thirty-Five

Drums beat in the distance. I pulled the pillow over my head to drown out the morning noise, but my attempt to sleep that little bit longer was useless. After a soothing shower, I stretched for my towel. In the shiny beads of water of the shower screen, I saw Kosigo's face. I wrapped the towel around myself and looked again, but this time both the screen and the mirror were covered in misty film.

The drums were still beating when I greeted Josh in the kitchen. I had not mastered the language of the drums, but I knew that they usually told of something vital to the community.

'Can you read the drums today?'

He put his head to the side. 'The message is sad. That's all I can tell.'

I looked out of the window. The ground was wet from overnight rain but the sun was out, smiling.

'Any phone calls while I was in the shower?' I asked, wondering if Arnie had phoned.

Josh shook his head.

Since charging Jake for Kosigo's murder, Arnie had not contacted me. He was making a major error and I was through making allowances for him. I dialed his number and the receptionist put me through to him. I was angry enough to tell him how disappointed in him I was, that he was carelessly ignoring important clues to the investigation and blindly insisting on charging Jake.

'You invited me to join you on the investigation to

help you find the murderer. What investigation… a dog's breakfast! There's more than that one murder, probably committed by the same person and you take the convenient way out. You'll do anything to close the case …anything to tell your boss you've charged someone… anyone.'

'Hey, cool it, Linda! I don't agree with you about Jake at all. He's the guilty one and as far as I'm concerned the matter of Kosigo's murder is closed. I'm not as certain about Raymond's death but I can't devote further time to it.'

'Well I'm out of it, then.'

'Don't walk away yet. Please. We may still need your help if the case doesn't go to trial.'

I had not heard the pleading little boy-like tone in his voice before. I mumbled a few words about him closing his eyes to the facts and clicked off. The conversation had frustrated me, and I had achieved nothing. He had not promised any positive action at all. All he was after, was to keep me on a string in the event he needed me. Over a cup of coffee, I made my decision; I would not withdraw from the investigation completely, but I would have as little to do with the police team as possible and continue to work alone. Once I had decided on this course of action, I felt more at ease than I had for days.

With Arnie no longer a thorn, I returned to the farm to talk to Esiekiel. I was sure that he had more to tell me about the feud between Moeketsi and Tagoe. He was amongst the orange trees, surrounded by young workers. I walked towards the group softly, so as not to disturb them. His head bobbed in my direction and he held up both hands with his fingers splayed. He would be free in ten minutes.

I sat on a ridge of new grass observing him as he worked with the young men. From the Setswana language I remembered, I understood that he was teaching them how to prune mature trees to increase their yield. They watched him intently and answered reverently. He was well loved.

'Ja Missie,' Esiekiel said in his gravelly voice, waiting for me to speak.

'There is something I want to ask you, but you look tired.

It can wait.'

'I sit first and rest.' He sighed as he slowly lowered himself onto the ridge next to me. Then he rubbed his legs and sighed again, dropping his head before straightening up.

'I am ready. Now you can ask.'

I asked if he knew about the argument between Moeketsi and his neighbour Tagoe. He looked at me sharply and nodded. 'I know, but it is a long story.' His jaw had that tight look. I knew his dislike of gossip.

'Please Esiekiel. I'm working with the police to catch Kosigo's killer and I need your help.'

'Okay, okay I will tell you.'

He explained in his detailed way that Moeketsi owned several hectares of citrus and grazing land. As his farm was too large to manage, he decided to let a portion of it to another farmer. When Tagoe, who was also a Tswana, showed interest in the land and was prepared to meet his price, Moeketsi agreed to rent him the property. The main conditions Moeketsi set were that rent was to be paid monthly and the orange trees maintained in prime condition. Within days of signing the agreement, Tagoe drove his cattle onto a paddock and moved into the du Toit's former farmhouse.

Esiekiel talked fast as he explained that after unseasonably heavy rains, Tagoe's oranges were not as juicy or as sweet as Moekesti's. There was no logical reason for the two neighbours oranges being of different quality but that's exactly what occurred. The result for Tagoe was poor sales. He was already in arrears with his rent payments and after the disappointing harvest, he had barely enough to pay his workers. Moeketsi wanted to recover his money and rather than employ a solicitor, he approached the headman of his area for help.

'Tribal justice is good and cost little.' Esiekiel rubbed his legs again. 'We can walk to the hut now. This a very long story.'

At the hut he wriggled in his favourite chair until he was comfortable. In spite of the hot day he tucked a worn blanket over his knees. I waited patiently for him to continue. At the hearing, the chief took Tagoe's low producing yield into consideration and ordered Moeketsi to reduce Tagoe's rent. In addition, he ruled that Tagoe was to give his neighbour one cow in lieu of back payments. Cows are valuable assets and Moeketsi was pleased with the ruling. Tagoe had a small herd that was his only source of wealth and grumbled angrily to his daughters all the way home from the court.

While Moeketsi put up with receiving a lower rent, Tagoe's crop of tobacco increased. Moeketsi saw the successful crop and approached Tagoe about a rent increase, but Tagoe laughed and refused to pay the extra.

Esiekiel cackled. 'All the time Tagoe is gambling the extra money at Sun City.'

I wondered how old Esiekiel was. Fast calculations put him in his late eighties or possibly early nineties. Like his Father Zacharias, he had not lost his sharpness even if his body had grown weaker.

Esiekiel went on with the story. Furious that Tagoe had gambled away the owing rent money, Moeketsi returned to the chief with his complaints. After another hearing, Moeketsi was delighted that the chief ruled that his neighbour was to give him a second cow. But this time Tagoe refused the ruling and the neighbours were deadlocked.

Esiekiel stared into the distance. 'One year there is no rain…poor Tagoe got no oranges. He is sitting at Sun City crying and pissing the last money on gambling. Now he got very big trouble – he must give the cow to Moeketsi or the farm is gone.'

I was unable to contain my curiosity. 'Well, did he give the cow to Moeketsi?'

Esiekiel slapped his bony thigh. '*Aikona*! No cow for Moeketsi.'

In the same way Manie du Toit reacted before him, Tagoe dumped manure outside the entrance to Moeketsi's farm. Moeketsi responded by putting thorns all the way down Tagoe's driveway. This incensed Tagoe. He waited in the dark for Moeketsi to slow down before turning into his driveway and pelted his car with stones. This then turned into a police matter.

'What happened next?' The story was exciting.

'Tagoe is scared of White law and he goes to very, very bad sorcerer, Jairus to help him. This Jairus makes dark magic.' Esiekiel shifted in his chair. 'I am tired now.' His eyelids fluttered and he lay back in his cane chair. His scrawny hand rubbed the greying stubble on his head. 'Tagoe is very weak man. Does Missie think he killed Kosigo?' he asked.

I shrugged. 'Maybe. He had a good reason.'

Esiekiel's face puckered. 'Missie will never find the killer of Kosigo if she is sitting talking to old man.'

I laughed. 'You're right.'

Esiekiel yawned and shut his eyes.

I took his hand in mine and whispered, 'thank you.'

Thirty-Six

I was surprised to hear Arnie's voice. 'I have some bad news for you.' Arnie sounded more worried than usual. 'We've discovered another body ....in similar circumstances. A young woman was found dead during the early hours near the entrance to a platinum mine.'

'Oh no!'

'And she's a cousin of Kosigo's.'

'How was she killed?'

'I'm not sure. I'm leaving now for the crime scene. I can pick you up in half an hour.'

'Thanks, I'll be ready.' I had forgotten my decision not to work with Arnie and his team. I was putting on my sandals when the horn beeped.

Amita was in the front of the car with Arnie. 'The dead girl was called Sunshine,' she said in a tight voice. 'Apparently she was the family's last child, born on a sunny day.'

We passed the saddle shaped football stadium and pulled up in front of a platinum dump. Gauging by the number of police vehicles, several officers had arrived before us. We were out of the car in seconds and joined a group of policemen next to the mineshaft. They were bent over a partially clothed body of a young woman. She was lying on her back, her small breast peeping from torn clothing. The smell of blood and death was in the air but I forced myself closer. Deep cuts slashed her stomach and blood stained the ground. About a metre from the body a single smudgy indentation marked the earth. It was a print, the size of an elephant footprint and though similar to those near Kosigo's body, it was not as clearly defined.

The coroner examined the body briefly and announced that Sunshine had died approximately six hours earlier. Then she was zipped into one of those dreadful plastic body bags and placed on a stretcher, to be transported to the morgue for a post mortem.

Meanwhile, Arnie had called in an extra unit of police and a ranger from the National Park to search for elephants. It was a brief search and within an hour, he was satisfied that no elephant prints flattened veld in the vicinity of the body and elephant dung was not seen either. According to the ranger, elephants had been cited six kilometers away but no one could account for the print close to the body.

As a nurse I knew death well yet this body, cut and brutally slashed, was nothing like the bodies of dead hospital patients. The horror of it shocked me. I walked away from the violent scene and stared at the mountain. At that moment, I grasped why Nathaniel stared at the mountain at moments when life became inexplicable.

In the car we discussed Sunshine's murder. She was the third person stabbed in a similar way to Kosigo, that is, counting Rethabile. And there was the footprint, though not as clearly formed as the others. Amita said that she noticed Sunshine's stomach had been stabbed and not her pelvis, as was the case with the other victims.

Amita clenched her fist. 'Bloody hell, boss, is this a copycat murder or what? '

'It's possible.' Arnie replied. 'It could even be a try at covering up a virgin rape. She's young enough, only twelve or thirteen. It's all getting much too complicated.' Arnie passed his hand over his eyes. 'We'll have to wait for the post mortem.'

Close to the mine was a sprawling squatter camp. Apart from the ancient mountain, the Rustenburg of my youth had disappeared. Mines and slums had taken over. The camp had originally sprung up in the nineteen eighties to provide miners with booze. More recently, people looking for work on the mines who could not find a place to live, put up shacks and settled there. The camp spread and most of the people who lived there were destitute.

'Time they fixed this dump of a place up,' Arnie said sharply. 'No running water, electricity or sanitation and disease is raging. It's terrible!'

'Apparently the government is doing something about it and the Catholic Church is contributing a hospital and AIDS education, but it's hardly making a dent. The mining companies should do more, but its money not people that counts,' Amita added cynically.

'The health and crime situation is so bad that they'll need mountains of aid to make a difference,' Arnie said.

※

Phyllis Green had left a message on my answering machine and I returned her call immediately. 'Those chocolate samples you gave me are saturated with a plant poison. It's a rare one and I had a heck of a time identifying it. It's from the bulb of a hyacinth plant.'

'Hyacinth again?' I replied.

I explained that the police laboratories had located hyacinth poison in both Kosigo and Raymond's blood. No wonder they were so ill.

'Whoever did this must've ground the poison up finely and added it to the chocolate to mask its taste.'

I thought of the quilted gold boxes and the chocolates with their sweet centres. The strong flavours had hidden the taste. Immediately I dialled the Moeketsi's number to warn them all about the poisoned chocolates. When no one answered the phone, I drove to the house. The family was in mourning again. Dark marks streaked the windows, under the sills ash lay like ant heaps. Beloved Sunshine was dead.

The new maid, Sybilla opened the door but did not ask me in.

'Madam Galani is praying.'

I looked at my watch. I could not wait much longer. 'Is

Thabang here?' I asked.

'Miss Thabang is very sick in the stomach.'

'I have to see one of them. It's important,' I demanded.

If I had to choose between the sisters, I preferred to talk to the clear-headed Thabang.

'Please come inside. I will ask Miss Thabang to talk to you,' Sybilla said leading the way.

After sitting on an uncomfortable stuffed chair in the hall for some time, Thabang stood before me in her dressing gown. She held her stomach and looked ill.

'Black tea, toast no butter, please,' she called out to Sybilla, scurrying past us. 'Tea and toast for you too?' she offered as an afterthought. I thanked her and shook my head.

'Come into the sitting room. It's more comfortable there.'

When I told Thabang about Phyllis Green's analysis of the chocolates, she was horrified that someone could have intentionally poisoned members of her family. We agreed that the chocolates had made each member of the family ill to varying degrees. Thabang said that Kosigo had experienced the worst reactions, while she and Galani had relatively mild symptoms in spite of the amount of chocolates they had eaten. She had no idea who the culprit could be.

'I'm feeling like a sick cat and cats are worse patients than dogs.' She attempted a weak smile. 'And we mustn't forgot that Keneuoe went home ill from the chocolates.'

I nodded sympathetically.

'Thank you for alerting us all. Now we know what herbal medicines to take so that we can detox.'

We discussed Sunshine's murder briefly. Thabang could not think of anyone who had a reason to attack, let alone kill the young woman she described as sweet tempered, affectionate and fun loving. I stood, ready to leave, when Galani entered the room. Thabang explained my presence and repeated my warning about the poisoned chocolates.

Before Thabang had finished speaking, Galani sank into an armchair. 'You wanted to know about Chi, my cat. The vet opened her up and analysed the contents of her stomach. He found some plant poison mixed with her food. It could've been the same one you're warning us about. The poor darling suffered because someone wants to hurt us. And now the latest horror, Sunshine's been murdered. You tell those detectives to get on to it.'

Thirty-Seven

When I visited *Masego* again, I was armed with sweets. A group of children ran up to the car and followed me like the Pied Piper. I doled out the sweets and each ran off with their loot. I found Nathaniel tending to vegetables he had propagated from seed. He rubbed the soil off his hands and stood to greet me.

'Look how big the vegetables are growing after the rain.' He pointed to shoots in the rich earth. Though the vegetable garden was twice the size it had been three years ago, it still wasn't large enough to feed all the workers.

He shook his head sadly. 'Sunshine is dead.' He gave the stones a sharp kick

I nodded sympathetically.

'Come to the house. Mina will make tea and cake for us.'

As we walked to the house, I thought of Oupa who had owned the farm when I was a child, a kind, burly man with whiskers that scratched when he kissed me. He carried odds and ends in his pockets. Whenever I visited he would pull out a cork with a usual head, some nails or string for me, his *kleintjie* or little one. .

When my grandpa was alive, the iron roof of the whitewashed farmhouse was green, and a feature of the house was the stained glass front door with a central four-leafed clover. The house was the heart of the farm in those years, but after my grandparents' death it became uninhabitable. That is, until Nathaniel moved in and renovated it. The roof became scarlet, the walls a buttery crème and the glass door

I had loved was gone. It was an African house now but I had not made up my mind if I liked it.

We sat around the table and Mina dominated the conversation with personal news. She served tea and chocolate cake. Eating Mina's rich chocolate cake jogged my memory about questions I wanted to ask.

'Do either of you know if anyone around here makes really good chocolates?'

Mina told me proudly that she had entered her own chocolates in the agricultural show and received an honourable mention from the judges. A man with the name of Tagoe won the top prize.

'Tagoe makes chocolates? Do either of you know anything about him?'

'Everybody knows he and Moeketsi argue. They are very stupid people. What if big trouble comes - locusts or floods; everybody needs a good neighbour to help,' Mina said.

'Does Tagoe sell his chocolates?'

'My sister bought a big box of chocolates for us Christmas time. They were yummy.' She closed her eyes at the memory. 'I have still got the box.' She disappeared for a few minutes and returned with a gold quilted box exactly like the one in Galani's sitting room.

'I need to get hold of a box of Tagoe's chocolates.'

I would take them to Phyllis Green. She would be able to establish whether the basic composition of Tagoe's chocolates was the same as the poisoned ones Raymond, Kosigo and the others had eaten.

Nathaniel, who had been silent for some time had a suggestion. 'I will buy a box of chocolates for you from Tagoe. I will tell him that Mina's birthday is coming soon.'

'Excellent idea, Nathaniel!'

'He stood and pushed his chair aside. 'Now I must work before the sun is dead.'

Before he left, I opened my purse and handed him some large notes, more than enough to cover the cost of the chocolates.

My phone buzzed. It was Phineas offering me free tickets to a soccer match. His pleasantness lulled me into compliance. I told him about Phyllis' discovery of poison from the hyacinth plant found in the sample of both Galani and Raymond's chocolate, and that she believed that it was that poison, that caused their dizziness and nausea. I made a point of reminding him that the police department's toxicology report had also cited hyacinth as the poison in Kosigo and Raymond's blood.

'And you're doing all this on your own?'

How could I explain that I was driven to uncover Kosigo's murderer, that I sensed her inner beauty, even now that she had gone. She was one of those special people that one did not say no to.

I laughed. 'I have no choice. You know that I can't rely on you and that boss of yours to investigate the crime thoroughly.'

'My hands are tied. I have suggested to Arnie that we look deeper into the crimes but he's put the investigation on hold since finding Sunshine's body, and won't even talk about it until we get pathology results – the stubborn bastard.'

Phineas had changed too. He had lost respect for his boss, that was clear. Where was the cop who wrote every detail in his black book? Was his former attention to detail a pretence, a front?

'So, do you want the tickets or not? The game between Australia and Germany will be fantastic.'

I accepted the tickets with thanks and replaced the receiver before I said something I regretted. The late afternoon light dulled the sitting room. Josh had left a tasty nibble of nuts and fruit for me on the table, but I barely touched it. I poured a glass of wine, drank it and then another, but the wine did not have the relaxing effect I anticipated.

I was expecting George for dinner at 7.00 P.M. Josh had decorated the table with candles in a well of pink roses and prepared a delicious dinner for the two of us, the perfect prelude to romance. In Melbourne, I was used to making easy but appetising meals in the shortest time possible. The allure of food preparation, popular with others, had passed me by. I thanked Josh for his trouble and suggested he use my ingredients to make dinner for himself and Karel and leave me to serve the dinner.

By 7.30 George had not arrived. This time, instead of becoming irritated or annoyed, I read. When I heard a knock on the door half an hour later, he was full of apologies and placed a bottle of champagne on the table. He had been sorting through his photographs and slides and lost track of the time, he said.

He was in a cheerful mood. That afternoon he had discovered another well-preserved cave painting and was already visualizing a book with glossy prints. When I told him about Tobias' eland, the largest and most dominant of the elands I had seen, his eyes shone eagerly. I promised to talk to Josh about a visit to Tobias. After the meal, we shifted to the sitting room and sank lazily into the couch.

'Sorry, all I seem to talk about lately is the eland. Work fills my head, keeps me going.' He put an arm around my shoulder. 'Tell me what's been happening with your investigation?'

'It's moving far too slowly.'

'Oh come on, update me.'

'OK, you asked for it,' I laughed. 'Now you'll find out about my obsession.' I gave him a summarized version, starting from the findings of poison in the chocolates to Sunshine's murder.

'Absolutely riveting. I'm a detective story freak, in TV and in books. Love it, but I don't know if I would want to be a real investigator. Too much hard work and bloody frustrating.'

'You said it.'

'If you have any of the crime photos, I'd love to see them.'

His eyes begged and I could not refuse. Phineas had made me copies of all the crime site photos. Though showing evidence to members of the public was against the rules, I bent them. I removed the photos from the locked cabinet and spread them on the carpet.

He paled and swallowed. 'She's ripe and round, isn't she? Like an eland that's been hunted down.' His eyes were glazed.

The elephant footprints near Kosigo's body fascinated him and he had several questions. Had the ranger mentioned the width and depth of the prints closest to the body, and how fresh they were? Were there more prints in the veld, further from the body?

I couldn't answer his questions and told him so.

'There's something about these footprints that doesn't seem quite right.'

'What do you mean....not right?'

'I'm not sure...and I don't want to say too much...not yet' He pointed to photos he had selected. 'Bring these to the dig tomorrow and we'll show them to Ivan. He has a brilliant scientific mind and you must've noticed what a stickler he is for detail. He will sort it out. You'll see.'

'Sort what out?'

'I'm not saying a thing yet, let it go until tomorrow.'

'Tomorrow, it is, then.'

I locked the photos away and sat next to him.

'The bedroom,' he whispered through a kiss. 'No more cramped and lumpy couches.'

Thirty-Eight

When I woke at sunrise, George had left. I promptly fell back into a dream sleep with George again, relishing our lovemaking.

Josh prepared my favourite breakfast of croissants with strawberry jam and coffee. I was giving my sticky jam fingers a last lick when the doorbell pealed. Thabang stood outside looking embarrassed. I invited her in and she sat stiffly in a lounge chair.

'Sorry to worry you and so early, I'm here about Galani,' she blurted out hastily.

'Something to eat and a cup of coffee or tea?'

'No thank you,' she replied.

'How can I help?'

'This week Galani has been a wreck. She's been threatened... and before you suggest it, I won't go to the police. They won't be interested or have the time for that sort of thing. That's why I've come to you... so that you can help us put all the pieces together. We think it could be related to Kosigo's death.'

'Threatened? What happened?' I prompted.

'Two days ago a small package addressed to her was dropped outside the front door. I was there when she opened it. Goat bones. Seven neck bones, all cut vertically,' she said, covering her face. 'It's an obvious threat. For us the goat is a sacrificial animal...it's awful. Since the package arrived she's been crying and shaking. We were arranging a thanksgiving for the rains, but she's not up to it now.'

I put my arms around her. 'Whoever did this will be pleased with the result of his evil deed. As I see it, the intent is to paralyze your sister with fear and stop her doing her good work.'

'It's the connection between the bones and Kosigo's murder that's worrying me. Someone is out to destroy us.'

'Yes, I think there is a connection.'

'Talking to you has made me realise that we have no option but to pretend nothing has happened. In time the sender will reveal himself. Evil waits it's time to do harm.'

Thabang's unexpected visit held me up. I intended to be at the dig early enough for the morning tea break. Driving fast, I arrived at the recreation tent just in time to discuss the crime photos with George and Ivan.

George was panting slightly from a rushed climb down from the ridge. He wiped his hands with a crumpled handkerchief and kissed my cheek. 'I told Ivan about the photos. Have you brought them with you?'

I patted my handbag. Ivan joined us and the two men found a spot under a shady tree. Once the ground was covered with a blanket, I laid down the photographs George had chosen – six from Kosigo's murder scene plus a further five from Polokwane.

Ivan whistled through his teeth. 'Unbelievable what so-called human beings do to each other?' He said, looking at George.

'Anything you notice about those elephant footprints, Ivan?' There was a note of professional upmanship in George's voice.

Ivan turned the pictures this way and that. I was looking at them too, but could not find the fault. Finally, he pointed to an enlargement of the footprint. 'There's something wrong alright. I don't know if it's your finding too, George, but all these footprints are identical. And what's more they're all facing in the same direction - left.'

'Yeah, I picked up that they were all facing left too. You noticed something else I didn't pick up - that they are identical. Each true elephant foot, like the human foot is different,' George said.

I studied the photographs. I was embarrassed and grateful all at once. It had taken two archaeologists to notice something so obvious. I was usually far sharper.

'Since there's no such thing as a one legged elephant, what are the implications?' Ivan said, stroking the side of his face.

'The killer could've made a cast of an elephant's foot or carved the foot from wood, and pressed it into the ground to confuse the police,' George suggested.

'He did a bloody good job,' I said. 'Those footprints look real.'

'Any idea who he could be?' Ivan asked.

I shrugged.

The thought of trying to encourage Arnie to listen to this new information made me sigh. It was enough of a struggle to hold his attention, now that had lost interest in the case... and possibly lost interest in policing. Just then my cell phone rang. I recognized Amita's voice.

'I'm calling to follow up on the poison... the hyacinth, found in Galani's chocolates and in Kosigo and Raymond's blood. The boss thought we'd better follow it up.'

I suppressed a sarcastic remark.

'The plant analysis...did you...err... have it done privately?' she asked. 'The boss wants to know.'

'Yes, through someone who used to work in your forensic department...before your time. Her name is Phyllis Green.

Would Amita take me seriously and pass on the message to Arnie, this time? My tone was stern. 'Please Amita, I must talk to Chief Detective Inspector Swart urgently. I have crucial new information about the elephant footprints and I must inform him about it. Make certain that he gets this message.'

'I'll tell him,' she replied.

Later, I added the new information about the footprint to my crime sheet. Tagoe remained pencilled in as a possible suspect. Frustrated I threw down the pencil and poured a glass of red. Where was Nathaniel? He promised to bring the chocolates I needed for testing. I emptied most of the bottle of wine as I browsed through a bunch of tempting travel brochures promoting the Cape. A trip would be a real holiday with friends to catch up with and places I wanted to revisit.

I slept restlessly and awoke remembering only one dream. I was on a raft in the ocean. With one hand, I clung to a brochure advertising the Cape and with the other, I held on to a cardboard box containing a peacock feather, chocolates, hyacinth bulbs and cigarette butts. When a gigantic wave washed over me, I almost let go of both the brochure and the box. Another huge wave and I slid off the raft. The soggy brochure had gone but I was still hanging on to the box. When I woke cold and shivery, I knew that my plans of visiting the Cape were a distant hope, and that I had a great deal of work to do before I went on a holiday.

The day was humid and the sky dense with clouds. Like Melbourne weather, I thought, feeling a twinge of homesickness for my wild native garden, the Magpies nesting in my roof and my two cats I had placed with a friend. Both cats would have been vying for a place on my lap after their breakfast. At least my life in Australia was ordered.

I was about to go onto the *stoep* to read when Phineas arrived. He apologised for any intrusion and pointed to the phone. 'The phones are out for the day, the computer is down but at least they are fixing the roads. That's something, I suppose.'

Sunshine's family had not yet been interviewed. As he intended to visit the family that morning, he asked me to join him. Perhaps it was his apologetic tone or my own curiosity, but my resolution to distance myself from the case melted yet again. In the car, he handed me the coroner's report on Sunshine's murder. I was not surprised to read that she had been raped and that the slashing of her stomach with a pointed blade had caused her to bleed to death.

'Why have you been putting off this interview? It's days since her death,' I said accusingly.

He was silent and then I heard him gulp. 'It's just too hard sometimes. With all the tests not in yet, I didn't want to have to tell the family that we couldn't release the body for burial. Now we have the coroner's report, I can give them hope of a funeral soon.'

The Ditsele's lived in a wooded valley on the outskirts of the town. The house was small and narrow but the tiny garden was well tended. Mrs Ditsele showed us into a simply furnished front room. She hovered, uncertain what to do or say until her husband, Morris joined her. When Phineas told the couple that the coroner had confirmed that Sunshine had been raped, Mr Ditsele's face puckered and he put his arm around his wife. She talked in a choked voice of the hopes she once had for sweet natured Sunshine. As expected, Morris was distressed and angry that his daughter's body had not yet been released for burial. Phineas tried to placate him with excuses and promises, but it was useless.

Morris shook his head sadly. 'New powers for blacks, eh. Still, nobody cares.'

'Yes, unfortunately democracy doesn't necessarily bring equality or even fairness.'

While Phineas talked to Morris, I looked about the room. A group of elaborately framed photographs on a corner table caught my attention. One of the photos was of a slim, smiling Sunshine. I took a closer look at the teenager standing between what appeared to be her two older sisters. There was another photo of Sunshine as a child with three older men smiling at her. Grace confirmed that the two girls were sisters and the smiling older men were Sunshine's uncles.

Phineas voice took on its serious tone, as he asked the couple if they could think of anyone who could have murdered their daughter. Grace answered as best as she could in a thin, tired voice, that she knew her daughter was loved by all. When Phineas asked if Sunshine had a boyfriend, Grace shook her head vehemently and began to tremble.

Phineas scratched his jaw and quietly observed Grace. 'Take a few minutes to calm down and then I want to hear the whole story ...everything that happened on the day Sunshine died.' Phineas insisted.

'But we've already told the police woman what happened,' Morris said, with his hand forming a fist and his eyes blazing.

A lengthy story eked out. Grace had been at the shops on the morning of Sunshine's murder. Later, she visited her elderly mother and spent the afternoon with her. Sunshine had school holidays and was alone at home.

'So she was by herself all day?' Phineas confirmed.

'My brother Petrus is sick with AIDS and he comes by here every afternoon when Sunshine is home from school. She gives him some food and they talk.'

'Was your brother Petrus here the day Sunshine died?' Phineas persisted.

Morris jumped from his chair. 'We know it, for sure... he's the one who raped and killed her. I know inside here.' He patted his chest. 'Justice of the tribe and the family is sometimes stronger than police justice.'

Phineas and I looked at each other.

'Shut your mouth!' Grace nudged her husband with her elbow.

'I think you'd better tell us what's going on,' Phineas said, his voice rising.

The story unraveled of how Morris and two friends had cornered his brother-in- law, Petrus and accused him of killing Sunshine.

'We took a cricket bat to scare him. Petrus cried like a baby and he admitted it, *'yes, I raped and killed Sunshine.'* Morris wiped away his tears and added. 'Poor Sunshine was a virgin,' he sobbed.

'Petrus thought she would cure his AIDS?' Phineas said in a gentle voice.

'He's a stupid man.' Tears continued to course down Morris' face. '

'Where is he?' Phineas demanded.

Morris made a dismissive gesture with his arm. 'Gone.'

'You better tell them the rest of the story, Morris,' his wife said sternly.

'Okay, okay. When we scared Petrus with a cricket bat,

two men held him. I took off my belt and give him the best hiding he had in all his life. After that I kicked him into street, told him he didn't belong to our family anymore and not to come back ever to tribal land or we'll tell the police he killed Sunshine and then he'll go to jail. That's justice!'

'He's lucky, he wasn't killed. Nobody knows where he is,' Grace added. They both shrugged.

'Right then, let's move on for the moment. How come he tried to make the murder look like an elephant attack?'

Morris explained that Petrus had attended Kosigo's burial and probably listened to the gossip about the elephant killing, and most likely heard about the footprint and the slashes on her abdomen. 'It was simple for him to copy it.'

We left the Ditsele's house knowing that even if DNA tests proved Petrus to be Sunshine's killer, he was unlikely to be found.

The visit to the Ditseles that morning was emotionally draining. I longed for a quiet afternoon and a sustaining lunch but I knew that the fridge was empty. I stopped at the shops nearest the house. At the fruit shop, cherries were on special and a crowd gathered around the boxes of glossy, fruit. As I filled my plastic bag, I listened to the conversation of two Tswana women. The women complained that the drought had pushed up prices of all food and that they were battling to survive. The plumper of the two women said that her daughter was visiting from Johannesburg and that as a special treat she would buy her a handful of cherries. The other woman said that even at the low price, she could not afford the cherries and would buy the packets of slightly spoiled fruit and vegetables that were selling cheaply. The plumper woman spoke softly but I overheard her. 'Maybe the people who say that things here were better under the Whites, are right. They kept the prices down and at least the country was organized.'

'Maybe the post came on time, and the roads weren't full of pot holes but that's not everything. Are you forgetting apartheid?' the other answered crossly.

'You're right. Most of us are poor but we have our

freedom. Thank the fathers that *Madiba* is still with us.

I smiled at the affectionate name used for Nelson Mandela.

The plumper woman clicked her tongue. 'May *Madiba* live to be a hundred!'

The women's comments did not shock me. I had read articles about Black dissatisfaction with the government's management of the country.

🐘

I fell asleep immediately that night but my dreams rolled from one frightening scene to another. First I was running over grass - faster and faster until I reached the edge of a chasm. From there I hurtled into the past, into painful and scary parts of my life that I rarely thought about. I was a spectator as I slipped down an embankment onto my missing fourteen year old brother Hannes' dead body. It was a horrific experience and I doubt it ever left me. I heard again Ma's wail and Pa's sob and the sound of the coffin being lowered, the clods of earth fall on its lid. I curled up inside and froze.

Then I saw myself coming home from school on the day of the mine subsidence, when the earth opened and sucked me in. Luckily I fell onto what must've been a ridge that was stable and not very deep. I heard myself calling for help in a terrified voice, and then I saw the kind faces of the Black women who formed a human chain to pull me out.

I woke slippery with sweat and went straight into the arms of a warm shower. The dreams were too vivid to be incidental. It was not a time when my hormones were crazy. Unwinding in the warmth of the water, the answer became clearer. I was being warned of danger with snap shots of terrifying past experiences. It was all very well my protectors warning me, but how could I ensure my safety?

Thirty-Nine

Mist clung to the house and even with the lights turned on, I could barely see.

'Josh, Josh what's happening?' I called out.

'I've checked the hot water and taps. It's just a bit of steam, I think,' he reassured me. 'Everything's ship shape now. It'll settle soon, don't worry.'

I returned to my bedroom. Under the doona it was warm and I felt safer. Josh must have completed his morning chores and I heard the back door bang shut. It was so quiet that the trees swooshing in the breeze carried me into sleep.

Josh's excited voice woke me. 'Come and see! Beautiful flowers arrived for you!' I threw on my gown and followed him into the sitting room. He carried in an exquisite arrangement of orchids sheathed in cellophane and tied with a huge cerise bow.

'They're magnificent! Please put them on the table where we can enjoy them.'

Josh removed the covering and turned the magnificent arrangement this way and that for maximum effect. He searched for a card from the sender but could not find one. I stretched out on the couch admiring the orchids. Suddenly I felt a needle-like stab on my arm.

'Ouch!'

'What's wrong?' Josh rushed into the room, dishcloth in hand.

'I think I've been bitten,' I said, rubbing the raised red bump on my arm.

Josh looked worried. 'A spider bite, for sure. Must've come from the flowers.'

I sat petrified while he searched the couch. He eventually found the spider lodged between two of the cushions.

'Shit, shit, shit! A Black Button Spider!'

He raced to the kitchen for a Tupperware box and spoon. He lifted the spider into the box and sealed it so that its venom could be identified. Then he called the ambulance.

I thought of Pa and Connie often bitten by spiders, stung by mosquitoes and bees. Once Pa had been bitten by a snake. They must've built up immunity because they didn't have to go to hospital. Though I had lived on the farm as a child, I had been careful, possibly lucky. Only a few nasties had bitten me.

'You'll be very sick soon, maybe die if you don't get a special injection.'

I looked at the cellophane bunched up near the sink. The sender must've placed the spider on the bouquet and then covered it with the cellophane. I shuddered. Perhaps there were more spiders, roaming the house, now that the covering over the orchids had been ripped off. I loathed spiders as much as I feared them. As lovely as they were, the orchids would have to go.

Within minutes I began to sweat, feel dizzy and my stomach muscles stiffened. When the ambulance arrived, I could not understand the fuss. The paramedic told me that soon I would feel a lot worse. By the time we reached the hospital, I heard a doctor say that my blood pressure was extremely high due to the poison in my body. He hooked me up to an intravenous drip feeding me antivenin and then I slept.

Hours later the uncomfortable sensations had almost left me but I was weak and wobbly, drifting in and out of a restless sleep. In a cloud, I saw Arnie's and Amita's worried faces and heard them asking questions I could not answer. Two mornings later I was discharged.

When Josh brought lunch up to my bedroom he was emphatic. He and Karel had moved all the furniture, vacuumed the carpets, pulled the curtains down and shaken them out in the yard. 'We've killed five spiders and we're sure we got all of them.'

How someone had crept through the locked security gates or climbed over the electrified fence to deliver the flowers remained a bothersome question. I asked Josh if the gate had been open.

'The place was locked up like Pretoria Central Jail. Only a bird or spirit could fly through.' His brow crinkled with his serious look. 'I should've warned you. The star…Sirius was very blue again in past days.'

The question was the same as the one I asked when the garage door closed and other strange things occurred. I waved his comment aside with my arm. Still in my dressing gown, I paced the house. Logic receded, and my fears of further assaults grew like mushrooms popping up from dark soil. I felt afraid and alone. The evil was in the air and the water. Kosigo's enemy was my enemy, I knew it. Until her killer was caught I would not be safe.

The ringing doorbell startled me. Quickly I patted down my messy hair and pulled the cord of my dressing gown tighter round my middle. It was George. His face was almost obscured by a huge bunch of pink flowers. I took a step back when I saw the flowers.

'Something to cheer you up. And this time I promise no nasties.' He beamed.

'How did you know about the spider bite?' My voice faded.

'Josh told me when I phoned.'

He put the flowers on the hall table and then took both my hands.

'I know I look awful.'

'Shush, shush.' His arms were around me. 'I can't bear the thought… of anything horrid happening to you,' he whispered.

'I'm from tough stock,' I said, dragging him by the hand. He picked up the flowers and followed me. 'I'm about to have dinner, join me? Josh always makes too much.'

He agreed to stay. Over coffee in the sitting room,

the unspoken words hung between us. 'You've had an awful time.'

I swallowed hard and brushed away tears with the back of my hand. He stroked my hair and I moved closer. 'There's been one attack on me after another – vile attacks, attempts to harm me. I don't like using the word 'evil', but it applies here.

'Josh is here some of the time and is doing his best to keep an eye open for your safety but it's *not* good enough.' He thumped the arm of the chair.

'You're right and I don't feel safe... but then this isn't the safest of countries to be in.'

'It has nothing to do with that. It looks to me as if someone's doing his best to terrify you into giving up that case you're working on.'

'Well, I'm not going to be intimidated.' I recognised the sound of rebellion coming from a steely childhood place.

'I understand, you're just as hooked on the case as I am on those elands. Threats wouldn't stop me either but it's your safety we're talking about.'

I pushed stray hairs into place.

'I could move in with you for a while ... at least until this passes. It's bloody miserable stuck alone in that motel room and I'd be the luckiest man to be here with you.' His normally tanned skin was tinged pink.

'Oh George!' I gave him a hug.

'Well, what do you think?'

I didn't answer immediately; I couldn't. 'We're new at this, but I'd like you to stay with me for the weekend.'

The room and the furniture grew fainter. All I was aware of was George kissing and caressing me and tingling all over. The nervous jarring was gone. We were accustomed to each other's bodies now and less awkward with our knees and elbows. Words were no longer necessary as we flowed together with our own rhythm.

Soon he was asleep on his back and snoring. A gentle prod and he responded by turning to his side. I touched his head, kissed his ear and shoulder with the overwhelmingly tender feelings for him that I once called love. Since my split with Wil, I was no longer certain of precise names for caring feelings.

Forty

I noticed a parcel on the kitchen shelf. 'What's that?' I asked Josh

'Sorry, I forgot to tell you. Nathaniel brought it for you yesterday. Tagoe's Chocolates.'

I ripped off the brown paper and a gold box glinted. 'There's such a lot going on at Tagoe's place. Wish I could have a peek,' I said.

'It's easy. Stand on a ladder on the Moeketsi's side of the fence and look over.'

'I can't do that.'

'At night you can. No one will see you.'

'No, I couldn't.'

Crime detection interested me, but I was not used to the snooping angle yet. It carried dirty connotations. I tried to prod myself into action but it did no good. Peeping over fences or creeping through a hole in the wall was not for me.

I phoned Phyllis Green to tell her that I had the box of chocolates. Intrigued, she agreed to compare a sample of the chocolates from the box with the original chocolates she had already tested and found poisoned.

Later that morning, she had a sample from the new box in her fridge. The task was uncomplicated, she said, and she would have an answer for me the following day.

Dark clouds had devoured the blue, and by the time I pulled out of Phyllis' driveway, droplets of rain spattered my windscreen. I was close to the Rustenburg turn off when my cell phone buzzed. Travel was too fast to even consider taking the call.

The call was from Arnie. I dialled his number as soon as

I arrived home. He cut straight to the point. 'My apologies for not contacting you. Can I come past tomorrow morning, around 9.30?'

🐎

'Let's move into the sitting room. We'll have coffee in there,' I suggested to Arnie.

He removed his coat slowly and rubbed his eyes. I waited.

'I believe you wanted to discuss something important with me?'

'I'm glad Amita gave you the message.'

'Anyway, I guess this gives us an opportunity to catch up. I enjoy our chats.'

Speaking a little too rapidly, I said, 'Petrus admitted to his relatives that he raped and killed Sunshine, but we only have their word… and it won't stand up in court.'

He opened his bulging brief case, extracted a file and placed it on the table. 'We've put out an alert for him but no luck in finding him so far. If he has disappeared, there'll be fewer problems for us.'

'Ah … but.'

He ignored my hesitance and continued. 'This should interest you. Sunshine's post mortem and tox reports are back.' He was selecting passages to read aloud. 'Definite signs of rape …her vagina torn and bruised. The slashes on her abdomen were from a knife with a wide blade… a hunting knife.' He looked up. 'It looks like the blade is far wider than the one used to kill Kosigo and that witchdoctor in Polokwane.' He turned the pages. 'The toxicology report indicates no poison of any kind was found in her body.' He opened another slim folder. 'And then there's that elephant print …not as clearly defined as the others. And as you know, no elephants found in the area.' He stood to make his point. 'Definitely, a copycat killing.'

Josh arrived carrying a tray. 'Coffee and cake is served. I'll put it on the table.'

'I understand now why Chief Menitjies gave up this job

in just over a year. At the time he said he wanted to spend more time with his family, but the truth was that he couldn't wait to leave.'

'Work stress?'

'Of course. I know I'm doing a poor job, and to be honest even covering the basics in crime detection is like climbing that mountain.' He nodded in the direction of the mountain range.

I watched him pull his slice of cake apart with his fingers and take a slug of strong coffee.

I cleared my throat. 'Now that we've caught up, I have something very important to tell you.'

'If you must…get on with it, then.'

I related George's findings about the elephant footprints as succinctly as I could, and added that Ivan, his colleague had agreed entirely.

Arnie stretched for his briefcase. 'Hang on a minute while I hunt for those photos of the crime scene.' He fumbled and then withdrew an envelope. 'Just as well I don't file things away as I should,' he said as he spread the photos on the table. Once the photos were laid out he asked me to repeat George's findings.

'They're bloody right… they're all front feet with identical indentations and facing the same way. I don't know how we missed it.'

I reminded him of Ivan's suggestion that the footprint could've been made by pressing a cast into the ground. A cast made of concrete, or more likely a carved piece of wood, could have created all the typical lumps and bumps found in an elephant's footprint.

'A smart deduction but it doesn't take us anywhere. We've found no evidence of a cast or bit of wood so far.' His neck had turned pink and his voice rose. 'You'll have us hunting for casts all over bloody Rustenburg. And with the Cup almost on top of us!'

'So, Jake is charged for murder, while someone else is guilty? Nothing new about that story.' A burst of anger fired through me, my words tumbled out. 'This time I mean it Arnie, I'm out of this investigation. You can blame it on stress if you want to, but I don't like what you're doing. I've had enough of your slipshod approach to policing. I won't be part of it any longer.'

'Hang on!'

'We've spent a lot of time on this murder. When there's some new evidence, a bit more work and you're not prepared to even open your mind to it.' I walked to the end of the room.

'Cool it Linda, you know we're always interested in what you have to say. That's why I wanted you on the case but what you're asking is massive. I'll have to think about it.' His phone beeped. 'Sorry, got to go. A body's been found in a car park. We'll talk.'

I was too angry to speak and let him go. When I heard his car accelerate and race away, I felt like kicking the table leg. After another cup of coffee and more of Josh's cake, my fury had fizzled out.

I was sitting in the back garden enjoying the sunshine, when Josh appeared looking concerned. 'There's a very old woman in the front who wants to talk to you. She says her name is Nandi.'

'Oh yes, she's the sister of my old nanny Tansie. Please show her into the sitting room and bring her some tea. She doesn't like coffee.'

Nandi's spare frame was clothed in the black of mourning. Her face was as tired and cheerless as it had been at Tansie's funeral. She looked about, taking in the size and relative opulence of my home. Then she placed her large brown carry bag on the tiled floor and sat stiffly in a wicker chair.

In the past, Nandi and I had little to say to each other and I knew her only as Tansie's sister. What had made her come to my home? She had not visited me before, nor had she been to the farmhouse when I lived there. Once Josh had brought the tea, I poured her a cup. She came to the point of her visit. Spirits had come to her at night to tell her that evil forces were threatening me. Now that Tansie had gone, she said it was her place to look after me. When she asked me if anything unusual had happened lately, I listed the recent unpleasant attacks made on me. The frown on her forehead deepened.

'Bad *tokoloshe* is causing big trouble for Missie,' she muttered in Setswana

She suggested I needed more powerful protection and made a sweeping movement towards the sky. I ought to have what she called special muti to frighten off the *tokoloshe*. She felt in her bag for a jar and opened it. The pungence of camphor escaped. I pulled away but she was insistent. With her index finger she dipped into the camphor and drew a line across my forehead. I coughed and wrinkled my nose at its strength. With the jar left open, she made an incantation in such fast Setswana that I couldn't grasp it.

'Missie must rest,' she said lifting her bag and zipping up the contents. 'I will go now.'

I wanted to wash the camphor off my face and close the jar but something stopped me. Though I didn't really believe it could help, I didn't know that it wouldn't. The smell of camphor was on my clothes, in my hair and the house reeked of it for hours. The intention I guessed, was for it to seep into every crevice and root out the evil that had taken hold. Smearing on camphor was an ancient method of healing and protection from illness and a sure fire way of burning out unwanted spirits. When we were children, Pryia my Indian friend who lived next door, had often talked of camphor sticks burnt with other herbs in their shrine during morning *puja*.

The camphor drove the sun away, leaving the house gloomy. I closed the jar and the overpowering smell lifted by mid-afternoon. The experience of the wet, pungent swipe of it across my brow confused me. I grew up with the Tswana and was used to their tribal customs. I knew about *ngakas*, witchcraft and spirits. My life was entwined with members of the tribe, but understanding another culture did not mean believing in all their magic.

Forty-One

We had developed a pattern of spending time together several times a week and talking on the phone at least once a day. We were melding as a couple and being together was more natural than being apart. Fear of rejection had almost left me, but I was still uncertain whether I wanted George to move into the house on a permanent basis. I was uncertain of so much. I wasn't even sure yet if wanted to leave all I had in Melbourne behind to live in Rustenburg. I hated the poverty in South Africa and I could not help thinking of all the urchins queuing for water in the shanty slums. Could I live with the disparity between rich and poor? Then there was the violence and talk of corruption in high places. The beauty of the country was seductive but the slipping standards of everyday life and threats to daily safety still left me uncertain. Should I follow my heart and stay with George? I knew Tansie would have laughed at me and told me to *jump in and swim, life's too short.*

That night we agreed to meet on the patio of his hotel. I waited for George in the narrow reception area, watching couples go in for dinner. Fifteen minutes and then thirty-five passed. At last, a tap on the shoulder and I turned quickly.

'Sorry I'm late again. So, sorry.' He had a naughty look, that he knew was irresistible. 'I was caught up on the phone,' he said, 'talking to an archaeologist, a world authority on cave paintings and it went on longer than expected.'

He was fixated on his work and there was nothing I could do about it. I'd have to accept that or move on. I cannot recall how many glasses of wine I had consumed when I noticed his hesitance in pouring me another. 'You're drinking more than usual,' he said gently.

I felt my throat tighten.

'Having Josh in the yard part of the time isn't sufficient protection for you.' He stroked his beard. 'The offer still stands, but if you're not comfortable with me moving in yet... you'd be safer staying at your brother's farm for a while.'

'Thanks but I'm not quite ready to relinquish my independence and I refuse to hide away at the farm, even though it would be safer there. I will watch my step,' I said placing my hand on his.

As soon as we had eaten we left the restaurant. Holding hands, we hurried down the hotel passage and up the two flights of stairs to his room. Deftly he lifted a poster size enlargement of a ruby eland and two files he had been working on from the bed, and placed them in the corner of the room. Before I could unzip my skirt, his coat was over the chair and his shirt unbuttoned. Gently, tenderly he stroked every part of me just as I had seen him stroke the elands on the rock wall. We could barely wait. We made love urgently with our eyes on each other.

I woke in his arms an hour later. Carefully I extricated myself so as not to wake him. Hungry and thirsty I padded to the bar fridge. An icy Mars bar and a diet Pepsi did the trick and I sank back into his warmth.

⁂

Still sleepy, I rubbed my eyes and pushed my hair behind my ears. Another clear day but I felt like a sponge that had absorbed its limit. Unease gripped me. My foundation stones, my loved ones were dead and I had spurned George's offer of moving in with me. A large part of me wished I hadn't. I was accustomed to being alone and there was a barrier of fear hindering me. I was acting foolishly but I was afraid of him moving in with me in case it didn't work out.

The investigation was at an impasse *again* and impatient

by nature, I wanted immediate answers. Pa used to say, *this is Africa where things happen slowly and in their own peculiar way.*

Connie and Raelene were away for the weekend. The farm was mine to roam and tease away my tension. Almost automatically, I drove there. I longed for two mind-numbing days of not having to face my fears or think about the investigation limping along. As if in a trance my feet followed well-known paths. The sunlight that followed the downpours had healed the veld and the abundance of flowers seeded by winds created a vivid garden. I embraced the delightful scene. Ducks and geese returned, creating a playground of the overflowing dam. They squawked and fluffed their wings as they dipped in and out of the water or hid behind reeds and water lilies. Lazing on the new grass, I watched the tall trees swaying in the breeze to their own tune. I appreciated it all.

Forty-Two

Josh hovered near the table. 'I have something interesting to show you,' he said chirpily as he passed me an envelope.

When I opened it, I gasped. Photographs of four peacocks, three males and a female. The flash had caught the male's feathers spread in an arc of iridescent colour, the famous intense blue, gold and saffron. The peahen was dull in comparison.

'Did you take the photos?'

He nodded with a wide grin. 'Tagoe keeps peacocks and a big cage of parrots.'

'Heavens! How did you get these pictures?' Josh's initiative surprised me. He had taken over my role of detective quite naturally, and in this case, performed far better than I could have.

'A friend of my mother's, Janet Bogopane, lives on the other side of Tagoe. She's got plenty trouble with him. He keeps peacocks and forty, maybe fifty parrots of all kinds in a big cage and they all make one hellava lot of noise.'

'Yes... but how on earth did you take the pictures?'

'Easy, I went to Janet's house, got a ladder and looked over the fence. And then I photographed what I saw.' He said, with a cheeky grin.

'How did you know I was interested in peacocks?'

'Ahhhh! I saw your sheet with the writing about the murder and the peacock feather. I was sure you'd be happy when you saw Tagoe's peacocks.' He gave me a meaningful look.

I didn't know how to thank Josh, even if he was a snoop. Reluctantly I phoned Arnie. If I could've taken a route around him I would've, but he was in charge.

'It can't wait this time. I have something important to show you in connection with Kosigo's murder. You must see it. It's up to you now. If you don't or won't follow it up it's on your head.'

He sighed deeply and then was silent for a second or two. 'Alright…I'll come round some time tomorrow.'

Josh had left my lunch in the fridge ready for me to warm up in the microwave. I was dozing on the couch when George visited unexpectedly. He placed a baked cheesecake on the table. 'Something sinful with our coffee.'

After an hour, he rushed off. His work on the ridge was over but he had to begin the task of compiling his photographs for a book.

⁂

Arnie arrived the following day as promised. His car sent the gravel of the driveway flying. He knocked loudly on the back door. Before answering the door, I flicked on the kettle.

'I've only got half an hour,' he said consulting his watch.

'Let's sit in the kitchen while I make coffee. The water's boiled.'

He placed his brief case on the floor, perched on a stool and eyed me expectantly.

'Right then, I'll tell you about my findings,' I said, placing two cups of coffee on the marble bench top.

I began by linking the homemade chocolates in the gold box to the nausea and dizziness that members of the Moeketsi household had experienced. I included Raymond's vomiting as a result of the chocolates in his gold box. I then backed up my findings with the tests Phyllis Green had performed, confirming that the poisonous chocolates were made by Tagoe, Moeketsi's next-door neighbour. I made the point that though the poison had made them ill, how it was connected to the murders was still unclear.

Once Arnie had finished questioning me on my findings, I moved on to describe the long-term feud between Tagoe and the Moeketsis that had developed as a result of Tagoe's failure to pay his rent. I then told him how the headman of the clan's ruling had resulted in Tagoe's loss of cattle.

He pursed his lips. 'No wonder Tagoe retaliated.'

'You don't know the half of it,' I said, thinking of the loud bird noises forced onto the Moeketsi's. 'That's the background to the next bit,' I said, as I laid my crumpled analysis sheet on the table.

'What's this?' He fingered a corner of the sheet.

'Hold on... I know it's a bit messy but bear with me. It's easy enough to follow.' I pointed to the lines I had drawn from Kosigo's, Rathabile's and Raymond's murders, to connect with bits of evidence: the chocolate poison, peacock feather, elephant footprint and cigarette stubs. Of course, investigation into Raymond's murder was not nearly as well developed as the other two.

His look was one of amazement. He was about to speak, when I reminded him of George and Ivan's finding about the fake elephant print.

'Those friends of yours, they're experts are they?'

'They certainly are. Scientists – archaeologists. I go by what they say but naturally your pathology section will have to back it up.'

'So, you're saying the elephant footprints are definitely fakes?'

I sighed, but buttoned my lip. 'Let's put that aside for the moment. I have something else to show you before we discuss it.'

'Shit. Just when we've covered the entrée next comes the main course.' He shifted his position and the stool squeaked with his weight. I replaced the crime sheet with photographs of the peacocks. I didn't tell him that Josh had taken the pictures.

'Peacocks! Where are they from?'

'They're from Tagoe's farm. Easy to confirm.'

He scratched his head. 'I guess this takes Jake out of

the picture.'

'True. The tie between Jake and the cigarette stubs is shaky. And as far as I know, pathology hasn't come back with anything conclusive implicating Jake.'

'Right, time to get hold of Phineas and have him follow through with all of this.' He fumbled in his coat pocket for his cell phone.

It didn't take Phineas long to organize a warrant to search Tagoe's house and farm. Arnie cancelled his appointment and had another cup of coffee while he waited for Phineas to arrive. At least this time Arnie was prepared to act. Phineas arrived with two constables to assist him and we left for Emmanuel Tagoe's farm. Though Tagoe's farm was next to Moeketsi's, his crops were failing. Somehow his orange trees survived and the groves held shiny leaved trees with fruit that was just about ripe for picking. We pulled up outside the Spanish styled farmhouse.

With no answer at the front door, we skirted the house to the back, where we found Tagoe filling a bucket with water.

'What do you lot want?' Tagoe said, his face furrowed in shock.

'We've come with a warrant to search your place. We'll work around you, carry on with what you're doing.'

'Search! Why? What have I done?' When he spoke his hands moved nervously, picking dirt and fluff from his jeans.

Phineas didn't bother to answer him. With the lines on his forehead deepening, Tagoe slouched against the doorframe, watching the police rifle through his possessions. The house was unbelievably messy with papers and clothes strewn on the floor. Two pet cockatoos out of their cage flitted about leaving their sticky muck on surfaces. The search revealed that shelves in the pantry held an interesting variety of glass bottles, containing dried bulbs and powders. Gold boxes of chocolates filled the lower cupboards.

'Bag some of the roots and the powder,' Phineas instructed the younger of the two constables.

'Look Sir, there's writing on the side of the cupboard with this lot of chocolates... and it's marked in black texter with

X , but there's no marking next to the taller lot on the other side.' the other constable said excitedly.'

Tagoe interrupted from his position at the doorway, 'They're divided into two sorts – liqueur filling and nuts.'

'You keep your trap shut,' Arnie snapped.

'We'll take one of each then and in two separate bags and I'll put labels on them,' the older constable suggested.

Meanwhile Phineas searched the kitchen for the knife that killed Kosigo. Spoons, knives and forks covered the kitchen floor. I doubted whether he would put them back where they belonged.

Arnie, Phineas and I went into the yard. We heard parrots screeching and squawking well before we passed a clump of trees shielding a large dome shaped aviary. It was constructed from steel and wire mesh, high and wide enough for the birds to fly and flap their wings. Noticing us, the cockatoos showed off by tossing their heads and fluffing their crests. There must've been at least eighty birds in the aviary, yet it was clean and the birds appeared to be healthy.

'Quick, come and look,' Arnie shouted. Bedside a wire pen, an exquisite crowned peacock with his tail feathers flared, strutted past us. The photograph had not done the magnificent bird justice. The other peacocks were in the pen behind him.

I realised then, that Josh must've climbed over the fence and entered Tagoe's property to take the photographs of the peacocks. The enclosure was hidden by trees and several metres from the fence line.

'With his oranges, the sale of baby parrots, peacock feathers and chocolates, Tagoe must be doing very well,' Phineas said, as he bent to scoop up peacock feathers for comparison with those at the crime scenes.

Though no knife was found capable of inflicting the wounds on the two women and Raymond, the two policemen did find two packs of Benson and Hedges cigarettes in the bedroom. It was almost dark by then, it had begun to drizzle and the temperature had fallen. I draped my cardigan around my shoulders and waited, while the cops formed a huddle to discuss their findings. As the cluster broke, Phineas made straight for Tagoe. 'Right then, Emmanuel Tagoe we're taking you in for questioning in connection with Kosigo Moeketsi's murder.'

'Bloody hell... I didn't kill her.'

'At last, we've got our man,' Arnie said, as he watched Phineas escort Tagoe to the car.

I had no appetite that night and put the dinner Josh had prepared aside. I longed for a few glasses of red wine and a long shower to wash away the events of the day. When I did sleep, it was fitfully. Towards morning, I dreamed that the afternoon's drizzle was transformed into torrential rain. Water gushed through Tagoe's dry farm sending the peacocks scurrying. Golden chocolate boxes dotted the flooding water and rows of hyacinths were ripped from the ground. Caught in depth of the churning water I struggled to find higher, safer ground. Somehow I made it to the car, parked on a rise, but not before a wave dumped on me and almost drowned me.

I woke with a sense of dread. Throughout the day, I pondered over the dream and its message.

By the following day I was certain, I had been too hasty leading Arnie to Tagoe. I had come to a rushed conclusion that he was guilty without thoroughly investigating the facts. It was my fault, my inexperience. The pieces in the puzzle appeared to fit but I had forgotten the key to the murder, the footprint and Rathabile's murder. Now that I had told Arnie about Tagoe, he was likely to build up a case against the man without further investigation. Though Tagoe was implicated in the murders, I doubted he was the killer.

I had no idea then what to do, where to look for further clues that would untangle the muddle I had created. Arnie was too inflexible and I had to admit, too busy, to consider looking deeper into the case.

Forty-Three

Raelene had invited George for a *braai* on Sunday, his first meeting with my family. I was as apprehensive about the meeting as a teenager taking her boyfriend home. I tried to convince myself that it would not matter what they thought of my 'English' lover but, the cultural divide was a constant stream beneath the surface, no matter how hard one tried to deny it. Though I considered it too soon for a family meeting, George insisted on accepting the invitation. At least these family matters diverted my thoughts from Tagoe and the investigation.

Once introductions were made, Connie disappeared to cook the meat with Vince assisting him. The rest of us had beer on the *stoep*. Soon Connie appeared in his navy and white striped apron carrying a platter of meat. He placed it on the table with a flourish. All Raelene had to do was to ring a bell for Emily to present the salads. Before we ate we said Grace. I thought of Pa saying his special prayer on Sundays.

The family tip-toed around George at first, and instead questioned me about my life in Melbourne. The conversation moved on to local issues and it amazed me how quickly South African politics became the topic of our discussion. When I was living on the family farm, the White government and apartheid was on everyone's lips, now the Black government was the talk of the day.

It wasn't long before Connie launched into fiery criticisms. 'The place is going to rack and ruin and violence wherever you turn,' he said vehemently.

'Things here aren't that bad,' Vince said.

'Aren't they?' Connie retorted angrily. 'You read the papers like I do.'

In his polite, easy way George made his comment. 'The country's gone through dramatic upheaval, for the better, mind you, and it'll take ages for the dust to settle. There's a new government and one would expect mismanagement. As far as the dire poverty, crime and serious health problems are concerned, it's going to take a very long time for any government to change that. Other than help as many individuals as one can, there's not a thing any of us can do about it. I wish we could. But we have a beautiful country, wonderful weather and for me the cradle of civilization is here to study. I'm getting on with it.'

My brother's stared at George for a few seconds before they commented.

'I like what you're saying and I agree wholeheartedly,' Vince said.

'You've made some good points, but I don't agree entirely. Things should be moving far quicker,' Connie added.

I thought of Ma, accepted on the surface by Afrikaners. George's colouring was typically Anglo-Celtic. He was lean, his cheekbones prominent and his eyes set deeply. He spoke with the less guttural vowels of the anglicised South African. It didn't take my brothers long to focus on George's past and his work, but he handled their questions smoothly.

Connie passed around the bowl of nuts and dried fruit, and for the next hour the conversation moved safely onto the soccer in the new stadium. Not that the three men could agree on that either. In spite of their differences about most things they continued to drink beer and laugh at the same jokes. Predictably, Connie nodded off and Vince's eyes began to close. Embarrassed, Raelene battled to make conversation.

I grasped George's hand and yanked him from his chair. Childhood places on the farm were special to me and I wanted to show them to him. We held hands down the leafless jacaranda path, and I did my best to describe how years ago, I imagined the delicately perfumed mauvey blue mass was heaven. I skirted past the farm's cemetery as I did not trust my emotions sufficiently, to take George to the family graves. When we reached Tansie's hut, I had to stop there. My tears trickled on to my blouse as I told George of Tansie's recent death. He nodded and swallowed hard when I described my attachment to her.

On the way back to the farmhouse, he picked a handful of daisies and handed them to me. 'I'm glad I've met your family and that you showed me where you grew up. Thank you, it fills out the picture I have of you. I understand more than you think. I'm like you in many ways… and I appreciate that you feel you must see the investigation through to its conclusion…. Once I'm set on a course I can't be shifted either.'

We left the farm at sunset and returned to the house, where blasting reggae and laughing voices greeted us. Josh turned down the sound after I'd knocked on his door several times. Stevie slipped out, ran from the din and slinked into hiding in the house.

Once we were seated on the couch, Stevie crept from his hiding place and lay at our feet waiting to be petted. I brought chips, cheese and biscuits and a bottle of wine from the kitchen. We were spoiling Stevie and gave him the first taste of crackers with cheese. Then George opened the wine. He sipped pensively and stroked his beard.

'Well, have you decided whether you're staying in Rustenburg or going back to Australia?' Before I could answer he continued. 'Come on; stay here for a few years. You could easily rent or sell your place in Melbourne,' he said, taking my hand. 'We have the beginnings of something, don't we?' Once we had kissed I felt as if my questions were answered.

Forty-Four

Early on Monday morning, I phoned Arnie and insisted on seeing him. I fought his reluctance and made an appointment with him later that morning. My visit to the Rustenburg Police Station was not a pleasant event. The weekend's collection of drunks and druggies had been let out of the cells and hung around outside. They were a verbal bunch, complaining loudly that they had been locked up over the weekend. I pushed past a woman arguing with a young policeman, blocking the entrance to the building and made my way to the crowded waiting area. At the reception desk I asked for directions to Arnie's office. I found him easily.

He put down his pen and stood to greet me. 'I'll have to mark this visit in my diary as a special occasion.'

I smiled.

'I suppose you're here about the case again.'

His voice was tired. 'We've checked out most of your findings and you're spot on. Just amazing'

'I'm not so sure about that.'

'And so, we've released Jake. We won't be able to charge Tagoe until we get the toxicology reports … and we've been promised them … soon. '

My reply was a grunt.

After Arnie once again complained at length about his staffing problems, I interrupted him and asked if he had heard anything further about the murder in Polokwane. This time I was determined to tie him down.

'Why are we going down that track again? Let's not waste

time, Tagoe's our man. You led us to him.'

'Yes, it was my fault...but I've had second thoughts about his guilt.'

'Playing games now?'

'No, I'm admitting that I made a serious mistake...and I'm asking you if there's any news from the cops in Polokwane.'

'No, nothing from them at all. And in case you ask, so far, we can't link Tagoe to Rathabile's murder. His alibi for Rathabile's death holds. He was at a citrus farmer's dinner and meeting at the time of her death and many people saw him there. His farm workers say he was on the land soon after dawn and worked all morning. It's definite, he couldn't have killed Rathabile.'

My stomach lurched. We had agreed that Rathabile was murdered by the same person as Kosigo.

'We need to recap. You're saying that at this stage Tagoe is our main suspect for Kosigo's murder, but you can't charge him until all the tests are back. And you're certain he didn't murder Rathabile?'

'That's how it looks.'

'Not much of case is it?'

His reply was a splutter.

'Have you found a carving or cast of the footprint on Tagoe's property? Or anything else to tie him to Kosigo's murder?'

'Not yet, but we have enough on him without it. He smokes Benson and Hedges cigarettes and thanks to you, there are all those peacock feathers.'

I was too frustrated to reply. It was my fault, I had given Arnie all he needed to patch the case together. Finally, I spoke, but the tone of my voice was accusing. 'How the hell can you charge him without proof that he engineered the footprint? The footprint is the *key* to the murder?'

'Don't upset yourself, Linda. It's not worth it.'

'That is the point. You don't seem to think finding the truth is worth the trouble. But I do.'

'Come on!' He was sounding edgy.

'Well, have pathology compared the cigarettes from his

house against the stubs found at the crime scene … and the stubs in my garden?'

'Not yet. You know very well there's an overload. We've been advised to send only key items for testing … and I can't do a thing about it.'

His expression was sulky.

If only I had waited before showing him the pictures Josh had taken of the peacocks. In my eagerness to nab the murderer, I had set Arnie on this course and he was too overwhelmed by work, and his own exhaustion to care.

***

I sat under the shade of a fiery acacia and plucked at the rough blades of kikuyu grass. For so early in the day I felt much too weary. I looked up at the sky through the lacy pattern of the branches. I desperately needed to right my mistake. Perhaps if I talked to Tagoe I would uncover a lead, find something to persuade Arnie he was on the wrong path.

The next day I phoned Arnie. 'You want to talk to Tagoe? It's highly irregular,' he said, accompanied by one of his long sighs. 'Only solicitors and cops visit suspects, but since you're one of the team and in view of your help, I suppose we can make an exception. But I can't see what you'll achieve by it.'

Tagoe was due to appear before the magistrate that morning to set a date for his hearing, but Arnie agreed that I could see him after that. The Rustenburg police station was as crowded as before, with insufficient seating, which forced unhappy looking people to hang about outside. I waited in a windowless, stale smelling room. Eventually Tagoe arrived accompanied by a guard.

'What you want? I already told the police everything.' He glared at me and refused to sit. Finally, confusing me with a solicitor, he asked me to help him to prove his innocence.

He spoke in an agitated voice. 'Ja, I do some bad things to the Moeketsi's. I put cattle shit outside the house and poison in the chocolates. I want them to be sick… to suffer much pain but I never kill Kosigo. Never.'

He told me that the feud between himself and the Moeketsi's began years ago, when first Kosigo and later Galani placed curses on his land.

'They fix it so my tobacco will never ever grow. Plenty oranges grow ... but no tobacco.'

He insisted that due to Galani's spells his tobacco developed a fungus that made the diseased leaves soggy when it rained. He grew citrus instead.

'Your oranges look healthy and I heard they brought in good money.'

He muttered about people who had no idea of the full story. It was just as well Esiekiel had given me his version of the story; the one that was likely to be closest to the truth. Tagoe failed to mention his gambling habit, or that he had not paid Moeketsi the rent owed to him.

'I go to the Moeketsi's house and beg Galani to break the curse she put on me. I even send two big baskets of fruit and flowers for Galani but she send 'em back. So, I go to the tribal chief but he not want to listen. When I cry already for much too long, my cousin takes me to see Jairus.'

'Jairus?'

'He make very strong curses.'

'Ah hah.' I remembered Esiekiel telling me that Jairus was an evil sorcerer.

'To make the curse, first Jairus burn a goat. Then he make me eat the heart of the goat.' Tagoe took a deep breath. 'And then he take the roots of the blue poison flowers and chops 'em up very small. He tell me to feed the Moeketsis the poison root so that they will be sick and they will cry ... like they make me cry.' Tagoe wiped his eyes.

'Then what happened?'

'I make beautiful chocolates for maybe six years. Last year I win a big prize for chocolates at the show.' His half smile was momentary. 'One day I am fed up with the Moeketsis again. So, I pull out the poison roots of the blue flowers from the garden and chop them up like powder. I make a rich chocolate mix and when it is ready for the fridge, I put the blue powder inside.' He made a stirring motion with his hand. 'I made plenty, pretty poison chocolates. Then I put 'em in the special gold boxes, and send one box to Kosigo and one box for Galani... pretend they come from ...er...'

'An admirer?'

He nodded. 'But I never kill Kosigo. Never... Never.' He made a fist and thumped the arm of chair.

I waited until he lifted his head to look at me. 'When did you last go to Polokwane?'

'Five years ago for the funeral for my Auntie Lettie. She look after me when I am small.'

'You're saying that you weren't in Polokwane this year?'

He shook his head. 'No, definitely no.'

While Tagoe sipped water, I ticked off my mental list of questions. I thought of Raymond and was puzzled. 'Tell me about Raymond from the Cameroons? Why did you send him one of your poisoned boxes of chocolates, when he had nothing to do with Kosigo or Galani?'

He looked at me for a second or two and cocked his head. 'From the time Kosigo and Galani give me all this trouble I hate *ngakas*. They only make more problems. And this one from the Cameroons, never stop talking... a smart arse ...know everything better, even when he not live in this country. So I want to teach him a lesson ... not to kill him.'

Tagoe was a liar, a gambler and someone who was capable of exacting revenge, but I did not think he was a murderer and there was no clear evidence to show that he was. I was about to call the guard to return him to his cell, when I realised I had not asked him about the peacock feathers.

'You keep peacocks don't you?'

'Ja, I farm peacocks.'

'So, how come peacock feathers were on the ground near Kosigo's body and in the clothing of another *ngaka* killed in Polokwane?'

'Peacock feathers? I not put feather near Kosigo ... and not near any dead woman in Polokwane.' His eyes were moist again.

'Well then, did you give or sell the feathers to anyone?'

He wiped his eyes and stared at the edge of the metal table for some time.

'When Jairus visit the farm, he take a big box of peacock feathers. He say he will look very smart wearing peacock feathers.'

After a few more questions, I ended the interview and knocked on the glass. At first the guard didn't respond but after a round of sharp tapping, he opened the door and took Tagoe back to his cell. In the long passage that led to the reception area, a constable stopped me. 'Please wait ma'am, Chief Detective Inspector Swart wants a word before you go. I'll take you to him.'

Arnie lifted his head from a mass of papers. 'You've spoken to Tagoe. Do you agree he's the one we're looking for?'

'He's a poisoner, but not the murderer you should be looking for. They are two different people. I'm sure about that now.'

'But everything points to him.'

I held up my hand. I could feel my cheeks burning and my voice rose. 'As I've just said, Tagoe didn't murder Kosigo, someone else did.' I closed my eyes and swallowed. 'I haven't the proof yet but I'll get it.'

'That's not good enough and you know it. We can't wait. Tagoe's being charged for the crime and will stand trial in four months.'

I left the police station angry with myself. Why couldn't I have been less impulsive, be more measured? Why had I led Arnie down the wrong path?

I looked through the windows of the sitting room at the gathering clouds and at the mountains that seemed to glare at me. Logic. Use logic, analyse the facts carefully and you will unravel this mess, I told myself. I found my crumpled crime sheet and spread it on the sitting room floor. I added the point that Tagoe was responsible for only the poisonings, but not the murders. Then, I wrote Jairus' name in bold letters. Nothing had shifted my belief that both women were murdered by the same person. But all that linked Jairus to the murders so far, were stories about his evil intent and the peacock feathers he had taken from Tagoe.

I thought of the glorious feathered eye, glimmering in the light. Peacocks had decorated many royal coats of arms and their myriad eyes were viewed by the ancient Egyptian, Greek and Roman civilizations as symbols of wisdom and immortality. Did they have a special symbolism for sorcerers?

I wondered if Rosie had heard of Jairus. She did not answer her phone and when she returned my call hours later, she had just come in from work. 'What's up?' Her voice was gravelly with fatigue.

'Have you a minute?'

'Hold on. I'll just get comfortable.'

'This is a long shot in connection with the murders. Have you heard of a sorcerer called Jairus?'

'Jairus Mogatle. Sure. I know him. He was in first year medical school with me. Bright as a button but kind of moody and he had this habit of switching off and staring into space. As clever as he was, he didn't complete his first year. He could've been a vet with his vast knowledge of large animals like elephants and hippos. Elephants in particular interested him and he used to say they were more like humans than gorillas. Some unkind folk called him the Elephant Man.'

'Sounds like a strange guy.'

'Weird. Religious in a crazy way too. He was big on bible quotes about evil and God's wrath. But we took no notice and had great fun with him. I heard that he dropped out of medicine to go back to his *kraal*.'

'Oh?'

'In Botswana he studied to be an *ngaka* and after a while left the healing side for witchcraft. Plenty money in it.'

'That's interesting! Anything else you know about him?'

'I heard from a friend, he was diagnosed with epilepsy, the temporal lobe kind. It would account for his weird behaviour. Who knows if he's been treated?'

'Please explain.'

'It's a huge field to go into especially late at night, but believe me it can cause some bizarre symptoms. Staring into space for one. Then there are delusions and all sorts of craziness.'

'Um, do you think Jairus could kill?'

'We can all kill if we're pushed hard enough.'

Later I tried to distract myself with wine, chocolate and after that, a large slice of cake but I couldn't rest. My thoughts clung like the last dribbles of the night's rain. At best, I could hope that an idea or a dream would trigger a shift.

It was late when my phone rang. Phineas was on the phone. 'I've got some news for you. We picked up Sunshine's uncle in a pub brawl as far away as Durban. We had an alert out for him and the cops there contacted us. He arrived here with an escort late this afternoon.'

'The bastard! I'm glad you've got him.'

'They tested him in Durban and he's got advanced AIDS. That could be why he reverted to the tribal belief that a virgin would save him. He admitted killing Sunshine in a sworn statement.'

Forty-Five

A week of gentle rain was a perfect preview to Galani's rain thanksgiving ceremony. From the snippets of gossip Josh had gathered, he was sure that Galani would present a ceremony based on Christian as well as African thanksgiving rituals. The concept was unusual and I looked forward to attending the ceremony that evening.

George was interested too, and we left for the Moeketsi farm well before sunset. With an umbrella between us, we joined the mob. Excitement swelled through the crowd. The belief that Galani had delivered rain in abundance had bolstered her reputation and from throughout the region, families swarmed to the farm to praise her talent and thank the ancestors for the life giving gift of rain.

We found seats close to the stage, behind a family with young children. None of the children sat quietly. The youngest, a toddler in a frilly dress perched on her father's shoulders, blocking our direct vision.

'Let's move, those kids will be jumping up and down through the ceremony and we won't see a bloody thing.' George suggested.

I turned to look for seats further back. Two rows behind us were six *ngakas,* in their full regalia of skins, bones and feathers. Galani must have made a name for herself if the inner circle of *ngakas* were attending the ritual. George pointed to empty seats and we moved.

The rain had stopped and the dying sun hung low in the caramel sky. I stood to remove my raincoat, using the opportunity for another glimpse of the *ngakas*. Was the light playing tricks with me, I asked myself. I whispered to George to check what the second *ngaka* was wearing on his head. George craned his neck.

'Peacock feathers. A whole bunch of them.'

'Are you positive?'

He laughed. 'Never been more certain. Couldn't miss them even in this half-light.'

'Shut up! Shush! It's starting,' people sitting near hissed. A spotlight fell on a white robed choir. Everyone stood for the choir's rendition of the national anthem, *Nkosi Sikelel'i Afrika*, God bless Africa. I particularly like the beginning of the anthem, a haunting hymn that had become popular during the apartheid years and was sung at resistance meetings and rallies.

Once everyone was seated, drummers in tribal dress ran onto the stage followed by a group of young girls dressed in animal skins, gyrating to the beat. A drum roll announced Galani's arrival and she entered amidst rapturous applause. We were close enough to see her green satin robe and dazzling crystal headdress. As torches lit the sky and sparklers sizzled, Galani held out her arms to the audience. The drummers and girls left the stage and the choral group joined Galani. With guitars as backing, they sang traditional songs and gradually jazz crept in. We all clapped to the catchy blend of music.

Then the singers left and she faced the audience alone. She led the crowd in prayer, entreating us to join her in thanking the ancestors and the highest entity, *modimo* for the gift of rain. The end of the ceremony was marked by the return of beating drums. More incense was lit as Galani made her exit.

'What a dramatic performance, just like a musical show,' George said. 'The crowd is loving it.'

'No ox on the spit this time, thank goodness,' I said.

George felt for the umbrella lodged under the seat, and we stood, waiting for our row to edge towards the exit. A loud and surprised wail came from the crowd near us and people pointed to a dart of light in the sky. Everyone looked up. '*A shooting star! Galani has made fire in heaven with her power!*'

George the cynic commented. 'She's a lucky woman. This is the time of year when meteoroids fall through the earth's atmosphere. They're just bits of dust or rock left behind by a comet when it orbited the earth.'

'You've got the scientific background, but to the rest of us Galani is a marvel.'

As the crowd thinned, we noticed that the group of *ngakas* had formed a tight circle under one of the large torches.

'Let's walk past the *ngakas*,' I said to George.

I stared at their earnest faces and their colourful attire that foreigners would have found strange but fascinating. I was accustomed to the sight of animal skins draped around their well-fed bodies, the feathers, beads and odd shaped dangling bits from waists and necks.

The suddenness of a hand shooting out to touch my arm gave me a jolt. 'Hi lady from Oz,' a voice shouted over the din.

It was Moses, an *ngaka* whom I had consulted on my previous visit. Back then, I was desperate to find my brother's murderer and used whatever help I could find. He had set me on the right path. His hair was still in dreadlocks and he wore a necklace of teeth and bones together with jeans and a checked shirt. With a truncated wave he left the group and came to talk to me. I introduced him to George and we found a quieter spot, away from the medicine men.

'I can tell, you're busy with another murder case,' he said as he studied my face closely. 'Stuck again are you? The police force is so overworked that they could do with your help.'

I smiled and ignored the puzzled look on George's face.

'The answer you are seeking is near. I sense it,' Moses said. 'If you hit major problems working with local police, take the matter to Commander Nkakabinde. He won't put up with second rate police work. I know it; he's a pal of mine. Mention my name and you'll do fine.'

'Thanks. I'll remember that.'

I turned and pointed to the *ngaka* with the bunch of peacock feathers in his hair. 'Can you tell me his name?'

'Jairus is his name but he's a sorcerer not a healer, a person I advise you to keep well away from.'

There was a black aura around Jairus.

'Is he giving you trouble?' Moses asked.

'Someone is... and it could be him, I guess. Some unexplained, unpleasant things have happened.'

I glanced at Jairus lighting a cigarette as he talked to the man next to him. He looked in my direction as he inhaled, held the smoke and exhaled slowly. Hot and clammy and trembling all over, I looked away.

'I'm not surprised.' Moses' expression was one of dislike.

I began to tremble.

Moses looked concerned. 'You're sensing his evil. Take a deep breath.'

Moses' friends were beckoning. 'I must go...keep far away from Jairus,' he said with a wave. As we walked on, I told George about Moses. He was dismissive about my words of praise for the young *ngaka*.

As tired as I was after the ceremony, I struggled to fall sleep. My mind traced and retraced anything I knew about Jairus. The longer I thought about him, the more my intuition told me that he was the killer – the peacock feather, Rosie and Moses' comments and my gut feelings. But I had made a mistake with Tagoe, and I had no rational explanation to corroborate my intuition about Jairus' involvement in the murder. This time I would be more cautious. When I had proof, I would make Arnie listen, insist he questioned Jairus and search his property.

Towards the morning, a shattering crash jolted me from sleep. I groped for the bedside light, flicked it on and looked about the room. A photograph of Ma and Pa taken on their tenth wedding anniversary, that had decorated the wall above my bed, lay smashed on the floor only centimetres away from me. Slithers of glass glistened in the light. The frame was buckled but at least the photo was undamaged.

How could it have fallen, I muttered to myself as I gave the hook a tug. It had been secure on the wall and the picture wire was unbroken. It did not add up. As I tried to sleep, pounding rain struck the roof and windows. The room was dark but a peek at the illuminated dial of the clock told me it was 5.30.

Sleep was out of the question. I was up in minutes, sweeping the glass away. I heard a clatter in the kitchen, dropped the dustpan and brush on the carpet, raced down the passage and down the stairs. A clay pot of violets I had placed on the kitchen windowsill was rolling on the floor. Not a rat or cat in sight. One thing falling of its own accord in such a short space of time was strange but two was scary. Before replacing the pot on the windowsill, I checked behind the kitchen blind and in all the cupboards. All was in place.

The sky rumbled. A burning smell accompanied by hissing green sparks from the oven drove me into a corner as dense acrid smoke filled the kitchen. '*Out of the kitchen! Get out!*' The panicky voice in my head ordered, but my legs barely moved. *This is not a power cut, it's something more sinister*. Gasping, I forced myself out into the hall and collapsed. Part of me could feel the hard edge of the table beneath me, while the rest faded. When my eyes opened, I clasped the leg of the table and forced myself up. Terrified, I made for the door and I was out of the house and on the *stoep* breathing fresh air again.

Could it be a troublesome spirit sent by a sorcerer? It was not the time to ponder if the *tokoloshe*, of countless tribal legends, was in my house. I thought of the recent episode in the garage and shivered. Tansie once told me that her cousin Seraphina had a spirit in the house that would not rest. Cushions moved, salt flew into the stew to make it too salty to eat and the mielie meal kept boiling over, even though she had taken it off the hotplate. She decided that her ancestral spirits were not happy and after consulting a *ngaka,* she sacrificed her largest chicken, the one she had been saving for Christmas. She wrung its neck until the blood flowed and then burnt it on a rock. Seraphina's life quietened down after that, or so Tansie said.

At about 7.00, Josh found me under the covered part of the *stoep*.

'What's going on? Are you OK?

I related the events of the night.

Josh clicked his tongue on the roof of his mouth. 'Will there be no end to it? You're outside, the storm drains are blocked and we've got a dam in the back yard. I'll phone Connie right away. He'll know what to do.'

Within half an hour Connie arrived. 'I don't understand this.' He lifted his hands to the sky. 'First the garage now this. When your alarm was installed, Thomas checked all the wiring and the drains too. I'll get him back here,' Connie dialled the number. 'He'll be here in about an hour. I'll have to go back to the farm but phone if you have any more trouble.'

After a thorough check, Thomas found no fault in the wiring or the oven.

'You've got spooks in the place,' he said jokingly.

I had to speak to Rosie. Though she would be dressing for work, I would try to catch her.

'There's a bad spirit in the house,' I told her. 'It has to be a spirit ...It's virtually impossible to break through the new high tech security Connie organised for me.'

'Honestly Linda. Next thing you'll be putting bricks under your bed like we used to in the old days, so that a *tokoloshe* won't be able to reach you.'

My laugh was shaky.

'Sorry I'm late for work, got to run. Talk to you later.'

≈

In the two weeks that followed the strange happenings, I slept most of the day and my appetite waned. Even Josh's best chocolate mousse could not tempt me. Rosie and others phoned but I had excuses for avoiding them all. The investigation no longer interested me and Kosigo's face, so prominent before, had faded. My intention to check my facts about Jairus was forgotten. With complaints of exhaustion, I tried to dissuade George from visiting but he ignored my pleas and came daily. During that period, I barely responded to him or anyone else. I was as dead inside as a block of wood. Though he persevered, his gifts of fruit and flowers could not please me. Nothing could.

Flashbacks of the shattered glass of the picture over my bed and the oven spewing smoke kept recurring. I stayed in the narrow realm of the house with Stevie at my side. Twice a day, at least, I checked that the windows and doors were locked. None of this was rational. Spirits, good or evil could slip through locks and doors and Stevie was too friendly to be a guard dog.

One night much like the others at that time, I went to bed early after my checking routine. Sleep came more easily than usual and during the night in a vivid dream, Moses appeared. He cut straight to the point of his visit - to remind me of my commitment to find Kosigo's murderer. I had fallen into the trap laid for me, he said. A *baloi* with evil spells had nibbled at my life sap.

'Tonight you will sleep well and when you wake you will remember my visit. You will have the new strength of a young kudu buck. You made one mistake, a serious one, but this time you will be certain about Kosigo's killer. Soon it will seem natural to you to continue your fight to find Kosigo's murderer.'

Forty-Six

When I opened my eyes, Moses' voice was with me. He was right of course. I had to resume the search for Kosigo's killer but it was not going to be easy. I was still shaky. His voice in my head said, *Slowly. Take it slowly.* All I had on Jairus was the peacock feather. My mind darted, seeking ways of finding further evidence until Esiekiel's face came into my thoughts and smiled at me. I was dressed and at the farm within an hour.

Esiekiel was sitting in his favourite chair outside his hut drinking coffee.

'Morning Missie. Rain is gone. My friend the sun come back,' he said as he rubbed an arthritic arm.

'Yes, it's a lovely morning.'

'You wanting know something from old man?' He smiled.

'I ask you because I respect your knowledge and wisdom. I'm trying to find out about Jairus … a man people say makes curses. Do you know him?'

'Ooooh Jairus! If he come here, I hide inside hut. He a very bad man.' Esiekiel stirred several spoons of sugar into his coffee before speaking again. 'Two, maybe three years past, people tell Jairus that Kosigo is busy with studies and she is going to be *ngaka*. He know she is beautiful and people tell him she is very, very clever and that one day she be the best *ngaka* in Rustenburg. He is cross. So, he try scare her to make her give up.'

'What did he do to her?'

'My cousin Rafe work for Moeketsi as gardener. One day

he sees Jairus at the Moeketsi farm hiding behind big tree. When Kosigo is going to open the post box to check for letter, Jairus make the box green and white like electric fire. She is lucky, she only burn the fingers. She scream loud. Rafe hear her and he run to help her. And then he chase Jairus all the way down the street… but Jairus is too fast.'

'You're sure it was Jairus?'

'One hundred percent. Rafe, he always tell the truth… I know him.'

I wiped my clammy forehead as I thought of the creepy occurrences in my home.

The old man shuffled his feet and yawned

'Thank you Esiekiel, I must go now. You've helped me a lot.'

🦂

The sun was overhead when I reached the Moeketsi farm. Workers were planting rows of seedlings in the soft earth. I nodded a greeting to Baba and the others but I avoided the house and Galani, and went directly to Thabang's consulting room. She would be the most reliable person to back up Esiekiel's story about Jairus and the post box.

Thabang had finished her consulting for the morning and was about to take a lunch break when I knocked on her door. She greeted me warmly. We walked through the garden together. When I asked after her health, she replied that she would feel much better when Kosigo's killer was named and charged.

As soon as I mentioned the scary incident at the post box, she sucked in her breath and put her hands to her face. Her description of the frightening lights at the post box echoed Esiekiel's story. She said that she should have told the police about the incident but at the time she did not think it was important.

On the way home, my mind was on the murder and not on the traffic, and it was only due to the other driver's vigilance that I avoided a collision. The house was quiet and Stevie was with Josh. After a glass of wine, I made my move and phoned Arnie. His direct line was busy and I suffered what felt like an interminable wait at the hands of a switchboard operator.

At last a grumpy voice answered. 'Yes, Linda, haven't heard from you for a while.'

'Arnie I'm certain now… absolutely certain about the murderer this time… and please listen to what I have to say.'

'Look, I know you mean well and you're a very smart lady but I'm drowning in work and I'm satisfied…we've got Kosigo's murderer. The boys at the top are happy. End of story.'

I heard the gravity in my voice. 'But we can't allow this man to go free to kill again, while the wrong man rots in jail. Surely not!'

'Let me remind you that you said exactly the same thing about Jake.'

I was about to threaten to take the matter to Commander Joseph Nkakabinde when he replied, 'Oh, alright then, come in later. Somehow I'll make the time.' There was a moment of silence. 'By now you must've realised that I enjoy seeing you or I wouldn't be bothering with all of this.'

I didn't reply. By then I didn't care.'

A quiver ran through my hands. I badly needed a cup of hot tea with loads of honey before I left for the Rustenburg Police Station. I knew had to go soon, before Arnie changed his mind.

As I entered the police station, a surge of warmth radiated from me. I felt a sudden and new firming from within. At that moment I had no doubt that I would convince Arnie to question Jairus and that when he did, he would be as certain as I was of the sorcerer's guilt.

Arnie listened reluctantly as I presented Esiekiel's account of Tagoe's troubles, and his explanation of how in desperation Tagoe had engaged the services of Jairus Mogatle.

'But it proves nothing,' Arnie said impatiently, tapping the desk…

'We're getting to the juice of it. Hold on a sec.'

I explained that Tagoe hadn't been in Polokwane at the time of Rathabile's murder. He had a strong alibi to account for the time. Of key importance was that Tagoe had given Jairus a box of peacock feathers. By now Arnie was sitting up in his chair and was listening. I also told him how I had seen Jairus wearing peacock feathers at the Thanksgiving Ceremony. Finally, I added the information I had just gathered from Esiekiel and was verified by Thabang.

'Never heard of this Jairus character,' he said lifting the phone. 'I'll get Phineas in here … see if he knows him.'

Phineas knew the name instantly. 'Jairus, he's a bad bugger with a reputation for vengeance spells and curses. He likes to dress the part with the witchdoctor regalia – bones, leather feathers and the lot.'

'Well Phineas, what do you think?'

'Linda's opened a new window here, Boss. And this crazy bloke is out there, a danger to the community when he should be locked up. We can't ignore that this latest information weakens our case against Tagoe.'

'Time and resources,' Arnie said tapping the desk.

'We might as well bring a case we've spent so much time on to its conclusion. We don't always get that opportunity.' Phineas looked directly as his boss as he spoke.

Arnie sighed. 'Right then, let's go for it. I'll give you and Linda twenty-four hours to wrap this up.' He turned to me. 'That's it Linda, I can't give you more.'

'We'll get on to it straight away then. I'll get a search warrant signed and we'll find and interview Jairus,' Phineas said. 'I'll drop what I'm working on and see if Amita is available.'

A few minutes later Amita joined us. 'Did the Boss tell you that just before you arrived he received a hand delivered letter from the Moeketsi family? They demanded he set up an appointment with them to discuss progress on Kosigo's murder. There was some comment about making a complaint, up the line.'

'No wonder he was reasonable,' Phineas said.

Jairus' house was perched on a peak overlooking the dam, without trees or flowers to soften its starkness. Two large sculpted velvet monkeys, totems of the *Bakalanga* group of Tswanas guarded the gate. The three of us trudged up the steep driveway, and then climbed the stone steps to the front door. Phineas knocked on the door, while Amita took precautions by covering the back of the house. A servant led us into a small sitting area.

When Jairus appeared twenty minutes later, he was in full witchdoctor attire, topped by a red velvet cape and carrying the traditional fly whisk. He must've dressed up to impress us. Haughtily he refused to speak until Phineas flashed the search warrant.

'I'm just a medicine man, a healer with nothing to hide,' he whined. Phineas and Amita began the search in the sitting room, shaking cushions and lifting couches. I followed them into the room Jairus called his den. Phineas whistled through his teeth. There was barely space on the walls to hang another root or bulb, and dark bottles of all sizes and shapes were crammed into the rows of shelves. The smell was putrid. Boxes filled with papers and more plant material were packed in the cupboards. In the crowded room, Jairus had found space behind his desk to set up a piece of white hardboard, displaying his tribal clan's velvet monkey, a black mask and beneath it two crossed assegais. Amita laughed loudly about Jairus creating his own, homemade crest. While they riffled through drawers and hunted in the boxes, Jairus sat on a chair covered with a lion skin. Suddenly he shocked us with a quotation from the bible, *Touch not, taste not as a thief in the night.*

As he pontificated, I was aware again of the murky aura that draped his body. I had no doubts, he was Kosigo's killer and my tormentor. He had tried to unnerve me so that I would relinquish the investigation. Phineas and Amita ignored him as they dumped the contents of drawers on the stone floor.

When Phineas called out loudly. 'Peacock feathers…in here.' I rushed towards him.

'I bought those feathers,' Jairus said indignantly.

'Where did you buy them?' Phineas asked.

'From a street market… I can't remember … where,' Jairus replied.

'Sure you didn't get them as a present from Emanuel Tagoe?' Phineas replied, his face close to Jairus. We all knew that laboratory tests could establish whether the feathers were from Tagoe's peacocks, and whether they had the same characteristics as those found at the crime sites.

Amita shouted, 'Benson and Hedges smokes over here.'

She had found three cartons behind the desk. Obviously the cigarettes would have to be checked against the stubs from the crime scenes and against those found on my property on the night of the fire.

Jairus' desk was so cluttered with papers and bottles, that Phineas almost missed a pack of tarot cards. He passed them to me. The western mystical cards were out of place in Jairus' African den. On the underside of the box of cards clearly marked were the letters K M. 'Look at this.' I held up the pack pointing to the signature. 'The cards and some wooden divining tablets belonging to Kosigo were missing a week before her death.'

'Slipped them into your pocket, eh Jairus,' Phineas said.

Judge not that ye be judged, Jairus uttered with a scowl.

The two cops continued rummaging through the pile of boxes. 'I've found it! Over here,' Phineas called out to us excitedly. 'Just as you described, Linda.' He pointed to a large item behind the boxes that was covered with an old blanket. Beneath the blanket was a hollowed out piece of wood approximately a metre long and as wide as a medium tree trunk. It would've been unremarkable if not for its markings at the base, the indentations, swells and crevices that resembled the underside of an elephant's foot. It was a replica of a left foot.

'Tell us about this piece of wood?' Phineas stood arms akimbo in front of Jairus.

'Just a log, as you can see,' he sneered.

'Like the foot of an elephant, eh?'

Jairus spat out another biblical quote. *The way of sinners is made plain with stones, but at the end thereof is the pit of hell.*

'Crazy stuff!' Amita said shaking her head.

Phineas rubbed his hands. 'We'll take him and the fake elephant's foot back to the station with us, and we'll compare the indentations to the crime scene pictures.'

Jairus' red velvet cloak was draped over his chair. It was the red of my earlier vision.

'Don't leave the cloak behind,' I called out to Amita. 'We have a lot on him already, but I'm sure the red fibers will match those found at the murder scene.'

The fury of the search was over. This time we had the murderer and we all knew it. The pathology tests and comparison with the crime scene photos would merely confirm his guilt. Phineas phoned Arnie and a police car arrived to take Jairus to the Rustenburg Police Station. The three of us made our way down the driveway in silence.

⁂

Later Arnie phoned. 'To give you an update: We've charged Jairus for Kosigo's murder.' He hesitated for a moment. 'The underside of that fake elephant foot is a perfect fit to blow ups of the footprints we have from the crime scene. Right now, Amita is checking the dates he was in Polokwane. It looks like he performed at an alternative health show there around the time Rethabile was murdered.' He stopped to take a breath. 'As far as Raymond is concerned …Phineas has just returned from the Elephant Sanctuary. He showed two of the assistants a photo of Jairus and they remember seeing him near the tent. We'll have to look into that further, though.'

'A good result so far,' I added.

'There'll be a wait for pathology as usual, but this time we've definitely got our man.'

'Have you released Tagoe?'

'We're charging him for the poisoning. He'll get jail time for that.'

'That's it, then. A positive result,' I said, trying to end the conversation.

'Thanks for all your ...' His voice tapered off.

'We're a top team... and we've got our killer,' I said quickly.

Forty-Seven

Phineas' phone was engaged when I dialed his extension the next morning.

After a few tries he answered. 'Good news about Jairus, You're a crack detective, Linda. We were planning on interviewing him this afternoon. Let's make it 3.00 and you're welcome to watch.'

There was the usual delay at the police station, until I followed a young woman constable to the interviewing area. Within minutes Phineas joined me. We both wore microphones that kept us in contact with Arnie and Amita, who were in the room with Jairus.

Amita led Jairus in and Arnie followed. She set the video machine and made announcements similar to those I had seen on television and films. Without his feathers, bones and other bits of witchdoctor paraphernalia, Jairus was a thin middle-aged black man with a down turned mouth. His glares at his interviewers were a pathetic attempt at bravado. He made a last attempt at a biblical quote. *Your adversary the devil, as a roaring lion, walketh about seeking whom he may devour.*

Arnie conducted the interview. At first Jairus denied his involvement in the murders but as the evidence against him was presented, he slumped in his chair. Arnie threw photographs of the murdered women on the table but Jairus turned his head away.

'Bloody well look at them!'

Jairus pulled back, scraping his chair on the concrete floor.

'You… you murdered Kosigo, Rethabile and Raymond.'

Jairus looked at the floor.

'I want to hear it from you, you low life…and no more bloody quotes from the bible. I also want to hear that you lit a fire, sent spiders and perpetrated other evils on Mrs Linda Van Wyk, because she was involved in this investigation and you wanted to frighten her off.'

Jairus' malevolent glare should've warned me. He spat with such force that the glob reached the two-way window shielding me. 'White bitch… digging in the dirt, won't leave things alone.'

Arnie looked at Jairus with contempt. 'Now, you'll tell me why … why you murdered them.'

'He can have a solicitor present…if he wants one,' Amita said to Arnie.

If Jairus heard he didn't reply. He quivered and his voice grew shrill. A wild, violent creature emerged, outraged that a woman, especially a young woman like Kosigo, had dared to enter the circle of *ngakas*. On and on he railed irrationally about women - their bodies misshapen with breasts, fouled with menstrual blood. They deserved to die; elephants should stomp on them and kill them.

That wasn't all of it. 'Just because the bitches think they're beautiful,' he whined. 'They get their head so big they think they're too, too clever…. telling men what to do, how to do, where, when.'

Even Arnie was flummoxed for a few seconds. 'And what about Raymond? What did you have against him?'

'A foreigner, stealing my customers. I had to get rid of him before the World Cup, my busiest time.'

Finally Jairus was given a statement to read and sign. He took a long time reading it or pretending he was reading it and finally signed.

Arnie looked over to the glass behind which we were sitting.

'Any questions from you two?'

'He'll have a psychiatric evaluation, won't he?' I asked.

'It depends on his legal representation, I guess,' Arnie answered consulting his watch. 'Get him out of here.'

An important task awaited me, my private thanksgiving for those who had helped me to identify the killer or had interceded on my behalf. At the florist, I bought an armful of flowers. With the flowers on the seat next to me, I drove to Connie's farm. I passed the farmhouse and pulled up behind the huts. Though Tansie had barely departed, I sensed she had resumed the role that she had taken seriously during her lifetime, of looking out for my wellbeing. She liked all sweet smelling, brightly coloured flowers and lots of them. I kissed the bright bunch and placed them on the rough mound.

Along the path to the family cemetery, budding wild blooms and greenery were overtaking all signs of the dry. I opened the rusty gate and divided the remaining flowers into posies. After kissing each one, I placed them on my family's graves and whispered my words of love.

Then I left the farm and stopped at the shops, where I purchased salami, olives, cheese, pickles, nuts and chocolate biscuits for Nandi. I knew that she would not appreciate flowers. When I presented her with the tasty assortment, she kissed me. The kiss was a first from Nandi. Over a cup of tea, I told her the result of the investigation.

'The evil one is broken,' she said with a thankful sigh.

❧

George was still asleep at sunrise. I placed a butterfly's kiss on his neck and lay next to him, happier than I could remember for years. When he woke, we shared the events of the past days and ate brunch in bed, enjoying our laziness.

While I had been involved with tying up the case, he had been completing his photography for his book on rock art. 'I'll have all I need by tomorrow or the next day. It will be over after a fascinating but tiring exercise. Let's go away together for a few days.'

When he suggested hiking, I immediately thought of

a trip to the mountains and Tobias. I was convinced that George would be impressed by Tobias' eland. George liked the idea. After breakfast, I discussed the hike with Josh and he agreed to act as our guide on condition that Karel joined us.

The arrangements fell into place easily and we set the date for two days ahead. Josh sent a message to Tobias alerting him to our visit. As always, the bush telegraph was an effective form of communication but how our news climbed the mountain amongst the sparse population confounded me. Fortunately, George had all the necessary camping equipment stored with a friend. All I had to do was buy sufficient food to last a few days.

The four of us began our climb on a clear morning. We brought Tobias brandy, tinned food, a tin opener, a thick woollen blanket and warm jumper. Josh found a second-hand gas cooking ring for Tobias. Between us we shared the extra load in addition to our tents, sleeping bags and our own food.

The little I knew about Karel was from Josh. He was a short, wonderfully coordinated man, agile enough to be a circus performer. He was comical, in a slapstick fashion, pulling silly faces and making bizarre movements. He told a joke well, even if they were old jokes. With him entertaining us, we laughed too much to complain of our heavy load and the slippery patches made by the recent rains.

Tobias was seated outside his shack waiting for us. His smile told us he was pleased to see us and he was even more pleased with the brandy and provisions. Though he said he did not need the blanket and jumper, he took them. As before, he preferred to talk to the men but this time he did answer me if I asked him a direct question. George and I followed him to a flat piece of land close to the stream suitable for setting up our tent. Tobias could not have suggested a more idyllic spot, surrounded by trees, wildflowers and a backdrop of mountains. Josh and Karel had already selected their position lower down the mountain close to the stream.

Josh and Karel kept their distance, and only the smell

of their food cooking and the sound of Karel's laughter occasionally wafted up to us. We were prepared to bide our time until Tobias showed George his precious eland. During our first two days we took long mountain hikes and naked swims in the stream. We talked about everything, from the day's weather to the politics of the day. Though our backgrounds differed, we had similar values and ideas on most subjects.

The day before we left, Tobias called George. They talked and then walked to the eland's rocky hiding place. I watched George help Tobias lift the rock, and then drag it into the sunlight. George's face glowed like a delighted child's.

'It's a magnificent eland, possibly the most striking I've seen so far and in excellent condition. The colours are still bright and even the brushstrokes are visible.'

Josh broached the subject of photographing the eland with Tobias. Though the old man agreed, I doubted whether he knew anything about photography or cameras. He watched George set up the tripod and lights but when the flash sparked, he limped to his tent and hid there, sipping brandy and jabbering to himself about the spirits. George left his camera and went into Tobias' hut. He patiently explained how the camera functioned. Tobias relaxed but was sceptical that the photograph George promised him would enable him to look at his eland at any time, without having to drag it from its hidden place.

The days on the mountain passed like a camera flash. Our descent was in dim light and mist and this time the need to concentrate curtailed the chatting and joking of our ascent.

Forty-Eight

After my favourite breakfast of croissants, strawberry jam and coffee, I ambled into the garden, making my way along the stepping stones. Spikes of lawn, weeds and tiny white daisies had shot up.

I was aware of a hum increasing in intensity. Closing my eyes to an unexpected brightness, I felt myself spin, ever so slightly. When the movement ceased, I dropped on the damp grass. The hum receded and I opened my eyes to a paler light. Spirits were visiting. Their presence put me at ease. They had been with me in one form or another for most of my life and now they were back. Absentmindedly, I tugged at a mass of weeds. I licked the dew off my fingers and went back into the house.

Amongst the post that day, was a stiff envelope. When I opened it, out fell two tickets for a soccer match - the Cameroons versus Brazil. They were first row tickets in a prime position. Attached was a brief letter of thanks from the Cameroons team manager, for the work I had done with the police in pin pointing Raymond's killer. George had already bought our tickets and my brothers had their tickets as well. The two prime seats from the Cameroons manager were earmarked for Josh and Karel.

It must have been a week or two later, that Arnie phoned to tell me that all the pathology tests had confirmed Jairus' guilt, and that he would appear in court at a formal hearing in four months.

I was still on leave from the hospital in Melbourne and

a few weeks of holiday stretched before me. No longer was there a crime sheet to ponder over or policemen to hustle me. The events of the past weeks required time to find their own spaces in my memory. The image of Kosigo had at last left me and Tansie's death no longer burnt so painfully. George moved into the house. Each day we spent a few hours together viewing and arranging his photographs of the rock paintings. The photos had to be in order before he could consider writing an accompanying text. He had captured the animals, mainly elands and the occasional human figures with amazing clarity. The picture of Tobias' magnificent eland was the finest of the rock paintings and George decided to place it on the cover.

The house had ample space for both of us to maintain our interests and yet be together. It was a more successful arrangement than either of us had imagined. Though we talked about living together indefinitely, I was still undecided as to whether I would return to Melbourne or stay with George in Rustenburg. Staying felt right but it was a risk. If I returned, I would resume my secure but regimented and comparatively dull life without George. If I stayed there were risks to my physical safety but at least I had a second chance at a real relationship. When I drove to *Mosego,* fields of ripe mielies were ready for picking. Nathaniel ran up to me, swiped his hands on his shorts and shook the dirt from his shoes. It was my first visit to *Mosego* since Jairus was charged.

'You've got plenty healthy looking mielies! You'll all have a big job picking them,' I said.

Nathaniel grinned. 'We don't mind. We'll be thinking about the money.'

We both laughed.

'The fathers will rest now the one who killed Kosigo will go to jail.'

'I hope so.'

He took both my hands. '*Ke a leboga,* thank you,' he said, and then gave me a hug. The workers laid down the shovels and hoes and stared. '*Ke a leboga*' he said again, loudly this time. It was loud enough for them all to hear it. A wave of chatter and then they resumed their work.

A week before my leave ran out, I wandered into the garden as I had most mornings. In the soft light, the air was sweet with petals, the mountains a fuzzy green and the earth had the rich warm smell that I remembered from childhood. How could I leave all this and George? There was no decision to make. My heart and my gut knew I had to stay.

I padded over the stones in my wet slippers and surveyed my land. Yes, there, in that open space between the bushes, a birdbath would look splendid and possibly a sundial a little lower. I marked the spots with handfuls of pebbles. I would visit the nursery later that morning to buy plants for a flourishing garden.